Miss Mary Investigates
Book Three

Death of a Dandy

A Mansfield Park Mystery

RIANA EVERLY

MISS MARY INVESTIGATES BOOK 3

DEATH OF A DANDY: A MANSFIELD PARK MYSTERY

Dedication

To everyone in this crazy world who fights for justice.

Contents

Acknowledgements

In difficult times, we learn that the heroes are not those who say the right words, but who do the right things. All too often, the ones who shout the loudest when times are good are the furthest from the fray when trouble strikes. To those who stand up when lesser people run, I applaud you, and take inspiration from you.

This book is the result of a great deal of research and discussion, and I have a great many people to thank. I shall name just a few, because there are far too many people whose names belong on my list, and I am certain to forget someone.

First, I want to thank Mikael Swayze, who listened and suggested and guided and edited. Then I have a fabulous team of beta readers whose comments and advice have been invaluable. Celia Martin, Heather Robinson, and Jeanette Ford deserve a round of applause. And even more so do I owe a great deal of thanks to the tireless work of fabulous author Liz Martinson.

Thanks also to Hadassah Swayze for her work on the silhouettes, and, as always, to Mae Phillips for her beautiful cover art. They say not to judge a book by its cover, but having something eye-catching and beautiful on the front never hurts, does it?

Cover design by Mae Phillips at coverfreshdesigns.com

Chapter One

Breaking the Journey

The house was quite fine, grand, even. Mary Bennet gazed around the drawing room, appreciating the clean, modern room with its elegant furnishings and accoutrements. It bespoke both wealth and taste, a combination most frequently distinguished by its absence. Pale butter-yellow wallpaper was broken into panels of pleasing proportions by mannerist columns in fresh white paint, which also covered the carved archway that led to the study beyond and the mouldings that flanked the high white ceiling. She closed her eyes and leaned back in her comfortable chair, ignoring for a moment the cup of tea and plate of biscuits that sat on the small round table to her side, and let out a long breath of relief.

"Is everything to your satisfaction, Miss Bennet?" Mrs. Meldola leaned forward in her own chair, keeping her voice low. She was a petite woman with dark hair and bright eyes, and possessed of a gentle manner. Her dress recommended her station as mistress of this beautiful house—elegant and modern and expensive, with none of the excess of the first circles of society. She was about thirty years of age, the wife of a successful businessman in Northampton who was a particular friend of Alexander Lyons, Mary's friend and her escort on this journey.

"Yes, yes indeed, I thank you." Mary stifled a yawn. "I am merely fatigued by the journey. The tea and biscuits will certainly revive me."

Her hostess gave a sympathetic grin that promised understanding and turned to her husband and Alexander. This small, kind gesture was as welcome as diamonds to Mary, allowing her to enjoy the sweet nourishment without the necessity of providing sparkling conversation when she desired only quiet and a few moments alone, in mind if not in body. She sent a grateful smile back towards Mrs. Meldola for her consideration and sank further into her chair.

If one required sparkling conversation, Lizzy was the one to provide it. Mary had been parted from her dear sister, now Mrs. Darcy, for only two days, and already she missed her. But after more than a month at Pemberley with Lizzy and Mr. Darcy and the new baby, it had been time to return home to Longbourn. How fortunate that Alexander had been passing through Derbyshire exactly when Mary was preparing for her return journey. He had spent three days at Pemberley to visit his friend Darcy and bring a present for the tiny heir to the estate, and had offered to accompany Mary home.

It was a remarkable coincidence, Mary now considered, that Alexander had been called to Yorkshire as part of one of his investigations six weeks before. He had accompanied Mary northward then, when he had learned of her planned visit. The investigation, he informed her at that time, was one driven more by a need for accuracy and attention, and less by the need for haste, and he was able, therefore, to time his own journey north to coincide with hers. And now, just over a month later, he was returning from his home near Glasgow. It was rather too convenient, and she mentally chastised her brother-in-law, Mr. Darcy, for arranging matters thus. For she was certain it had been his fingers stirring this pudding. She let out a huff, half in exasperation and half in gratitude for his consideration, and hoped that none of her companions had heard her. They all seemed quite immersed in their conversation about Alexander's visit home and the wedding.

Mr. Meldola pressed for details. "Tell me, Alex, of Sarah's husband. I can hardly imagine her as a married woman, for in my mind, she is still a girl of thirteen. Can it really have been so long since last I saw her? And was your cousin Kathryne there?"

Mrs. Meldola leaned forward with a smile. "I recall Kathryne Lyons with great pleasure. And your mother? How does she do?"

Mary sat back with her eyes half-closed and listened to Alexander talk of the event and his family. He spoke of Abel Miller the goldsmith, now his new brother-in-law, and of various aspects of the wedding, as the Meldolas asked questions about others they knew. The details seemed strange to Mary's inattentive ears, but things might be different in Scotland, she presumed. Her eyes fluttered closed and she allowed her thoughts to wander as the conversation washed over her like a warm blanket.

This was not her first stay at the Meldolas' house, for this is where she and Alexander had stayed on their journey northward. It had been a pleasant, if quick, stay at that time, and she was pleased to return. She had liked Mrs. Meldola when they had met some weeks before, but had had little time to converse with the lady for the night of their arrival had coincided with a gathering of local merchants in the large salon at the front of the house.

She recalled her prior visit as if it had been just days before, rather than weeks. The carriage which Alexander—or Darcy—had hired for the length of their journey had arrived at the house shortly before dark, and already some early comers for the gathering could be heard talking. With all due attention, Mrs. Meldola had shown her to a small but comfortable bedroom and had extended an invitation to dine with her in her chambers whilst the gentleman convened below. Mary had demurred, citing a wish not to intrude on the lady's time and privacy, but Mrs. Meldola had glanced around her and then whispered, "perhaps we may creep down to the kitchens then, and pretend to be children hoping for some of the extra tarts and treats from the cook's table." She had emitted a giggle most unbecoming to the wife of an esteemed leader of the merchant class, but which had endeared her to Mary, and the two had followed through on this plan.

They took their meal of a tasty pie with bread and vegetables and a selection of fruits for afters and had talked of such inconsequential matters as the state of the roads and the comfort of the inn where they had stayed, and whether Mary's maid Alice, who also served as chaperone on the journey, was in need of anything.

This pleasant conversation was interrupted by Mr. Meldola, who burst in with all apologies, but, "Bertram is here once more, quite uninvited. He followed Framington to beg for the loan of more funds to repay somebody or another and fell down quite drunk on the floor. Oh, dreadfully sorry, Miss Bennet!" Mary had been sitting on the side of the table furthest from the door, out of the direct line of vision of a newcomer, and Mr. Meldola only seemed now to notice that his wife was not alone. He executed a neat bow, but kept to his task. "Shouldn't discuss such matters before company, but…" his eyes wandered around the very informal environs of the kitchen and he shrugged.

"Again?" Mrs. Meldola huffed an errant curl of black hair from her high forehead, then tucked it into her cap. "I shall ask Mrs. Graham to set up the brown room for him. Can some of your companions help carry him upstairs when the room is ready?"

These were not the manners of the upper classes, but Mary did not mind them, finding them comfortable rather than forced and by no means disrespectful. Although she wished to leave the couple alone to discuss their unwelcome guest, the doorway to the stairs lay at the far end of the kitchen and she would have to pass by both master and mistress to achieve it. Instead of calling attention to herself by interrupting their hurried discussion, she willed herself to vanish into the walls. She had often considered herself nigh on invisible, knowing how her presence was so often ignored by those around her, and already once this evening Mr. Meldola had failed to notice her in the room. She shuffled backwards on the bench upon which she sat and fell into herself.

As if her wish had become reality, the couple continued their conversation as if she were not there, discussing whether to send for Bertram's valet or whether to keep his whereabouts quiet for the evening. From what Mary gathered, it was not the first time the man had required a place to sleep off his drink, nor the first in which he was hoping to avoid a creditor or other such person. Who he was, Mary could not determine, but he seemed rather a wild and unsavoury sort and she wondered at the connection with the respectable and amiable Meldolas. Whoever he was, her hosts were most kind to attend to him in his less decorous moments.

At last, a decision having been reached, Mr. Meldola looked up once more and, noticing Mary, blinked. "You must think us quite uncivilised, Miss Bennet..." he began, but Mary assured him she thought no such thing.

"Your civility is better demonstrated in your wish to help this man than in any display of outward polish... which is by no means lacking!" she hurried to add.

"Go on to your guests, Elijah," Mrs. Meldola squeezed her husband's hands. "I'll ready the room. Oh, Mrs. Graham..." she called through an open doorway on the far side of the hearth.

Mary took this as her opportunity to escape and bid both master and mistress a good evening before disappearing up the stairs to her own rooms as quickly as she could, wondering all the time about the unfortunate Bertram.

That had been the last of her conversation with Mrs. Meldola until her arrival once again this very evening. The journey from Pemberley back to Longbourn was five and sixty miles, too far to travel in one day, but very easy to complete in two, and there was no need for an early start in the morning. There would be plenty of time to converse at leisure tomorrow before their carriage was called.

The hum of conversation pulled Mary out of her reveries. Of course... she was back in the comfortable yellow drawing room, her tea growing cool at her elbow, Alexander still telling his old friend Elijah Meldola about Sarah's wedding and his mother and sisters back in Glasgow. Alexander glanced up at her and gave a quick smile. Had she fallen asleep? Had he noticed? They had their differences, she and he, but he was far too much of a gentleman to draw attention to her faux pas.

He now turned the subject to his days spent at Pemberley with Darcy and Elizabeth and the babe, allowing Mary to ease her way back into the conversation, and by the time she had told her new friends of the sweet young infant and her sister's glowing health and exultant joy, she was feeling very much back to full vigour. Those few moments of reverie had revived her completely.

Therefore, she was quite alert when, a few minutes later, the housekeeper Mrs. Graham bustled into the room, leading a rather distraught-looking man of middle years and the mannerisms of a valet.

"Barnaby!" Mr. Meldola exclaimed.

"Most dreadfully sorry to disturb you in such a rude manner." The man's accent was impeccable, his gestures perfect. But his voice and face were laden with a panic, which must surely explain his unbecoming intrusion into a man's private drawing room.

"Speak, please." Meldola rose from his seat.

"I have been seeking Mr. Bertram. He did not return to his rooms last night, and has not been seen in any of the…" He cleared his throat and reddened. "In any of the usual places. I hoped he might have taken some refuge here, as I know he sometimes does." His eyes pleaded with the two Meldolas.

"I am afraid I cannot help you," Mr. Meldola replied in a tight voice. "I have not seen him, nor heard word of him, in about six weeks, not since the last time he, er, requested a bed for the night."

Barnaby staggered to a chair and seemed about to collapse into it before remembering his status as a valet in the house of an esteemed merchant.

"Then I am most afraid," he choked, "that Tom Bertram has disappeared."

Alexander refrained from emitting a disgusted huff before his friends. He recalled this Bertram from his last visit here, six weeks or so before. What he had seen then did not recommend that man at all.

On the journey northward to Yorkshire, through the course of which he had escorted Mary to her sister and brother-in-law's estate at Pemberley, he had been invited to sit with the local merchants as they took their port and whisky and apprised each other of any unusual occurrences within the local markets. For an investigator, no tidbit of information is ever extraneous, and frankly, the matter interested him, and so he had accepted.

Part way through the evening there had come a crash at the door, and the clomping of boots upon the marble floors had heralded the entry of a tall, thin man. By the quality of his clothing, so well cut and of the finest fabrics, he was well-to-do. By the dandified style of it, he was more likely of the upper classes than this sedate and sensible group in Elijah Meldola's salon. But here any intimation of superiority ended, for he was clearly quite inebriated and in quite a bad state. The man's hair was dark and in considerable disarray, and he might have been handsome were his looks not so dissipated by ill living; There was no knowing what colour were his eyes, for no sooner had he entered than they fluttered closed and he reeled before landing against the door jamb.

"Framington," the intruder drawled as he struggled to keep his balance. "Did I see him come in? I need that silver, or at least a note. I need..." The words trailed off and he collapsed on the floor. The cause of his distress was obvious, even from across the room. Ale, by the smell that began to permeate the air, and a vast quantity of it, to be sure.

He was not yet unconscious, for even from his crumpled position he called for Meldola and had some words with the man, most of which were quite unintelligible. And yet, even slurred and garbled as they were in the man's besotted state, they were the tones of Quality.

How Alexander laughed to himself. This! This was Quality, this reeking, filthy, drunken excuse for a man. How his class would jeer at the company assembled in the salon, these fine upstanding citizens, whose hard work and industry allowed the toffs to live the luxurious lives they did. These men who strove forward with talent and sheer determination, whose children were leading the way to the future, sober, intelligent, educated. It was remarkable that the drunken gentleman even deigned to enter the abode of a mere merchant.

And yet, here he was. Alexander watched as Elijah Meldola straightened the man's limbs to prevent injury and rushed off, muttering about putting the blighter to bed.

"That's Thomas Bertram," one of the other merchants explained in a low voice. He had introduced himself as Jeremy Nathan, and was in attendance with his son Avery, a young man with bright eyes and a quick wit. Their vowels were a bit muddy, but the words crisp and clear, the eyes behind them sharp and honest. Genuine quality if one were to judge by character rather than birth, Alexander mused as Nathan continued his explanation. "Heir to the baronetcy at Mansfield Park, not ten miles from here." He tsked. "More's the pity. The current baronet is a decent sort, if standoffish. Son's quite a disappointment, I should think."

"Yes. So I see." Alexander's Scottish brogue seemed more out of place here than in London. He ignored his companion's raised eyebrows. "Is he like this often?"

"More so than he ought," the man replied. "He drinks and gambles away his father's wealth, and is as often found in Newmarket with the horses as he is at Mansfield, learning to manage the estate. There are rumours, all sorts of them, some quite unpleasant, and one never knows which might be based on truth. I suspect Bertram owes some unpleasant people a lot of blunt." The eyebrows waggled again, and this time not at Alexander's accent.

The conversation was interrupted by Meldola's return. "Apologies, friends," he announced to the room. "We're setting up a room for him. Framington, Nathan," Meldola gestured to Alexander's companion, "help me carry him upstairs, would you? My wife will arrange for someone to tend him there."

And that, six weeks ago, had been Alexander's introduction to Mr. Thomas Bertram, heir to the baronetcy seated at Mansfield Park.

Now this same man was missing.

"What do you mean, exactly, that Tom Bertram has disappeared?" Meldola asked the valet, for valet he must certainly be.

The man's next words confirmed Alexander's supposition.

"He was expected back after dinner last night. He had requested I set out his green coat, which he deemed to bring him luck at the tables." Barnaby reddened again. It was not quite done to confess the shortcomings of one's master, and especially not to do so before the lower classes. The valet cleared his throat and continued. "He was to dine with some friends from school—he did not inform me as to the particulars and it was not my place to ask— but I certainly expected him back by eight o'clock. When the clock chimed ten, I presumed he had found other arrangements, which he has done in the past. But he did not appear this morning, nor this afternoon, and nobody I have asked has seen him at all."

Alexander glanced at the clock on the mantel. It was about to chime six o'clock. "At what time did you last see him?"

Barnaby's eyes flashed towards him and Alexander recognised his mistake. He was not investigating a case; he was merely a guest in a friend's house, and the valet had no idea who he was.

"You are in luck, Barnaby," Meldola addressed the situation. "Our friend Mr. Lyons here makes his way in the world investigating exactly such instances. You may speak freely before him, and heed his questions, for he knows which ones to ask."

Barnaby's shoulders eased fractionally and he nodded. "Thank you, Mr. Meldola. Mr. Lyons." He furrowed his brow and then answered Alexander's question. "He was at his rooms to dress at four o'clock, and called for his chaise a half an hour later. Although this is a town, people keep country hours and dine early."

"Why did he not dress in his lucky coat before heading off to his friends to dine?"

The valet chewed his lip. "He never ate in his coat. He had decided it was only to be worn for gaming. It was something of an irrational superstition, but it is not my place to question him."

"Then he has been gone for over a day."

Barnaby nodded. "I sent a messenger to Mansfield. But I knew he had come here on occasion, when he needed sanctuary from those he had crossed. It was my last hope." His breathing was so shallow and rapid that Alexander feared the valet would swoon.

He caught his friend's eye, then glanced at the chair by Barnaby's side.

"Do sit down before you collapse, Barnaby," Meldola responded at once. "Hannah, I am certain the man would appreciate a cup of tea. Take a moment to catch your breath." The lady got up at once and prepared a cup, which she set at the valet's side. He swallowed it with a single gulp and his breathing calmed.

"I would beg you, if you don't mind, to write down all the places where Mr. Bertram might have gone." Alexander rose and walked the few paces to sit on the tall chair beside the one where Barnaby had crumpled. "Elijah, have you some paper and a pencil?"

His friend scurried off and returned in a few moments, setting the requested supplies on the escritoire that stood against the far wall. Barnaby struggled to his feet and crossed the distance to complete his task.

"If my friend Meldola does not object, Mr. Barnaby, I shall also have him send messages to all of his associates asking for news of your master. Are we to assume this is a sensitive matter? We must ask our questions, but I am certain Mr. Meldola will request discretion from those he asks." This was met with nods and grunts of approval from both men.

"Aye, that is fine, then. Do not worry yet, Mr. Barnaby. It is most likely that your master is sleeping off an overindulgence somewhere safe but unknown to us. Does he..." He glanced towards the ladies, and thought of how to phrase his question. "Does he have any particular, uh, friends or establishments he likes to frequent?"

"You may speak bluntly, Alexander," Hannah Meldola's calm voice cut through his fumbling. "I know of what you speak, and I would warrant that Miss Bennet does as well, no matter her youth and sheltered upbringing."

"I stand corrected, ma'am." Alexander returned to the valet and repeated his question with less careful language.

"I... I do not know... I do not believe so, but I am not privy to his activities when he is out of an evening. Some might confide such things to their valets, but he is not such a sort. I might have smelled perfume on his clothing from time to time, but any crowded ballroom or gaming house will provide such. I had wondered..." He stopped short and turned his attention most markedly to the blank sheets of paper before him.

"Finish your list, and Mr. Meldola will write his notes—we can all assist—and you can return to your rooms in the event that he returns as if nothing happened."

Barnaby spun his head around, taking note of the two women in the room for the first time.

"Both are most trustworthy, Barnaby," Meldola assured him.

The valet sighed and turned to his task, and departed shortly, somewhat less in a panic than when he had arrived.

"What will you do with his list?" Hannah Meldola asked when the front door had closed.

"I shall keep it for my information," Alexander smiled, "but the purpose was more to calm the man by giving him a task than for immediate use. But as for those messages, let us begin. Mary, we can talk of this later on; for now, let us begin our inquiries."

Chapter Two

A New Case

Morning broke cool and rainy. Alexander was pleased not to be in a hurry to depart the warm and welcoming house. In mid-October, such weather could be unpleasant for travel. They could tarry till noon, perhaps later, and still arrive at their destination before nightfall. Banishing all thoughts of a damp and draughty carriage, he turned his attention instead to the cup of steaming coffee before him.

"Sleep well?" Elijah Meldola spoke from the other side of the table where he sat with his tea, a plate of kippers, and yesterday's *Times*. Of all the benefits of living in London, the timely arrival of the newspaper was one which Alexander appreciated the most. Being accustomed to such, having to wait a day or more for the news would be a difficult adjustment to make.

"I slept well, I thank you. We were awake late enough writing out those messages. Have any responses arrived?" The clock had only minutes ago struck six o'clock, but merchants seldom had the luxury of slow mornings, and all work would cease by four in the afternoon, for the Sabbath was soon upon them. The question, therefore, was not unreasonable.

"None had arrived by the time we retired last night; I shall ask John if any have come since we sat down to our coffee." He called through the breakfast-room door to a servant, who glided in a few minutes later with a small stack of papers on a tray. Meldola perused the pile, mumbling names as he did so.

"Seven responses, of the twenty-three messages we wrote and dispatched, and before the sun is completely risen. My associates are an industrious lot." He passed half of the notes to Alexander and set about reading the other half himself.

Alexander pulled his notebook and pencil from a pocket in his coat and set about preparing a sheet to record the results. He was not engaged in this matter, but his habits were ingrained and had worked well for him thus far.

He wrote the date, October 15, 1813, at the top of the page, and then prepared two columns, one labelled *Name* and the other *Response*.

"If you wish, I can record the particulars whilst you read the notes." Mary Bennet's elegant tones contrasted coolly with the more earthy accents of Northamptonshire that otherwise surrounded him.

"Mary! I did not hear you enter. Good morning." Once more, his Scottish brogue marked him as separated by the widest gulf from the gentleman's daughter who was offering her services as his scribe. But this was Mary, and they had worked together in the past. Moreover, he knew she had a fine mind and a shrewd intellect, and any observations she might have would be valuable.

She settled herself at his side, closer, perhaps, than strict propriety allowed, and took his notebook. Alexander ignored Meldola's eyebrows, which threatened to disappear into his hairline. Taking turns, they read the names and responses, which Mary wrote in her careful hand.

Thompson, the mill owner, had no news of Tom Bertram, and had neither seen nor heard word of him since his unusual appearance at the gathering six weeks before. Framington, who had an interest in the canals, likewise had not seen Bertram the previous evening, but had heard from others that the gentleman owed a large amount of money to some unnamed person or persons. Harris, from the bank, had been approached for a loan, but had been unwilling to extend more credit without a surety from Bertram's father, who was unfortunately abroad in Antigua tending to his properties there, or failing that, from Tom's brother Edmund, who was managing the estate in Sir Thomas' absence. Edmund had refused. Harris, too, had seen nothing of Bertram last night.

By the time the initial pile of notes had been read and recorded, six more had arrived, and upon their completion, another five sat on the tray John brought into the room. Nobody had any news of Tom Bertram's whereabouts. Alexander let his eyes slip towards Mary, whose expression suggested she had expected nothing else. Neither had he. But this was a necessary step in the search, and it had to be done.

The more discreet message sent to the one brothel which Meldola knew about yielded a similar unsatisfactory result. There were surely others in town; that investigation would be left to others.

"It is nearly seven o'clock," Meldola sighed at last, "and I must prepare for my day. I have a shipment of spices due. I am afraid I shall not see you before your departure, my friend, and so I shall wish you a pleasant continuation of your journey..."

He did not continue his thought, however, for at that moment Mrs. Graham appeared at the door and announced the arrival of Mr. Edmund Bertram.

The gentleman who now entered bore such a resemblance to the missing man that he could only be his brother. Edmund, too, was tall and handsome, but without Tom's dissipated air. His hair was dark, his complexion fair. His clear brown eyes met them all with a steady regard, and Alexander would wager that the man had never overindulged in his life. There was little warmth emanating from the newcomer, but he carried with him an air of utter trustworthiness.

"Mr. Bertram," Meldola stood and bowed his head. "We are honoured by your presence."

"Sir." Edmund's voice was as steady as his eyes. Only the tic of his bottom lip suggested that he might be in any way concerned about something. "Please accept my apologies for intruding upon your private rooms, and at such an hour of this. I would never presume under most circumstances, but matters are such that I cannot be idle."

"Your brother?" Alexander spoke and Edmund gave him a curt brow.

"Indeed. You must be Mr. Lyons. It is to you that I have come to speak. Miss Bennet?" He looked at Mary and bowed more elegantly, allowing a smile to reach his lips, if not his eyes.

"That is correct, sir." She tilted her head. "How did you know?"

"I believe you must be included in my conversation with Mr. Lyons. I shall explain all."

Within a few moments, Mr. Edmund Bertram was seated with a cup of tea at his one hand and a plate of buttered fruit bread at his other, whereupon he began his speech. Meldola sent John with a message to his assistant at work explaining his delay, and he too settled back to hear the baronet's second son.

"I wish," Edmund announced, "to engage you to find my brother." He stopped and let his eyes settle upon Alexander, as if daring him to refuse.

When Alexander remained silent, Edmund continued. "You are not unknown to me. You did a great service to a former schoolmate last year when you saved the life of his wife. You must recall Mr. Elton, vicar at Highbury?"

Alexander nodded. How could one forget those frantic attempts to save a woman who was a hair's breadth away from succumbing to so dire a fate? It had been chance, more than anything else, that had brought him to her side at that moment. For months he had been haunted by the ghosts of what might have happened had he arrived just moments later...

"Recall Mr. Elton? Indeed I do," was all he managed to say. A similar event, just days later, had a much less fortunate outcome. That, too, haunted his sleepless nights.

Oblivious to Alexander's thoughts, Edmund Bertram continued. "Like Elton, I studied for the church, and am soon to take orders. Elton and I were not quite friends, for we saw the world in very different ways, but we were schoolmates and have kept up a correspondence. When Barnaby sent his message last night concerning my brother, he mentioned your names. Of course, I recalled what Elton had written, and hoping you were the same man of whom he had written, knew I must speak to you and implore you to consider this appeal. I shall, of course, meet your regular fees, and shall include a suitable gift for Miss Bennet from my own sisters. They are distraught and would be most glad of any assistance in returning their eldest brother to them."

Alexander saw Mary's mouth twitch into a smile. Edmund Bertram had executed his offer to perfection. He could not pay

Mary—a lady of gentle birth did not work for money—neither could he bestow upon her a gift himself. But a gift from his sisters would be acceptable, quite unexceptional even. He was a gentleman of good sense and very fine manners.

"Shall I leave you to confer?" Edmund began to rise, but Mary spoke before he achieved his feet.

"If Mr. Lyons wishes to take the case, I am certain my family will forgive my absence for a few days longer. However, I am loath to intrude upon Mr. and Mrs. Meldola's hospitality for more than the short time they had expected."

"To that, Miss Bennet, you need have no fear," Meldola offered. He had the expression of a man who dearly wished to laugh, but dare not. He most certainly did not look like a man anxious to return to his place of business. Alexander believed his friend was enjoying himself.

This hospitality was welcome; there were issues, however, which he could not raise at the moment. Later, he would speak with his friend, and then with Mary. That latter conversation was one he dreaded, and he determined to put it off for as long as possibly he could. A lump threatened in his throat at the thought, and he swallowed around it.

Instead, hoping for a reprieve from what he must say later, he turned to Edmund Bertram. "You have mentioned sisters; how many have you? Who else is at Mansfield Park?"

To his surprise, Mr. Bertram turned a rather unbecoming shade of red. Whatever could bring about this reaction? Alexander reached across the table for the notebook Mary had been using to record the replies to last night's notes and turned to a new page. "Everything you say will be held in the strictest confidence, Mr. Bertram. However, if you wish for my assistance in this matter, I must have information. If there is something you wish Miss Bennet not to hear..."

"No, no! Nothing like that." Mr. Bertram sputtered. "It is... that is, we are... Oh, dash it! We are engaged in preparing a theatrical performance"

"A play?" Mary's voice held the intimations of a suppressed chuckle. "But that is a fine endeavour. There is no need for concealment. At Longbourn, my family's estate in Hertfordshire, we often spend a winter's evening reading through *Hamlet* or *Lear* or one of the comedies, with the unsuitable sections removed, of course."

"Er, well, yes, Miss Bennet, but we have not chosen one of the Bard's plays, neither are we merely reading it, but acting it out like players on a stage. It is one matter for men to engage in such affairs, but my sisters... ladies! This borders on the disreputable."

"Surely there can be no harm in a simple amusement in the privacy of your house," Mr. Meldola soothed. "Reading, even acting out a scene, is hardly the same thing as setting yourself up as an actress on the public stage."

"There can surely be no harm," Mary added in her most prim voice, "in such a pastime, as long as one is not exposing himself to the eyes of the neighbourhood. Although acting can be seen as the entryway to less salutary pursuits, at home, with one's own family, there can be no danger."

Alexander could almost see her searching her mind for some quote from the sermons she used to read so assiduously.

Bertram cleared his throat and shifted in his chair. "Well, you see... Here is the problem. Tom, my brother, set off to invite some of our neighbours to come as an audience..." He ran a hand across his brow and cleared his throat again. "That is neither here nor there. You asked about Mansfield Park." His voice was steady and stoic once more.

He took a sip of his tea and spoke as Alexander scribbled his notes.

"My father is away in Antigua seeing to our holdings there. My mother remains at home, as do my two sisters. Maria is the elder of the two, Julia the younger. They are three and four years younger than me. I am five and twenty." He said this last as if admitting to some secret vital to the safety of the empire. "My aunt lives at Mansfield Park as well. She is my mother's sister, wife to our late vicar Mr. Norris. I was to have that living upon his death, but... circumstances intervened. Since his passing, Mrs. Norris has taken residence in the manor house."

"Very good." The pencil danced over the paper, recording all of these details for later contemplation. "Are there other residents at the moment?"

Edmund thought for a moment, lips pinched together. "There is myself, of course. Because I live at Mansfield, whereas Tom is more often in Town or at the races, or about the country with friends, I have taken over the management of the estate until our father returns.

"Tom arrived home from one such visit about two weeks ago. It was on the third of October, to be precise." Alexander made such a note. "He had been at a house party at Ecclesford in Cornwall, and he returned with one of his friends, John Yates. The honourable, I ought to say."

"Is Mr. Yates with your brother?"

"That would have relieved me, had it been so. Two men together are safer than one alone. No, Mr. Yates remains at Mansfield Park."

"His particulars?"

Edmund blinked. "I'm afraid I do not know. All he has spoken about since he arrived is this dashed play. The man is quite mad for theatre. His father is a baron, no one of any particular importance, from Cornwall. You shall have to ask him when you meet him."

"Very well." The pencil moved again. "Who else might I meet?"

"Down the lane, at the vicarage, are the Grants. He is the vicar now. Mrs. Grant has living with them her sister and brother, both of whom are also participating in our theatrical production. They are Mary and Henry Crawford. The Grants are hardly involved at all, but Miss and Mr. Crawford are quite often in the house."

"I see. And does that complete the list of inmates at the house?"

"Yes. Or rather," he expostulated, "no! I had quite forgotten about poor Fanny. My cousin, Miss Fanny Price."

Chapter Three

The Cast of Players

Edmund Bertram's carriage rolled down the long tree-lined drive and came to a stop before the imposing portico that guarded the massive front doors to the great country house of Mansfield Park. From the direction of the lane, which ran as straight as any Roman road, and through the curtained windows of the carriage, Mary had enjoyed little view of where they were going. The distance of eight or nine miles had been completed in about an hour, with Mansfield's team of fine horses pulling them along apace, and the scenery that had been available to Mary's eyes was lovely, even in the browning days of mid-October. But of the house itself, she had mere glimpses until the horses ceased their toil and the carriage door was flung open. Edmund murmured a word to them, then leapt from the conveyance and bounded down the stairs to command a servant to alert the housekeeper about his guests, leaving Alexander to hand Mary down from the coach. She allowed her hand to rest in his for a moment after she achieved the ground, taking confidence from his reassuring touch.

At last, she allowed her eyes to take in the grandeur that was Mansfield Park. She had thought Pemberley grand, and in many ways it was a more impressive building than was the building before her. But where Pemberley nestled into its environs, a natural outgrowth of the surrounding topography and as much an organic part of the landscape as the very trees that clung to the rocky hills, Mansfield Park seemed imposed upon the ground on which it sat. It spoke not so much of belonging to the land, as of the land belonging to it.

The house itself was not the Jacobean mansion Mary had expected, but rather it was a modern building, newly built on its site. If it housed the heart of an older structure, it was not visible from the drive. The front stretched across the lawns, with different sections breaking up the monolithic expanse. In the centre, a grand staircase swept upwards from the drive, through a phalanx of six Corinthian columns that soared heavenward to support a pediment above the portico. To the sides of this central block, vast wings promised elegant and well-appointed salons and parlours and ballrooms, with enough windows to keep the King's coffers full for many a month. At the distant end of each wing, another block arose in a smaller mirror of the centre. How far back the house extended, Mary could not discern from her current view, but proportion demanded an interior as grand as the outside. She imagined the house suitably large, a far cry from the modest country house of Longbourn, her own family's estate.

When, at last, her eyes had completed their survey of the yellow stone house and found the grand doors once more, it was to notice a young woman standing in the entry. As Edmund led them up the stairs, her features became clearer and clearer to Mary's eyes.

The young woman seemed to be about eighteen years of age—three years or so younger than Mary herself, perhaps Lydia's age, or a little older, but with none of her sister's girlish exuberance. She looked too well-dressed to be a servant, not grand enough to be one of the Bertram sisters, and far too young to be the housekeeper. Even at the distance, her face held every promise of gentle beauty, though held at bay by a need to stay hidden. This was a look Mary recognised.

As the small group reached the portico, the young lady dropped to a deep curtsy and spoke. "My aunt bid me come and welcome you to Mansfield Park." Her voice was sweet and soft, almost inaudible. Mary wondered if the girl had become so accustomed to not being heard that she had adopted such tones. Indeed, her entire demeanour, her shrinking posture, timorous expression, and simple clothing all bespoke a young woman more accustomed to being ignored than being seen.

Much like...

Mary blinked away the thought. She had enough of her own experiences of being passed over; only in the last year or two, since her older sisters married, had she found her voice and her place in society. She vowed to give all attention to this young woman.

"You must be Miss Price," Mary offered her most open and friendly smile.

The girl gave no response, but her expression spoke more clearly than words. To her side, Mary could see Edmund's look of amused wonderment and Alexander's proud smirk.

"Forgive me for my presumption. Mr. Bertram mentioned you, and there was nobody else in his account of the residents of the house that you could be."

Edmund flushed and cleared his throat and made the introductions before leading the small party to a comfortable and very beautiful parlour toward the back of the house. This room opened onto a great lawn that now was cold and brown, but which, in the spring and summer, must be glorious. Mary could envision a small canopy tent to protect the Bertram ladies' fine complexions as they took their tea out in the fresh air, the scent of roses from the manicured gardens to each side lending its fragrance to the warm summer breeze.

Edmund invited them to sit and called for coffee and cakes. Alexander stopped him with a raised hand. "I thank you for your gracious hospitality, Mr. Bertram, but we are not here to impose as guests. Whilst I would not refuse a cup of coffee, you have no need to entertain us. We are here to make our inquiries."

To her side, Mary could see another look of surprise upon Fanny Price's face. She even seemed about to speak, before closing her mouth with an almost audible snap. The girl would never be so bold as to ask the question which must be burning in her mind. Mary chose to answer it, regardless.

"I have," she turned to the timorous girl beside her, "been of some minor assistance to Mr. Lyons in his investigations in the past."

"Minor assistance!" Edmund fairly shouted. "My dear Fanny, allow me later to share what my former classmate Elton wrote to me about Miss Bennet. She is most capable, a most valuable asset to Mr. Lyons indeed. Why, Elton told me..."

Whatever Elton had told remained unexpressed, for at that moment the coffee tray was brought in by a colourless maid, a glamorous and very pretty young woman trailing behind her.

"Edmund? Company? And so early in the morning, and with Tom still not returned? What can you have been thinking? Oh, Fanny," the young lady added, her eyes alighting on the girl at last. "Aunt Norris was asking after you. Have you finished sewing the curtain hem yet?"

Fanny shifted as if to rise, but Edmund stayed her motions. "Our aunt and her curtain can wait. Finding Tom is of far greater importance. Julia, allow me to present to you Mr. Lyons and Miss Bennet, who have graciously offered to assist us in locating our brother." He turned to Mary and Alexander and continued the introductions. "My younger sister, Miss Julia Bertram."

Mary took a moment to examine the baronet's daughter. Edmund had given a very brief family history during their short journey and had explained his father's choice of wife some three decades before. Miss Ward, as Lady Bertram was at that time, had been a most inappropriate match, her family being of lesser means and no importance. Mary had assumed the man's choice had been made at least partly on the lady's loveliness, and seeing Julia, she understood Sir Thomas' reasons. Edmund was a handsome man, and Julia was exceedingly pretty. Unless Sir Thomas was an Adonis of his age, Lady Bertram must have been an unparalleled beauty in her youth.

She knew not exactly what to think of this, of selecting a wife on the basis of a lovely face alone. Her own father readily confessed to having been turned by her mother's high spirits and pretty face, and theirs was not a happy match. And yet, she could hardly begrudge her father's choice, else she would not exist. Rather, she hoped the Bertrams were better matched in temperament than her own parents, and resolved for the thousandth time that if ever she should marry, it would be to a man of sense rather than appealing looks.

Although, should such a man exist who would consider her for his bride, she would not object to a handsome face. Brown eyes tending to hazel in the sunlight would be fine, and an unfashionable but still attractive head of copper-red hair... Her eyes darted towards Alexander and she forced her thoughts back to Miss Julia Bertram.

The young woman wore a morning dress of excellent cut and obvious quality. The subtle ornaments and embellishments made a striking contrast to Fanny's work-a-day garment, or even Mary's simple frock. The dress, and the lady within it, seemed designed to show off this room to its greatest advantage, or perhaps it was the other way around. No matter the detail, they all seemed of a piece, elements of a greater whole.

Now that Edmund's sister had been informed as to the identities of the newcomers, her finely honed manners too were perfect for the company. Mary might be close to her rank as the daughter of a gentleman, but Alexander was a working man. He ought to be at the back door, not in this elegant room. Still, Julia greeted them as if they were royalty. "Miss Bennet, Mr. Lyons, you are most welcome. Thank you for your assistance. We are all most troubled about Tom. Coffee, Mr. Lyons? Sugar? No milk?" The latter clearly surprised her. Alexander made no comment, but thanked her as he took the cup and accepted a plate with a slice of buttered bread.

As Mary accepted her own coffee (with sugar and a lot of milk), Alexander began his casual interrogation. "Tell me about your brother, if you will."

Miss Julia paused. "Edmund has not already told you?"

"I would prefer your observations. Please be completely candid. I have no interest in spreading gossip and every interest in finding him. Absolute honesty is vital." He had retrieved his notebook and pencil from his pocket and prepared to write. Mary decided she really ought to equip herself likewise. She glanced down at her reticule and wondered what size notepad would fit comfortably therein. His pencil hovered over the paper in preparation to write as Julia began to speak.

"Candidly?" She looked to Edmund, who nodded his consent. "Very well. The truth is that I hardly know him anymore, and especially so since he returned from Antigua. He is so seldom at home, and when he is here, he is more often than not distracted with some plan or another. If not that, he is planning his next adventure."

"Tom is not known for his steadiness of character," Edmund interrupted. "If I may trust this to go no further—" he waited for his audience to nod their agreement "—I am concerned for the future of the estate."

"The local living was to be Edmund's," Julia rushed to add, "but such were the debts that Tom accumulated that father had to sell it. That is why Doctor Grant holds it now, and Edmund must do with Thornton Lacey."

"Julia!" Edmund's voice was scolding.

"Well, it is true, Edmund. If Tom was less extravagant and more restrained at the races and gaming tables, he would not have lost that fortune. I have heard you and Father talking when you thought the door was closed. It might not be a subject suitable for my ears, but it reached them nonetheless."

Edmund's face went white and then red. Mary did not need to ask if the story was true, for his visage told it all.

"What other habits does your brother have?" Alexander's pencil was poised above the paper to record the response, but Mary knew he had the answer already. They had both seen Tom Bertram falling down dead drunk at the Meldolas' house on their journey northward those several weeks before.

Edmund coughed and Julia flushed, but neither had a chance to speak.

"I say!" came a voice from the doorway, "Have you seen Tom anywhere? We were to talk about the hunt tomorrow, and I simply cannot find him. Is he not back yet? Or rather, still sleeping off last night's libations, eh what? I wonder where he went, for I hadn't seen him all day. Must have been a grand evening. Pity he did not invite me along. Pity."

The speaker sidled into the room and sat rather too close to Julia, who seemed uncertain whether to like it or not. He was, to Mary's eyes, the epitome of an overindulged nob. He was tall and lanky with a colourless, thin face and narrow chin, topped with straight blond hair and pale eyes that might have been blue or grey, depending on the light. He was dressed in the latest fashions from London with far too much embroidery for the country, and looked as if his valet had spent a considerable amount of time creating the appearance of casual nonchalance.

"Who are your friends?" he purred to Julia, who smiled and blushed before seeming to recall she was not supposed to like him.

Edmund quickly leapt to the introductions, presenting the gentleman as Mr. John Yates, one of Tom's friends and a guest at Mansfield Park.

"Mr. Lyons," he quickly explained to Yates, "is helping us to locate my brother, who seems to have gone missing."

"Missing, you say?" Yates tugged at his lower lip with his forefinger and thumb. "But I saw him only the other morning. He was setting off to Stoke to invite Maddox and Oliver to join our hunt tomorrow, and then to be audience for our attempt at play acting. I am to be Baron Wildenhaim, and Tom Bertram is Verdun, the baker. You must stay to watch our performance. Bertram was ever so delighted to perform the play here when our previous attempt was so sadly aborted. Sad of the grandmother to die like that. Most inconvenient."

"And Tom?" Edmund prompted.

"Right... Tom. When he was not back for dinner, I expected he had chosen to indulge with his friends and would ride back later. 'Tis only seven or eight miles from Northampton, I dare say, an easy journey in a carriage. It was only a sliver of moon, but the carriage was lit and the road broad and clear. I expected him to return last night."

"Did Mr. Bertram take the carriage?" Alexander's voice was light, but Mary saw the pencil hovering at the ready.

"Er, he might have. That is, I suppose it was possible, but, well, I do not rightly know. Cannot say, all that."

Alexander turned to Edmund, who clarified matters. "He did not take one of ours. They are all accounted for in the carriage house; I looked before I departed to meet you this morning. His horse is gone from the stables, though. It is eleven miles to Stoke, an easy enough ride. He has, in the past, left his horse there or in Northampton, and hired a carriage to return him home when he has been, er, less capable of riding."

By that, Mary surmised, he meant when his brother was too filled with drink to sit upright in the saddle.

"Have you sent messengers to his friends at Stoke?" The pencil flew over the notepad.

"I have. I expect a response within the hour."

Alexander stretched and narrowed his eyes. "I would like, if possible, to meet the other residents of the house. By then, I hope your message from Stoke will have arrived. Afterwards, if you will give me a description of your brother's horse and lend me another to ride, I shall return to Northampton to make my inquiries there."

Over the next hour, the remaining residents of the house were called into the parlour. Maria Bertram was, if anything, more beautiful than her younger sister, and more perfectly dressed. She batted her lashes at Alexander, but it was, to Mary's eyes, a gesture of habit rather than intention. Maria seemed to be a young woman who expected every man under fifty, single or not, to fall prostrate at her feet. That she sported upon her finger a ring set with a large sapphire surrounded by diamonds suggested that one of these men—and a wealthy one at that—had succumbed to her charms.

She was, so Yates informed them, to play Agatha, the wronged woman, in their chosen play.

Miss Bertram had little information to impart to Alexander, but her eyes darted around the room as she spoke and she chewed upon her pretty bottom lip. These might have been habitual affectations, but Mary wished to know more about this coquettish young woman.

The next to enter the room was the gentleman who wore Miss Bertram's noose. He was introduced as Mr. James Rushworth from a nearby estate. Mary quickly took his measure as a young man of considerable wealth and girth, and far less considerable intellect. He was part of the theatricals, taking the role of the scoundrel Count Cassel, and Edmund supplied that he stayed over at Mansfield Park more often than he returned the twelve miles to Sotherton at the end of the day. He was all pleasant of manner and amenable of intention, but he looked to his betrothed at every question, seeking the correct answer when there was none to be given. "So sorry, wish I could help. What's that? Bertram missing? But how could that be? For this is his house, and we were to put on a play! Gone since before yesterday? By gum. Missing? How very odd. Whatever should we do about it?" He paused. "Do we still hunt tomorrow, Edmund? I had so set my heart on it. I have sent for the hounds already; they do enjoy a good chase. Or ought we to wait for Tom? I would rather hunt."

As he spoke, Maria Bertram grew paler and paler and began to twist the large ring that marked their engagement. Her eyes darted more and more often towards the door to her right and the expanse of lawn past the windows to her left, and with every movement, Mary's questions burgeoned within her mind.

The only remaining residents of the house were Lady Bertram and her sister, Mrs. Norris. Lady Maria Bertram was, indeed, the beauty Mary had imagined her to be. Even after the passage of so many years as to have four adult children, she had the delicate features and freshness of complexion so as to appear more her children's sister than their mother. It was no wonder the Bertram siblings were so handsome. She was, however, vague and indolent, and seemed more concerned with her pugs than with her missing son.

Mrs. Norris was her sister's opposite in every way. Although handsome in her own right, her features were strong and her manner stronger. She was officious and bustling, and all but scolded Edmund for having the effrontery to engage an investigator in the search for Tom. She eyed Mary as if she were an unwelcome rat in the larder until Edmund made an obvious mention of her father's estate and her brother-in-law's great wealth. Perhaps to be related to the esteemed Mr. Darcy of Pemberley was the only thing that could instal her in the shrewd-eyed lady's good graces.

"'Tis only a pity," Miss Maria Bertram sighed as Alexander announced he must be off to Northampton soon, "that you should have to depart before meeting our neighbours. They are also in the play and are here almost the entire day as we rehearse our scenes."

"Neighbours?" Alexander raised his eyebrows. "Ah yes, your brother mentioned them. Mr. and Miss Crawford, if I recall. I should like to meet them."

"Mr. Bertram, sir, a message from Mr. Maddox," the butler announced from the doorway. Edmund leapt from his chair, followed by Alexander.

Mary now sat alone, surrounded by these strange and beautiful people who buzzed and chattered with an elegance she could never attain. She felt like a moth in a greenhouse full of butterflies, almost one of them, and yet separated by the greatest chasm. Only Miss Fanny Price, who had said not a word since Yates first entered, seemed of her species, and she gravitated towards the young lady. Mary sought some innocuous topic to coax the poor cousin into conversation and had managed to elicit a few words from her when Alexander and Edmund returned. Alexander beckoned her to join them at the doorway.

"Miss Bennet," Edmund bowed before her, "we would be honoured if you would grace our house with your presence until we locate my brother."

Alexander leaned close enough that his quiet words might not be overheard in the hum of conversation in the room. "He was not at Stoke. Maddox wrote that he arrived early on Wednesday, but departed shortly after noon, supposedly for Northampton. I would travel there too—to Stoke, that is—to speak with the two men, but they are expected at Mansfield Park later today to join in tomorrow's hunt. Stay here, Mary. You can be my eyes and ears. I have places to go in Northampton where I cannot take you, and I would benefit from your observations. Will you do it?"

She nodded quietly, despite her discomfort. She had been sufficiently uncomfortable last year when forced by circumstances to stay a week at Hartfield with Miss Emma Woodhouse. There it had only been the two of them, and the lady's elderly father who cared more for his digestion than the fripperies of society. To stay here, at Mansfield Park, with these glorious and alien creatures, would tax her to the limits of her being. She was about to beg a reprieve when she caught a glimpse of Fanny from the corner of her eye. Fanny Price was a young lady she could understand; perhaps she might befriend the girl. That alone gave her the strength to accede to Alexander's request. For him, and with the hope of a connection with Fanny, she would do it.

After a pause, in an audible voice, she replied to Edmund, "I thank you, sir, for your invitation. I would be delighted to accept."

Alexander grabbed her hands and gave them a squeeze. "Thank you, Mary. I know you'll learn something even if I don't."

At that moment, a hush settled over the parlour. Two figures could be seen walking across the lawn towards the house—a lady and a gentleman.

"How delightful!" Maria cried out. "They have come at last. They are the last two actors in our play. Come, Miss Bennet, our cast is complete. You must meet Miss and Mr. Crawford."

Chapter Four

The Investigation Begins

The horse Edmund had offered to Alexander was a calm and reliable beast, not the fastest in the stables, he was sure, nor the most handsome, but steady and calm and willing to take the commands of a new rider. "He'll see you to Northampton and back without complaint," Edmund had said as he gave the direction of a suitable stabling inn in the town.

As he rode, Alexander allowed his eyes to wander over the scenery, letting his mind work over the problem of Bertram's disappearance without his conscious contributions. The path wound through gently rolling countryside, sometimes open to view, boasting wide empty fields, the crop long since harvested, and sometimes obscured by trees and shrubbery that encroached close to the narrow lane. Here he passed a shepherd's lodge, there a church or a village or a bridge over a stream; it was pleasant countryside and would be quite beautiful in the greening days of spring or the lush growth of summer.

The journey took about an hour, and as promised, the horse was as strong at its conclusion as when they had set out. Alexander found the stable and, with Edmund Bertram's name and coin, ensured the beast would be well tended until his return.

The stables were only a short walk from The White Horse, the best inn in Northampton. Alexander had learned from Barnaby that this was where Bertram had taken a room, and it was here that his search would begin. The innkeeper, who gave his name as Houghton, eyed Alexander with a suspicious eye. He was quite unhappy at first at the request to see Bertram's room, and more so, it seemed, at Alexander's brogue, but once more a letter from Edmund Bertram and the flash of a coin made the proprietor more agreeable. The man led Alexander up a narrow flight of stairs and down a long passageway, and at last to a door at the very end of the hall.

"Best room we have." He narrowed his eyes at Alexander once more, but reached into an apron pocket and withdrew a key. "I run a respectable establishment 'ere," he scowled. "I'll stay and watch that you don't go off with somethin' not yours."

"A most reasonable request. I have no complaints. I have his brother's purse at my back and I do not need Mr. Bertram's leavings."

The innkeeper scowled again, but opened the door to let Alexander enter.

The room was clean and well proportioned, if unremarkable. This would be a pleasant place to break a journey if one had deep enough pockets for it. Aside from the expected furnishings, there was a reasonably sized sitting area, a separate room for bathing, and another room off to the side for a servant. A large window allowed ample sunlight to flood the space, reflecting off freshly painted pale yellow walls and dark polished furniture. This was clearly a room for the well-to-do.

Barnaby had unpacked Bertram's few belongings. Although only a short distance from his home at Mansfield, Bertram had clearly planned to spend at least one night in town. The wardrobe held a single change of clothing, and the dressing table showed off Bertram's shaving kit, each piece laid out with care. A quick look through drawers revealed nothing of note, other than that Bertram did not travel with a separate nightshirt. There was a bottle of spirits tucked into a valise, but this seemed nothing out of the ordinary. There were no papers, no scribbled notes, no half-crumpled notices or pieces of newspaper.

Alexander now moved back to the wardrobe to examine the clothing that hung therein. The innkeeper followed close behind. With slow and deliberate movements, so his guardian could see he meant no strange business, Alexander searched the coat, shirt, waistcoat, and riding breeches for pockets.

It was there, in a small pocket in the buckskin breeches, a small scrap with a name, freshly written.

"Who is Rollings?"

The innkeeper made a strange noise. "Eh! Don't like the sort of that one in my inn. This is a respectable establishment. 'E's not welcome here."

"Fair enough. I admire your standards. But would you please tell me who he is? If Mr. Bertram has his name written down, he might be of some assistance in locating the man."

"Owns the tavern down t'other side of the stables. There's rooms there too, but not the sort I'd want to stay at."

"A business rival?"

"Ptah!" the innkeeper spat. "Not by half. He draws a different sort than comes to this inn. I run a respectable establishment."

Hiding a chuckle, Alexander commented, "So you've said." He took a deep breath. "Lots of gaming there?"

"That's the one. And watered-down swill he serves too, but charges the full penny."

Alexander thought for a moment. "Is there anything counter to the law going on at Rollings' tavern?"

For the first time, the innkeeper's tone was not belligerent. "I've wondered myself about that. Nothin' I knows of for certain, but I don' like the types going in and out of there."

Alexander thanked the innkeeper for his time and gave him enough of Edmund's coin for another two nights so that the room would not be disturbed, and then set off for Rollings' unsavoury tavern.

Mr. Rollings, when Alexander introduced himself, was a genial man with a large middle and deep laugh. In his years of professional investigation, Alexander had learned never to assume a man's appearance would match his character or occupation, but he was nonetheless caught by surprise at the amiable manner and pleasant face that made up the questionable Rollings, especially after Houghton's warning.

The tavern keeper's bright eyes fairly twinkled as he spoke. "Yes, yes, of course. Tom Bertram. Come into my little office. Much more comfortable there to sit. Ale? No, you're on a case, I see. I'll call for tea, or would you prefer coffee? Bread and cheese? Be just a moment!"

And as promised, within a few minutes Alexander was settled in a small and shabby but comfortable chair in an equally small, shabby and comfortable office, with a pot of fragrant tea balanced atop a pile of documents and ledger books, and a slab of fresh bread with a hunk of sharp cheese on a tin plate at his side. He took out his notebook and scribbled as the tavern owner spoke.

"Bertram, eh?" Rolling repeated the name as he poured the tea into two incongruously delicate china cups. "Sugar? Bertram was a familiar face here for a time before he went to wherever it was with Sir Thomas. Barbuda? Jamaica? One of those places. I've heard the names enough, though I couldn't find them on a map. Sugar islands, they are."

"Antigua, I believe."

"Yes, yes, that's it! He kept me in business, that he did. The boy liked his ale, and I was not one to refuse his business."

"Did he wager at the tables?"

"What one of them doesn't? He won atimes, lost too. Always made good on his debts. I don't know what you've heard of me, but I keep an eye on the goings-on. We don't cater to the nobs, but I keep my nose clean. I won't let the stakes rise too high. A bit of sport is good for entertaining the lads, and good for business, but too much does no one good."

Alexander felt himself warming to the man and strove to keep his tone professional, lest he end the day taking the fellow out for a drink. "If a man were to lose a great deal of blunt—say, enough to cause his father considerable embarrassment and force him to dispose of some family property—where, then, might he have done so?"

"That would be at some private table, I'm guessing. Plenty of them around if you run in those circles. Or the races. Off in Newmarket, you won't believe what these toffs drop on the horses."

"Any names you might have for me?"

The man shook his head. "None, as I recall. I'll think, though."

Alexander reached into his pocket and drew out the scrap of paper. "I found this. Have you seen Tom Bertram of late? Have you any notion why he might have your name in his pocket if he knew your establishment of old?"

Rollings pursed his lips and wrinkled his nose. "Seems odd, that it does. Might it be meant for another?" He scratched at the side of his neck. "Or perhaps someone might not have known we've been acquainted and thought to send him here."

Alexander nodded. He had considered these possibilities as well. Then Rollings surprised him.

"But you asked if I've seen Bertram of late. That I have. He hasn't been around much since his return to these parts—busy with some business back at the manor, theatricals the rumours say—but he stopped in a while back for a drink and a gab. A month ago, maybe two? Asked if he could take a room for a few hours. No, no, not for that, for he was quite alone. He was avoiding someone and asked me to deny I'd seen him.

"Two fellers did come by asking after him as well. Well dressed, spoke like toffs, lots of fancy posh O's and fancier words. They said they were only looking to talk to him, but I sent them on their way, regardless."

Alexander's pencil stopped in mid-air. "Two men looking for him? Can you recall, more exactly, when this might have been?"

Rollings scratched himself again. "Let me think... 'Twas the first time I'd seen Bertram since his return; he's been scurrying all over the country from what I hear. Let me look..."

He moved the tea pot and extracted a ledger from the pile, seemingly at random, and scowled at columns of figures that to Alexander's eyes were a mess of illiterate scribblings. Once more, appearances were deceiving. Rollings stopped his finger on a single line of blotted black ink. "There. September the second. Six weeks past. Paid in coin for the room, he did, and not on credit as his type like to do. That's one reason I don't like them here. All that blunt, but can't remember to pay their debts. I'm happy for my bad reputation if it keeps that sort away."

Alexander stifled a snort of laughter. He had met a number of 'that sort' in his own line of business. The date was interesting, however, for that was almost exactly when he had been in town on his way northward, and had seen Bertram rush into Meldola's house, falling down with drink and escaping creditors. He made another note in his book.

"Can you recall what these men looked like?"

"Can't say they were much out of the ordinary. Well dressed, as I said, well spoken. Neither young nor old, but maybe on the younger side, between thirty and forty, I'd say. One was shorter than the other, but that goes for all of us in groups, don' it? Let me think. One—the taller one, though he wasn't so tall as a man would take note of it—was lighter in colouring than his friend. Just going blond from brown. I don't recall his eyes. The other was brown-haired, but again, nothing unusual. No scars that I saw, nor anything one of your Bow Street Runners would mark as special. Sorry I'm not of more help."

"That is more than I expected." Alexander made his last scratches in his notebook.

"They didn't stay here, I can tell you that much. Go back to Houghton at The White Horse. He might be able to tell you if they stayed there."

At last, his teacup empty and his page of notes full, Alexander thanked Rollings for his assistance and promised to come back for an ale before departing the town for London.

Mary sat alone in her room at Mansfield Park, writing her impressions down on the paper that Edmund Bertram had provided for her. This had been Fanny's room, tucked up at the top of the stairs as it was, near the nursery and the old school rooms. She had been offered something more elegant in the guest wing, near the room that Mr. Rushworth used when he did not return to Sotherton, but when Fanny, with tentative gestures and almost inaudible words, suggested that Mary look at the nursery room, she could hardly say no. And, to everyone's surprise, she had opted to take this as her accommodation during her stay.

The room was simply furnished, but it was clean and bright, with large windows and a selection of books on a bank of low shelves that sat across from the fireplace. Sunlight brightened the space, and the desk at the window, where Fanny had almost certainly written her own volumes of notes and letters, was perfect for Mary's purpose. Moreover, the room was quiet, being distant from the family's quarters, and it allowed her the privacy she required to collect her thoughts and gather her energy after a day in new company.

The fire now burned at her back, warming the space, and the autumn sun added its rays to the desk as she prepared the paper like she had seen Alexander do so many times.

Henry Crawford.

She wrote his name at the top of the page and began to record her impressions.

Henry and his sister Mary had appeared moments after Alexander had taken his leave. They had been the couple seen walking across the lawns arm in arm, a picture of bucolic elegance. In this, as in every gesture, they seemed aware of the image they presented and moved so as to display themselves to the very best advantage. Mr. Yates might have been the enthusiast and instigator of all matters theatrical, but Henry Crawford was by far the most natural in the execution of the art.

He was, in person, not so much handsome as profoundly appealing. With so charming a manner, any faults in his features must soon disappear, thereby to make him seem the handsomest man in England. He had entered the room and stopped at once upon seeing a new face, before demanding an introduction.

"Miss Bennet." He bowed low and kissed her hand like a chevalier from the ancient French court. "What is this that Edmund Bertram has done? But he has brought into our presence a beautiful and delightful young lady, a veritable rose into our blossoming greenhouse. Ha! You must forgive me, Miss Bennet, but I am all full of theatre and poetry, and you draw it forth from me. Look, Mary," he called to his sister, "a namesake of yours, and just as lovely. Two beautiful Marys in one room, and a beautiful Maria. What wonderful fortune."

To her chagrin, Mary blushed.

Having dispensed of these inanities, Henry Crawford laughed at himself and proceeded to sit by Mary's side and had with her a most pleasant and unaffected conversation. He inquired as to her presence in the neighbourhood, and upon being told she was returning from a visit to her sister and new nephew, he asked with all graciousness about the babe, his size and weight, the health of his mother, and the pleasantness of the journey thus far.

He and Miss Crawford, he explained, were enjoying the hospitality of their sister Mrs. Grant, whose husband held the living at the village church. "Mary—let us call her by her two given names of Mary Kate whilst in your company—prefers her sister's companionship to that of our uncle in Town," he smiled, "and I find the company here far preferable to that at my own estate of Everingham, which lies in Norfolk.

"Miss Bennet's companion, who is accompanying her on her return to her home in Hertfordshire, is helping us look for Tom." Edmund brought a cup of coffee to Henry and inserted himself into the conversation.

"Your brother is still not home?" Henry exhaled through clenched teeth, making a light whistling sound. "We all thought he would be back during the night. No signs of a fall from his horse on the road? It was dark last night. You have been into the village?" He gestured out the window, the way he and his sister had come. That must be where the village of Mansfield was. "And what about the town?"

Edmund sighed. "I have searched Northampton to the best of my ability; I feel quite ill at my present indolence, sitting here at tea as if nothing were wrong. But I cannot think what else I might do. I could revisit the same people and the same taverns, but I would receive the same information I had before, namely nothing. This is quite beyond me. I do not know what Mr. Lyons might do that I cannot, but he may well have avenues to follow that I cannot think of. He is now making the attempt where I have failed." He fell backwards into the cushions of his chair in utter despair. "Tom has never done anything like this before—not told Barnaby of his whereabouts, and just not come home."

Henry Crawford studied his cup of coffee. "Might he not have gone into Northampton at all? He would not have gone on to Newmarket instead, would he? I know nothing of the races, but if there is one drawing close..."

Edmund sat up straight. "I had not considered that Tom might have made for Newmarket. It would be unlike him, but I have long since stopped trying to understand his mind. But... but he would have to pass by the Wellingborough Turnpike were he to have done so. The man at the toll house knows him and would recognise him. I shall send a man immediately to inquire."

He leapt from his seat and ran from the room, leaving Mary and Henry Crawford together on the settee.

"I say," Mr. Rushworth wandered over, "You don't think we will have to cancel tomorrow's hunt, do you? That would be a pity. I had so hoped to ride after some fox with my hounds. I even have my new green coat that I had made for such occasions. It turns out it is exactly the colour of Bertram's, for my valet nearly confused the two when he took it below to dust and press. I can see my face in the brass buttons, and my boots are polished to a shine! I really should like to hunt some fox. I have sent for my hounds and all."

The man seemed more concerned about his clothing and the hunt than his betrothed's missing brother. Neither did he seem too concerned about Maria, nor she, from what Mary could see, him. Maria sat talking to Mr. Yates and Julia, casting the occasional glance in Mary's own direction, but not at the man she was to marry. This would prove an interesting matter to puzzle out.

"Really, Mr. Rushworth," the velvet sweet voice of Miss Mary Kate Crawford sounded from behind, "I am quite certain the others will make the best decision about the hunt. But I see no reason for it not to proceed as planned. If Mr. Bertram is here, he may join us. And if he is not, I see no reason for everybody to sit around staring stupidly at each other. A lack of occupation will hardly hasten his return. We had much better be entertained, and you may then regale us with tales of your adventure upon your return." She tossed a coquettish smile at Rushworth, who mumbled something unintelligible in reply.

"Now move along, Henry," she continued. "I have not had the opportunity to talk with Miss Bennet, and I shall not have you commanding all of her attention. Go, both of you." And just like that, she shooed the two men off with her pretty embroidered shawl and took her brother's seat next to Mary.

Now, in the bright sunlight of the nursery floor room, Mary blinked her eyes at the memories and finished her notes on Mr. Crawford. In her general comments, she wrote, *he is a flirt; pays more attention to Miss Bertram than perhaps he ought, seems always to seek every lady's attention.*

As charming as he was, it was no difficult feat to sketch his character.

Now Mary began a new section of her notes—*Mary Kate Crawford*—and set about to record everything she could recall.

If Henry were deemed handsome by means of his charm, his sister grew more charming because of her beauty. Even without her arch manner and sparkling wit, Miss Crawford must be considered very pretty, prettier even than the two lovely Miss Bertrams. In her presence, Mary no longer felt a moth in a garden of butterflies, but a lowly worm, not even able to fly. Why Miss Crawford chose to oust her brother and Mr. Rushworth from their seats in order to talk with her, Mary could not fathom. Perhaps she, too, craved the attention of a new acquaintance. Regardless, Mary had determined to learn what she could from the party at Mansfield Park, and consequently she had found her own polite smile that she donned in company and encouraged Miss Crawford's conversation.

"I do so enjoy meeting new people," Miss Crawford had announced as she settled herself onto the settee. "When one is consistently in the same company, even the most charming people can grow tiresome. A new face, or a new activity, such as our play, or a new flirtation is so dearly cherished, for this brings the variety that colours our every thought."

At the word "flirtation," Miss Crawford's eyes had flickered to the gathering near the doorway, but then returned to Mary with a shimmer of disappointment. Who could she have set her cap at? Surely not Rushworth. That left only one of the Bertram brothers. Mary determined to discover more as her visit progressed.

"And now," Miss Crawford's voice grew light and teasing once more, "we may have all three! Tell me, Miss Bennet, is your companion very handsome? I have heard talk about the investigator, but none can describe him. It seems quite unusual that a gentlewoman of your youth should be travelling only in company with a single man, and of the middle classes at that. I long to hear your story." She shifted closer to Mary on the settee, inviting her confidence. For a moment, Mary felt herself to be back with her dear sister Lizzy, for such was her new acquaintance's bright and teasing manner.

"I do travel with my maid—" Mary began.

"Well, of course!" came the reply. "I should never suspect anything improper. But do tell me of Mr. Lyons, for I believe that is his name. Is he handsome?"

For some reason that she could not name, Mary wished to keep some part of Alexander only to herself, so she answered circumspectly. "Some may say so, I suppose. He is, at once, ordinary and very pleasant to look upon. If a man may be handsome without being particularly striking in appearance, then perhaps he is. It is only his hair that stays in the memory."

"His hair?" Miss Crawford leaned closer still.

"It is dark orange, quite a striking copper in colour," Mary explained, "in the manner, I suppose, of so many Scots, although other than him, I have known almost none."

"Oh no!" The disappointed look on Miss Crawford's face was almost comical. "I could never fancy a red-headed man. There is something not very serious about a man whose hair is neither blond nor brown nor white. I'm afraid I shall not be able to flirt with him at all."

Chapter Five

A-Hunting We Shall Go

When Mary came down from her room for tea, she was surprised to see Alexander in the parlour talking with Edmund. She had imagined he would conduct his inquiries in the town and spend the night at the home of Mr. Meldola. He anticipated her question, for he answered it before she could open her mouth.

"I learned everything I could in Northampton. I shall tell the both of you in good time. Mr. Bertram has been patient enough to await your arrival, so I need tell it only once. I have also accepted a room here this evening; I shall relieve my friends of the burden of my company for this one night."

"The study?" Edmund asked. His eyes moved to the hallway at Mary's back.

Alexander nodded. "It might be best."

Mary nodded once. What he had to say, then, he did not wish overheard by others in the house.

Edmund led them through two sets of doors and into a room in a curious state of disarray. The furniture was all moved to the back and sides of the room, leaving the centre empty, with an odd assortment of objects and half-painted screens scattered around. At the far end, and through an incongruous fall of heavy green fabric, was another set of double doors, towards which Edmund made his way.

"The play," he apologised as he gestured about the room. "This is where we have been rehearsing and preparing the sets. It is… It is not what we are wont to do, what we have ever done before. Tom and Yates were so insistent…" He broke off and pinched his lips together.

"Through here." He opened the curtained doors. "This will be the stage, past the curtain. It is Father's study, but I have been working here to maintain the estates in his absence. Let me lock the doors, and we will have some privacy. One moment, first." He walked to another door and called for a tray, then closed it behind him.

The three sat and Alexander began his account without waiting for an invitation. "My first stop was the inn, where I examined Mr. Thomas Bertram's rooms…"

He spoke at length, describing both his findings at the inn and then, afterwards, at the tavern.

Edmund chuckled as he described Mr. Rollings. "He is all bark and no bite, as far as reputation is concerned. I would prefer an evening in his company than in Houghton's, to be certain."

Alexander agreed with a laugh and continued his account. "As Rollings suggested, I returned to the inn to inquire of Houghton whether he knew these two men who were seeking your brother. They had indeed stayed the night in his establishment, but the names they gave were Mr. Jones and Mr. Smith. We shall find no joy there. Neither could he give a better description than Rollings could. However, their trunks were labelled with their addresses in London, which Houghton considerately inscribed into his rolls, and I have sent a messenger to my associates in Town to conduct that line of inquiry." He paused as a maid brought in a tray with cold lemonade and biscuits. "Neither Rollings nor Houghton, however, had the sense that these were desperate men. That they wished to find your brother was certain, but they likewise seemed content to await him or return another time. Houghton thought they might have mentioned returning in mid-October…"

"Which," Mary interjected, "is now."

"So it is. And coincidentally, the man they sought has vanished."

There was not much more to discuss. Mary wished to pass her observations along to her friend, but she had no desire to do so in Edmund's presence. One cannot speak freely about a man's family and friends whilst in his company, after all. When she said nothing, Alexander smiled and murmured in an offhand manner, "Perhaps, Mary, you might help me transcribe these notes later, if Mr. Bertram can spare a space on a desk somewhere." He wished to speak in private.

"I will be pleased to help."

How well they understood each other! But for the time being, they must return with Edmund to the parlour. Alexander might be a paid agent, but Mary was a guest and must pay for the kind hospitality she had been offered with pleasant conversation. She and Alexander would talk about the case later.

When they returned to the parlour, the room was full. Maria Bertram was presiding at the tea trolley with Rushworth hovering at her one side and Henry Crawford at her other. The expression on Crawford's face implied he knew exactly what he was about, and the expression upon Rushworth's suggested he had not the first notion. By Maria's smirk, Mary suspected she was fully aware of the situation and was quite satisfied with it.

Julia Bertram sat on one sofa with Mr. Yates hanging on her every word. Across from her, her mother and aunt sat surveying the room, one with a complacent daze on her sweet face, the other seeming to look only to find fault. The fifth person in this small gathering was Miss Crawford, who looked up with a great smile as Mary and the two men entered the room. She rose from her chair and walked over towards them.

"Miss Bennet, Mr. Bertram." She smiled at Edmund, and Mary understood all. "And this must be the renowned Mr. Lyons. Do introduce me, please, so I may command all his attention. One of the things I miss about London is the chance to be admired afresh each day." With her beautiful and impertinent smile, how could she not be?

She did not wait for an introduction, but continued her charmingly inappropriate speech.

"Come sit awhile by me, gentlemen. Mr. Lyons, I do hope you have some interesting news from London for my poor starved ears. Since I left the house of my uncle, the admiral, I have had to rely upon Henry and those friends who remember me for my gossip, for my uncle and his... companion so seldom write."

With that, she grabbed Edmund's left elbow with one hand and Alexander's right with the other, and in her swaying walk led them both to a heretofore unoccupied grouping of chairs near the window, beckoning Mary to follow. This she very nearly did, until she noticed, sitting alone on a chair along the far side of the room, the last member of this party, Miss Fanny Price.

Poor Fanny. Once more, Mary felt a kinship with this girl, almost a part of the family and yet so neglected. Even the Crawfords looked more at home in this graceful parlour than did the young woman who had lived here for the last ten years. Mary moved to Fanny's side. "Miss Price, may I bring you a cup of tea?"

Fanny blinked and looked around her for a moment. Seeming to accept that there was no other Miss Price behind her, and still looking quite taken aback at having been spoken to, she nodded her acceptance.

"Thank you, Miss Bennet. Please sit, and I shall go."

"Nonsense," Mary smiled at her. "You are already seated and I am not. I shall return in a moment." This she did, balancing two saucers with their delicate teacups atop and a small plate of iced biscuits, which she placed on the small table at Fanny's side. Fanny still looked stunned at being the focus of somebody's attention. This feeling Mary knew well, for until not so long before, she too had been the forgotten sibling, seeming to fade into invisibility in the middle of a room of people.

"What have you been reading?" Mary nodded at the book on the chair at Fanny's side.

The young woman picked it up and Mary read the title. It was Thomas Gisborne's *Enquiry into the Duties of the Female Sex.*

"Are you a reader of books on moral improvement?" This was a book that Mary herself had read through many times in her younger days. When, she wondered, had she put such volumes aside? She used to have sermons and guides to spiritual improvement at hand wherever she went, but as for her personal copy of this title, she could not now even recall where she had last seen it. "I was once a great reader of Fordyce's *Sermons for Young Women.* I found his admonishments..." What had she found them? At the time, they formed the scaffolding upon which she had based her ill-formed opinions. She had not given up the pursuit of a moral and introspective life, but upon reflection, perhaps Fordyce had been overly dogmatic in some areas. She strove to finish her sentence, and eventually concluded with, "Instructional."

Miss Price seemed not to have noticed her hesitation, and spoke with quiet enthusiasm, if a habitual reserve of words, on her particular choice. "I find," she stated at last, "that I am often torn between doing what is asked of me and what is right. I am here upon my uncle's sufferance and do wish to be helpful and not a burden to the family, but there are times when I feel…" her voice dropped, and she continued with more suppressed emotion than Mary would have imagined her capable of, "…when I feel otherwise, when duty and integrity are at war."

Mary recalled that other than her aunt, Fanny was the one person not somehow involved in the play, and the girl's expression from their first discussion thereof came once more to mind. "These theatricals, for example?"

The meek and demur girl was back. "Yes. There are many circumstances which might make a private endeavour acceptable, but with my uncle overseas, and without his approval, it all seems so very wrong, as if we were toying with the edges of something almost immoral."

Mary would consider this more later. For now, she wished to put her investigation aside and further her desire to befriend Fanny, who reminded her so much of herself.

"How long have you lived at Mansfield Park?" she asked. "If you care to tell me of your life here, I would be pleased to hear it." She knew the broad strokes of Fanny's life, but wished to draw the girl out and possibly learn something new.

Once more Fanny gazed up at her with round eyes. She was unaccustomed to attention, and hesitantly, at first, but with growing animation, began her tale.

She spoke of her mother who had married beneath her to a marine lieutenant, now on half-pay, of her great number of siblings, of her arrival at the great house at the tender age of nine years, and of how she missed her older brother William, who was at sea.

"When first I came here, I knew nothing and my cousins would tease me for it, all but Edmund, who was so kind. He was the one who brought me paper and pens, so I might write to William, and he was the one who was my only friend. All through the years," she looked up towards Edmund, "he has been the one person who has never teased or belittled or cast me down." She sighed and looked up again. That look in her eyes was not one of familial adoration.

Oh... There was more going on under the polite surface at Mansfield Park than Mary would have imagined!

Her musings were interrupted by the arrival of Baddeley, the butler, at the parlour door. "Mr. Charles Maddox and Mr. Thomas Oliver."

Two gentlemen entered. Both were well but informally dressed, and both seemed familiar with the house and family alike. One—whom Mary later discerned was Maddox—was of medium height with dark hair and eyes, and looked a year or two shy of thirty. The other—Oliver, she discovered—was short and stocky and very blond with that pink complexion that must go very red with exposure to spirits or to the sun. He looked a year or two older than Edmund, about Tom Bertram's age. These had been the two men Tom had gone off to meet on the day he vanished, and they were here now both to enjoy some of the preparation for the theatricals, as well as to join in tomorrow's hunt.

Edmund was expecting them, for he hurried forward to greet them. "Oliver, Maddox." he shook their hands with a good-natured smile. They responded in turn, and were brought around the room to be introduced to Alexander and herself.

The groupings now inevitably changed around, and Mary had no more private conversation with Fanny, who retreated once more into her book. Had she, herself, been like this, striving more to avoid company than to accept it, and then feeling spurned when she was ignored? Perhaps, if she and Fanny both had made a bit more effort to enter into society, society would not have been so complacent about ignoring them.

The following morning the household arose early, far earlier, Mary suspected, than was its wont. Today was the hunt, which had been so anticipated, and which even the continued and mysterious absence of Tom Bertram could not postpone. Whilst the men would later ride for a time and then have breakfast in the fields near where a farmer had spotted a foxes' den, they were gathered in the breakfast room when Mary descended from her chamber, taking their early morning coffee and sweet buns.

None of the other women was awake as of yet, or at least, none had decided to take tea outside of her chambers. But Yates and Henry Crawford were talking together on one side near the sideboard, and the trio of Rushworth, Maddox, and Oliver were gathered on the other by the windows. The room was abuzz with excitement.

Foxes... the hounds are ready... my horse... fine weather... The words darted about the space as a swarm of bees, brushing past Mary's ears.

Alexander sat conferring with Edmund at the far end of the table, and Mary went to join them.

"We still have no word of Tom," Edmund replied to her query and rubbed the bridge of his aristocratic nose. "There is still no word from the toll booth, nor any from my acquaintances in Northampton."

"And the hunt?" Mary asked.

"Will proceed. These fellows would have nothing else. Miss Crawford is correct, I suppose, in that occupation is preferable to idling about the house staring at each other, but it seems wrong."

"Have you decided whether to join them?" Alexander asked the question Mary had been thinking.

"I imagine I rather must. Without Tom here, it would be improper to send them off across our land without a host." Now that Mary looked, she saw that Edmund, like the other men, was dressed in suitable attire for the event.

"My hounds have come by cart, and we shall ride with them. And then, perhaps, later this week we can shoot pheasant." Mr. Rushworth's voice came from across the room. "Do I have your permission, Bertram?" he called to Edmund. "I should so like to shoot some pheasant. You may hunt my birds next month if you wish; we can arrange a visit to Sotherton once our play-acting is over, and then you may shoot my birds, or stalk some deer."

Edmund nodded his agreement. "A gracious offer; we shall organise matters after we return, once we have our foxes."

"Excellent! I am right pleased. I wish to shoot pheasant. But today we shall ride after fox, and I am most pleased. I have not yet ridden out in my new hunting coat, and look forward to it. See how the buttons shine." He preened and puffed out his chest. The buttons, all brass rather than usual cloth-covered items, did indeed gleam in the morning light. How long had his valet spent polishing them? And all for a day out in the thickets, to return covered in dust and sweat and mud.

"And you, Lyons?" Edmund asked. "Will you join us on our ride?"

"I thank you, but no. I am not your guest, but your agent, and I have some more inquiries to make. If I may take the same beast as yesterday, I will ride out to as many of the other toll booths as I can to ask after your brother. Do they all know him? Have you a small portrait I can show?"

Edmund nodded and put a word in a footman's ear, who then disappeared to complete his assigned task.

Before long, the men were all ready to depart, the hunters in search of a fox, and Alexander still in search of some word of Tom Bertram. "We shall talk later, Mary," he had whispered to her before departing for the stables. They had not had the opportunity to talk the previous evening, despite their tacit plans. Today, upon his return, they would try once more. And then, as quickly as the noise of excitement had overflowed from the breakfast room to the hallway to the back door leading to the stables, the noise vanished, leaving Mary in a well of silence, and feeling strangely forlorn.

She found the library, which was off the room which had been cleared as rehearsal space for the play, then took her chosen book to the parlour. She selected a comfortable seat near the large glass doors that overlooked the wide lawn and gazed outside for a moment before reading. Past shaped hedges and manicured shrubs and the stand of trees at the far end, she could see the spire of the church. That must be the village, and the residence of the Grants, who were the Crawfords' sister and brother-in-law. The walk must be no more than ten minutes, a comfortable distance at any time of year. Why her thoughts tended towards the Crawford siblings she knew not, but allowed them a moment to wander as she surveyed the pleasant scenery.

Struck with a sudden whim of fancy, she laid down the book and went in search of her cloak and bonnet, and armed with a set of directions from the housekeeper, pointed her feet towards the village. Mansfield was very much as she had expected it to be. There was a church, a general store, a blacksmith, a tavern, and all the expected shopfronts. The smell of baking bread drew Mary around a corner, and when she emerged a few minutes later with a fragrant pastry in her hand, she continued walking down that same lane.

"Miss Bennet." She was startled to hear her name called, here in the place where she knew nobody, but of course, that was not quite true. For there, at the gate to a neat stone house, was Miss Mary Kate Crawford. "Have you come for a walk? And a lovely day it is for it too. How fine for the men to enjoy their hunt. Come in and have a spot of tea. You must meet my sister! Do come. I shall be ever so put out if you do not."

Within moments, Mary was sitting in a small but comfortable salon, which was occupied largely by a magnificent harp positioned perfectly so as to be seen through the window. Mrs. Grant, who was Miss Crawford's half-sister and the parson's wife, was fussing over her like a newborn babe. Was her tea too cool? Too hot? Had she found the walk tolerable? The weather too windy? The sun too strong? Or not strong enough? Of an amiable disposition, but not given to restraint, Mrs. Grant spoke on at length as thoughts crossed her mind.

"How lovely to have new company! It is this past summer that my sister came here to live with us—it was just early July, was it not, Mary?—and how Dr. Grant and I have enjoyed it. When Henry is with us, which he is more often than not, it seems, we are a merry party indeed. But my sister and brother spend so much time at the Park that at times, it seems they hardly stay here at all.

"Why, when Mary first arrived, she quite had her sights set on Mr. Bertram—that's Sir Thomas' eldest son, of course—for what could be better for my sister than to be the wife of a baronet?"

"Now Anne," Miss Crawford admonished, but Mrs. Grant brushed away the half-hearted complaint with the sweep of a hand.

"'Tis but truth, Mary, and no shame in it. Moreover, you showed your character when you settled your hopes instead on another, *whom I shall not name*, whose manner was more suited to your own."

"I shall not marry him, dear sister, for I could not be wed to a clergyman, for all that your own husband is of that profession. That is a life suitable for your temperament, but not my own. No, I should prefer a member of parliament, or a colonel in the army, or some figure of rank and distinction."

"Or a baronet?" Mrs. Grant teased.

"Or a baronet!" Miss Crawford teased back, before drawing Mary's attention to the harp. Made easy by the comfortable banter between sisters, so familiar to her from her own home at Longbourn, and more than happy to enter into a conversation about music with a skilled player, Mary spent a great deal longer at the rectory than she had intended. Neither her hostess nor Miss Crawford seemed in the least put out by this extended visit, and when, after a second cup of tea, a mid-day nuncheon, and a lesson at the beautiful harp, Mary took her leave, it was with sincere entreaties to return if she possibly could.

At last she returned to Mansfield Park and took to her room for a while to rest and change her dusty clothing. She was sitting at her sunny window seat, recording her thoughts and obligations, when a great noise filtered through the windows from the grounds below. She peered down to see the men returning, and seemingly not in good spirits. Shouts and calls and cries for help all filtered through the glass, and she rushed downstairs to find out whatever was the matter.

Alexander was there at the bottom of the stairs, his coat still dusty from the road, his forehead damp with perspiration under his mop of copper hair; he must have only now returned from his mission. Together, they hurried to the door where the hunters were crashing into the house.

"Baddeley! Mrs. Parker!" It was Edmund's voice, but it held a frantic note Mary could not have imagined. "A cart, and ale, and the doctor. Somebody summon the doctor! There has been a terrible accident. He is dead!"

Chapter Six

The Body in the Woods

Alexander groaned at these words. "Oh, no." He sagged against the door frame on which he was leaning. He had hoped not to be involved in another death, or at least, not now. As much as such events were a large part of his business as an investigator, he hated them nonetheless. He would gladly forego the income from these cases if it meant these awful occurrences would not occur. They were all too common.

Who was it who had died? His first thoughts went to Tom Bertram, whom he had been seeking all day. He had ridden to every toll booth he could find leading out of Northampton, but none had any news to offer him about the missing man, and whilst he would not say the words aloud yet, he was beginning to lose hope for the man's safety.

But no—Edmund had mentioned an accident. Surely Tom was not out in the field, was he? Was it Tom who had been the victim? Had he met with some accident while riding home the other night, only now to be found? Had he joined up with the others on their hunt and fallen from his mount? Or was it someone else? Surely, if it were Tom, Edmund would have said something, looked more distraught, rather than merely shocked. Alexander took a quick survey of the returning hunters. One was missing.

"Rushworth?" he voiced the name.

Edmund nodded, a picture of despair.

"He was called away as we gathered near the farm where the gamekeeper had spotted a den. He said he would find us, and left with the fellow, and at that moment the hounds caught their scent. We did not notice he was not with us until quite a bit later. You know how a hunt goes." He shrugged, as if it were a common pastime.

Alexander bit back his retort. He had never hunted a thing in his life, other than the clues he needed to solve his cases. Instead, he asked how they had found the dead man.

"When we returned to the field where we had gathered, where the cart waited with food and to transport the hounds, we realised Rushworth was not amongst us. It was his hounds who began to act strangely, circling around and straining. We thought he might have gone home after his business, whatever it was, but his hounds... He would not just leave them to us. We decided to look for him, in case something had happened.

"We knew the direction in which he had gone earlier, but separated in hopes of finding him more quickly, each with one of his dogs to catch his scent. Whichever of us came across him first would alert the others." Edmund's head dropped on his neck.

"I found him," Maddox interrupted. His face was white, but his voice strong. "We had been searching for a while. We thought he might have returned to Sotherton, but the dog's nose took me in a different direction. The beast was quite upset, but I could see nothing, and had no reply to my calls. I was nearly ready to turn back for the others when the hound went quite wild and I saw something by a thicket. It was a piece of fabric—turns out to be part of his coat. Almost didn't see it because it was in the branches, but it was the wrong sort of green, if you know what I mean. Not what grows on trees, especially not this far into autumn. I think I called out to the others, because Crawford rode up right then, followed by Bertram here. Past the thicket was a sort of a gully, and we followed the hound. Just past the scrap in the branches, we could see down the banks, and there was, well..." He stopped, his hands shaking visibly, his face draining even whiter as he recalled what he had seen.

"Mr. Bertram?" Alexander turned to his host in hopes of more explicit information.

"He must have taken the brush in a jump and not seen the gully. There was no sign of his horse. He was clearly dead. His head... no one could survive that. I..." He stiffened. "Oh no. I must tell Maria. I must..." He wavered on his feet and Alexander caught him before he fell.

"You must all sit. Where is that ale you called for? Mary," he turned to her, confident in her cool nerves, "help me get them to the rehearsal room, the one with the scenery and props. I shall see about the ale. Mr. Bertram, take a quick drink, but then I shall have need of you. We shall need the doctor and the coroner, and you must take me to the site. I presume Mr. Rushworth lies there still."

Edmund nodded, his face still as white as a sheet, and allowed the guest to lead him through his own house to the room. A maid and footman together brought in trays with enough tankards of beer for all the men, and two extra. Alexander refused his and noticed Mary eying one of the remaining containers with a strange expression. Did she disapprove of the drink, or did she wish to partake herself, but dared not for danger of being scorned by the others?

The returning hunters all drank deeply of the brew, and at last Edmund was able to continue. "Father is the magistrate outside of the town, but he is away. In his absence, we have referred everything to the judge in the town."

"Is he the coroner?"

"No. that's Harris…"

"The banker?" Alexander had met him at the Meldola's on his visit six weeks prior.

"Not him. His brother. His father was granted a knighthood for some service or another, and saw this older son into a career at law. The younger earned the family's disapproval by going into trade, if banking can be called a trade, but he earns more than the rest of them together, and so they forgave him. Francis Harris is the lawyer. He is capable, if not particularly interested. He has served well enough as coroner thus far."

"I do not like him at all," Oliver supplied. "Harris can be a fool. The man cannot tell a turnip from a cricket ball."

"Be that as it may…" Edmund began, but Alexander interrupted him.

"Whatever his character, we must summon him at once. I shall need his permission to touch the body, which I need to do should you wish for me to involve myself."

"Yes! Yes, of course." Edmund collected himself with a sudden burst of will. "Baddeley?" he called for the butler. "Baddeley, send a fast rider immediately to Northampton, on the fastest horse we have, to call Mr. Harris in his capacity as coroner. Maddox, you wait here, and as soon as he arrives, lead him to the fields past Easton where we found Rushworth. You recall the exact location? Good.

Mr. Lyons? Are you ready? We may leave now, if you wish to examine what of the place we can before he finds us."

Alexander glanced down at his dusty coat. He had spent all the day thus far riding around the county and his back was sore and his legs ached, but this was a duty that must be done. His comfort was secondary. "Of course. Let me retrieve my hat, and I shall follow at once."

It was a few minutes before they were off. Edmund went in search of his mother and Maria to break the dire news, and Alexander used those moments to have a quick conversation with Mary. "Keep them in the rehearsal room," he said. "Tell them what you must, that the coroner will need to speak to them, or that Edmund Bertram insists... I shall have him give such a command to the butler and footmen. Feed them, ply them with ale and coffee, and then sit and listen and let me know what they discuss. Can I trust you with this? I know I can."

Mary nodded her serious head and scurried off to find her paper and pencils, and Alexander completed his part of the task with Edmund and the butler. Then, at last, they found fresh horses and were flying across the fields in the direction of the gully past Easton.

Edmund was correct. There was no doubt that the man was dead. His body was crumpled in an unnatural position at the bottom of the shallow but steep trench, his head a red and bloody mess, with a dark substance oozing onto the surrounding earth. The man was lying partly on his side, with enough of the remains of his face visible to know his identity. Mary had seen violent death before, but Alexander was relieved that she had not asked to accompany him. This was a gruesome sight.

He scanned the area. This was a lightly wooded part of the estate, more scrub and low brush than trees, presumably kept free from agriculture for exactly the purpose to which it was being used today: for the sport of the owner. There, in the distance, he could see the scrub break way to neat brown fields, demarcated by dark green hedges, but here the land was rougher. The thicket which had caught Rushworth's coat—more of a low natural hedge than a stand of any height—obscured the depth of the little ravine from a cursory sight, and with the land rising again on the far side past the ditch and the trickle of a stream that had created it, a thoughtless rider might have assumed he could leap it. Upon further examination, Alexander considered that a skilled rider and strong horse might well succeed.

Edmund must have been thinking along those same lines. "Tried to leap it and fell off, I think, and landed badly with his head on one of those stones. A terrible accident."

Alexander's grunt was noncommittal. He glanced back to where his own horse was tethered to a convenient tree branch and then examined the ground. It was covered in moss and fallen leaves. If there had been any tale told by the hoof marks from Rushworth's horse, it was destroyed by the subsequent arrival of Maddox and the others on their own mounts. He could not blame them for a moment for obscuring what might have been important information. They had no notion of what they were trampling, and if there had been any hope for Rushworth, their assistance must take priority over every other consideration.

"Where is his horse?" He peered into the distance across the small gully, back towards the farmland. There was no sign of the creature. He had not expected to see it. "Was it his own, or one from your stables?"

Edmund frowned. "His own. We have not so many that they can all be spared for leisure. Some are still needed in the fields, or for taking goods to market, and are not good riding animals. Even of those accustomed to the saddle, not all are good hunters."

"Might it have returned to its home? Souther...?"

"Sotherton. Might have. It lies twelve miles from house to house by road, but across these fields, and this far out in the park, it is more akin to eight. An easy distance for a riderless horse."

"Hmmmm."

Keeping a good distance from the ghastly sight in the trench, Alexander scrambled down the incline and then, with difficulty, up the other side. The gully was not deep, but the walls were steep and made slippery by the recent rains that had drenched the area. He caught a tree root and pulled himself up with its help. He was muddy and wet from the rivulet whose course had carved the ditch, and he was certain he looked a right mess. Fortunately, Mary would not mind this.

He thought too much of Mary. She was in his mind too often, and he cared too much about her opinions. He had long since acknowledged his affection for her, but kept at trying to convince himself that they could be nothing but friends. He pushed her from his thoughts once again and proceeded to his task.

"I see prints here," he called across to Edmund. "Here is where the horse landed, and quite hard, to judge from the depth of the imprint. The ground here is clearer and damp... ah, there is the next set, and then next. He ran that a-way."

He pointed, and Edmund called back. "Towards Sotherton. I shall send a messenger as soon as we return."

"What is this?" Alexander stopped still as he gazed at the soft field. "More prints, and another set there." He dropped to his knees—his poor buckskins would never be clean—and then lowered himself further until his face was inches from the ground. He moved a few feet in one direction and repeated his actions, and then again and again.

"What in heaven's name are you doing?" Edmund's voice sounded from across the gully. "Have you seen something?"

"Do you have plaster of Paris at the house?" Alexander called back. "I may be wrong, but I believe we have more than one set of hooves here. I would like to make casts of the marks and examine them at leisure." He looked up at the sky. It was thankfully still clear. Rain would destroy what might be evidence, although of what, he was not quite certain.

"Plaster? Yes... I believe so. As soon as someone comes, I shall send a note for some." He paused for a moment. "Do you suspect something amiss?"

Alexander stood, careful not to disturb any of the prints. "I cannot be certain. It might be just as it seems—a dreadful accident. But why were there other horses here? They were moving in tight, random patterns from what I can see, whereas Rushworth's horse seems to have galloped straight on towards those fields, and then, presumably, home." He made a mental map of the area and found a twig to plant in the ground so he could locate the prints easily when the plaster came, and then walked back to the rim of the gully. "It could be something simple, two other horses escaped from their enclosure, or merely set free to graze and wander. If Rushworth's mount had seen or smelled them, it might have wished to join them or run from them. That could explain a poor jump. It could easily be something that straightforward." He did not elaborate on what else it might have been.

He walked about a hundred yards down the edge of the ditch in one direction, and then, after returning to the spot where the body lay, a hundred or so in the other direction and back. Heavier and taller trees lined the gully for a fair distance in either direction. "This is the only place one might cross." He spoke as much to himself as to his companion. He half-crawled, half-slid down into the gully again and approached the dead man, keeping enough distance that he would not disturb anything of importance. Crouching without touching the ground with his hands, he peered at the gaping wound that had once been Rushworth's head. A bloody stone lay directly to the side.

Then he found his previous track several feet away and hoisted himself back up the bank to return to Edmund's side.

"Is it as we thought?" Edmund was still frowning.

"Aye, could be. Could be indeed. And yet..." Something bothered him. Perhaps it was instinct; perhaps there was something he had seen which he had not yet understood, some perception borne of long years at this profession.

Alexander wandered closer to the hedge-like thicket. There was the scrap of fabric from the dead man's coat. There, some broken twigs where the horse's hooves must have caught them, there...

"What is this?" He heard Edmund walk up behind him.

"Take a close look," Alexander invited. "What do you see?"

The other man peered closely without touching the object under consideration.

"That stem is stripped."

Edmund was correct. The upper foot of one of the thick woody stems of the shrub was bare, stripped of all its small twigs and branches, almost as if it had been pruned, or if someone had fastened a tight noose about the base and pulled sharply upwards. Alexander's stomach twisted and a familiar sensation of ill ease settled upon him. He walked to the far end of the thicket, eyes fast upon the growth, until, just as the shrubs grew too high to see over, he found a similar stripped stem.

A dull thundering from behind him foretold the arrival of more men, and so it proved. With Maddox and Crawford and two grooms from the estate, rode another man. He looked about five-and-forty or perhaps fifty, strong and vigorous, with hard eyes and hair just now sprinkled with grey. He leapt from his horse with the agility of a young man and strode over to Alexander.

"You are the one I have not met. You must be the London investigator. Harris." Thus, he introduced himself. "What have we?"

Without waiting for an answer, he pushed through to the edge of the shrubbery, where he could see into the gully. Alexander watched as the coroner visibly recoiled at the sight. He did not blame the man. His reaction had been similar.

"Maddox here says he had gone off alone. Looks like he took the jump and didn't make the other side. His horse?"

Edmund explained their supposition.

"Sad accident. Well, there must be an inquest. Tomorrow at the Green Man at eleven. No, wait. Tomorrow is Sunday. Monday it is. I'll see to it when I get to the village. You will be witnesses. Sad accident. No other way about it."

"Pardon me, sir," Alexander stepped forward to speak.

"What is it, man? Lyons, is it? Well?"

This coroner seemed less than concerned about getting to the truth of the matter, so it seemed, than getting it over and done with. "I have some, er, minor concerns about the nature of the accident. I believe it warrants more investigation."

"Nonsense. You may speak at the inquiry, of course, but the evidence of my eyes—and yours, gentlemen, correct?—points exactly to an accident. What more investigation is needed?"

"May I point out a few inconsistencies....?"

"There's time for that at the inquest. I am confident it will be declared an accident. Let's bring the body up. Jury needs to take a look at him, and we can't have them all coming out here, can we?"

"Sir!" Alexander stepped forward once more.

"Lyons?" The voice was not friendly.

"May I make a request, sir, for one more day to gather evidence before holding the inquest?

"What concern have you in this matter, Lyons?"

There was no charming Mr. Harris. He was, as Edmund had mentioned earlier, uninterested. "I am always concerned when there is an unexplained death."

"'Twas an accident."

"I am not convinced."

At this point, Edmund inserted himself into the conversation. "Mr. Lyons is a guest at Mansfield Park and is under contract to me to pursue another matter. Since Mr. Rushworth was to be married to my sister, the matter is of personal interest to me, and therefore I am, as of now, engaging Mr. Lyons to investigate the nature of the events leading to Mr. Rushworth's untimely death." He stood up to his full height, which topped the coroner's by about six inches. "Mr. Lyons is not only a skilled investigator, whose opinions I trust implicitly, he is also a personal friend of Mr. Darcy of Pemberley, whose investment in the shoemakers' guild in Northampton is to thank for a great deal of the town's prosperity, and consequently, your own."

Edmund said no more, but as indolent as the coroner might have been, he was not unintelligent, and was able to come to the appropriate conclusion. "Very well. We convene the inquest on Monday, as per the law, but if I see cause, I will adjourn and grant you one more day before hearing evidence. Monday at twelve noon, and not a minute later. Have you an ice house for this poor man's body? Get him there at once."

"Sir..." Alexander stepped forward once more. "Do I have your permission to examine the body before it is moved?"

Harris cast another distasteful glance towards the gully and shuffled backwards. "Do what you must. Monday at the Green Man at twelve." Upon which words, he spun about and returned to his horse.

Chapter Seven

Things that Mary Hears

Mary cast her eyes to the large pendulum clock sitting atop the mantel. It read half-past six. Alexander and Edmund had been gone for nearly three hours. The sky was growing dark, and already the lamps had been lit to fend off the encroaching gloom. Around her, the room was now quiet, but it had not been so for long.

At first, immediately after Alexander had left, there had been the expected complaints about his orders. Mary had simply shrugged and opined that Mr. Lyons surely knew what he was about, and that a minor inconvenience was nothing when compared to the fate suffered by poor Mr. Rushworth. The men might not have felt the impingement on their liberties any less, but they were too well brought up to refute this.

When a second tray of ale and cheese was brought in a few minutes later and the men ate and drank their fill, their grumblings eased further. With a tankard in hand, Henry Crawford had wandered over to the corner where Mary sat, partly concealed by a half-painted screen for the play and an elegant Grecian half column, atop which sat some exquisite ornament that must have cost what her father's estate earned in a year. The sun had still streamed in from the mid-afternoon sky and lit the area where she sat.

Mr. Crawford scanned the blank paper on the small table to her side. "What do you write, Miss Bennet?" His voice was easy.

She turned an innocent face at him and lied, "Poetry, sir. I am no proficient, but I hope I may improve with diligent practice. Mr. Lyons has asked me to remain here as he has you, so I shall, I hope, use the time productively. I merely await some inspiration." To that, he had given her an indulgent smile and then turned away, his curiosity suitably satisfied.

Mary's curse of invisibility, by means of which she had been so neglected and ignored as a child, was now become a gift. Despite being new to the company's acquaintance, she was neither beautiful nor interesting enough to capture their attention. Alexander had spoken not a word of her role in his investigations, rendering her no threat, perceived or otherwise, and consequently, the men soon seemed to forget she was present at all.

And so they talked, and under the guise of a visit by Calliope, she wrote what she heard.

Alexander and Edmund had been gone for only a short time and their absence was still felt. At first, it seemed none of the erstwhile hunters knew what to say. Engaging in idle chatter seemed somehow disrespectful when one of their number lay dead in the woods. There were long moments of uncomfortable silence before Henry Crawford mumbled, "Terrible, was it not?"

Mary's pencil glided over the paper.

"Awful." That was Maddox. He had found the body only an hour or so before, a fact that she noted in the margin she had drawn. There was a pause, then, "Do you think it was an accident?"

"Of course." Oliver's voice was a light tenor, strained now to a reedy thinness of timbre. "What else could it have been?"

Another pause; then Maddox spoke again. "Those men asking after Bertram in Northampton also asked for directions to Sotherton. You do not think...?"

"What's this, what?" Yates spoke for the first time. He had only today made the acquaintance of Oliver and Maddox, being new to the area and Tom Bertram's guest. He also had little knowledge of local goings-on, and if he would ask the questions, Mary would gladly record the answers.

Maddox relieved their curiosity. "There are two men who have been seeking Bertram of late. They mostly stayed in the town, where he spends many a night at the tables, but I was at the public house at the inn not so long past and I heard somebody provide the exact route to Mansfield Park."

"Whatever did they want with him?"

"That much I did not hear. They said they wished only to speak with him, but those words are often spoken and less often meant. Had I been Bertram and overheard them, I should have run."

"Then they asked after Rushworth as well? He is not... he was not a gambler, was he? Hardly knew the man, but," Yates lowered his voice and Mary had to strain to hear him, "he did not quite seem the type to lay down the bets. Not too much happening under the scalp, if you know what I mean. He could hardly remember his four and twenty lines of text for our play; he would be a right disaster if put up against habitual gamblers. If he cannot recall a smattering of text, he can hardly recall which cards he had, or which horse he bet on, can he?"

"Not to mention," Oliver drawled, "that with his twelve thousand a year, he could pay his debts immediately and not notice the difference in his pockets."

"Cannot have been about that, then, can it?"

There was silence for a few moments before Henry Crawford spoke again. "If there is something good to come of this, at least now Miss Bertram shall not have to marry the man."

Shocked exclamations filled the air, covering the light scratch of Mary's pencil on her paper.

"By God, Crawford!"

"You cannot mean that!"

"Come, now, man!"

Henry brushed them off. "Accept my apologies, gentlemen. I was trying to make light of a dire situation. Of course, I did not mean that. My words were ill-considered."

The other men seemed to accept Crawford's words, but Mary recalled his interactions with Miss Bertram the previous day and made a note of that as well. She wondered what Alexander would make of it all, and suddenly longed for him to return. But that would be a while, for he must only recently have reached the place where poor Mr. Rushworth lay dead.

It was then that the footman had entered the room with Mr. Harris, the coroner. Harris was in his riding gear and seemed anxious to be on the way to the site where Rushworth's body lay. He required Mr. Maddox, who had found the victim, to lead him to the exact place. He likewise requested, in a manner that was an order and not a request at all, that Mr. Crawford, who had come with Edmund, accompany them as well. These two gentlemen departed almost at once, leaving only Mr. Yates and Mr. Oliver in the room.

Now the silence was broken by female voices. "Well, no matter what Edmund told me, I do not see why it needs to be brought here!" Mary recognised the voice of Mrs. Norris, the aunt. "Surely

Sotherton has an ice house for Mr. Rushworth's body. And why did he have to die before the wedding? That was most inconsiderate of him, for now Maria shall get nothing." She gave an exaggerated sigh. "And after all my great efforts in arranging the match. Most inconsiderate."

"Aunt, surely he did not die on purpose. And Edmund said that since he died on our land, the inquest must happen here." That sounded like Julia.

"And I am equally certain he did not do it to importune you." This was Maria, who did not sound quite as bereft as one might expect from a woman who had only hours before lost her betrothed.

From her seat by the screen, Mary did not see them enter, but she did hear them as they walked through the doorway, their skirts rustling as they moved. Then came the unmistakable sounds of Mr. Oliver and Mr. Yates pushing from their seats as they rose to bow to the ladies.

"Miss Bertram, my most heartfelt condolences." Mr. Yates was the first to speak. He might be a dilettante actor, trained to dissemble with a convincing air, but his words and voice sounded sincere. "Miss Julia, Mrs. Norris, how have you taken the terrible news? Is there anything I might do, any task I can undertake, to ease your distress?" He had the manners of a well-bred gentleman.

It was Mrs. Norris who answered. "My dear niece has recovered from the worst of the shock, have you not, Maria? During the years in which my late husband was the parson here at Mansfield, I quite honed my skills at spiritual succour; I comforted many a bereaved parishioner over the loss of a loved one. I am most distressed that my own niece has need of my skill, but I am honoured to be able to offer it to her."

"Allow us to leave you ladies in peace," Mr. Oliver ignored Mrs. Norris' braggadocio, but addressed himself to the sisters. "I shall retire to my rooms."

"And I to mine, unless you have need for me. The coroner has come and gone and will have no questions for us this day." This was Yates again. With the ladies present, it seemed to Mary that little more would be said that might offer more insight into Rushworth's death, and so she said nothing as the men took their leave, Alexander's orders all but forgotten.

Maria, Julia and Mrs. Norris moved fully into the room. Mary heard the two sisters sit, but the swish of their aunt's heavy skirts suggested she was stalking the walls.

"Where is that girl with the tea?" she asked after a moment. "I most distinctly asked her to see to tea. Such a lazy girl, that Fanny is."

There was no response from either Maria or Julia, but at that moment, Mary heard somebody else enter the room, and Fanny Price's timid voice could be heard from the doorway. "I could not find Cook, and I had to search the stillroom and the gardens to request a tray. Maria, I have also spoken to Mrs. Parker about procuring some black shawls until the half mourning wardrobe arrives, as you asked. The green shawl which you left on my bed, I have now handed to your maid to clean and store until your period of mourning is over."

"Surely, Maria, you do not intend to keep from society for a full six months!" Mrs. Norris sounded more angry than concerned for her niece.

The ladies of the family clearly thought they were alone; Mary waged a momentary war with herself as to whether to speak and announce her presence, or to remain silent and invisible in the hopes of learning something.

Her decision was made when Julia chided Mrs. Norris. "Aunt!" She sounded as annoyed as Fanny was meek. "If my sister wishes to mourn her betrothed as he deserves, we must allow her that courtesy."

"But she had no particular affection for him, surely. Three weeks will be sufficient to exhibit her distress to the neighbourhood."

Maria interrupted. "Three weeks? No, ma'am. I may not have loved him, Aunt Norris, but he was a neighbour, and our engagement was of long standing, and he deserves the appearance, at least, of some devotion."

"Not to mention," Mary heard Maria's sotto voce comment to her sister, "that I shall wish for a lengthy period out of society, so my relief at being relieved of the obligation of this marriage should not be noticed."

For her part, Mrs. Norris seemed to be reconsidering matters. She had walked far enough into the room that Mary could see her face through the panels of the screen as she narrowed her eyes in thought. "That might do, Maria. It might do well at that. For if Mr. Rushworth's brother returns from wherever he is to claim the estate, your modest and devoted nature might capture his attention, and if we are fortunate, you might end up as mistress of Sotherton after all."

The conversation now turned to the details of Maria's mourning wardrobe. For a while, Mary recorded the number of grey gloves and ribbons and lilac-hued pelisses, but these minutiae seemed irrelevant to the case. What was of more interest was Maria's noted lack of distress at the sudden and violent loss of her intended husband, but this was a point to be discussed, not recorded on paper.

In due time, the ladies departed the room, leaving Mary alone. She had been still and silent for a very long time, and she groaned as she stretched her cramped legs. "You may come out of hiding, Miss Bennet," a soft voice sounded from near the door.

"Miss Price." Mary had not heard the girl at all, had forgotten she had even been in the room. Oh, how very like she, herself, had been so passed over by family and friends alike not so many years before. The irony was not lost on her. She stood in her place and could now see Fanny over the top of the screen.

"I am so accustomed to being ignored," Fanny explained to her. "I am always aware of others who are likewise. I shall not tell anybody that you were here. As soon as I collect my cousins' shawls and find Lady Bertram's embroidery, I shall leave you to your peace." She began to gather the items the Bertram sisters had left strewn about the room and then stopped. "Did you hear...?"

For the second time since she had been in the room that day, Mary lied. "I was working at some poetry earlier and fell asleep." She patted the pile of papers in her hands. "I recall the gentlemen lamenting the dreadful accident that claimed Mr. Rushworth's life, and then I knew nothing until you spoke. Perhaps it was your cousins' departure that awakened me."

How easily the untruths left her lips. She ought to be ashamed; such behaviour was so contrary to the strict moral code she had espoused not so long ago. And yet, a part of her rejoiced at her skill in dissembling, for surely this was a skill required by those who pursued investigations as a trade. A lady, of course, would never embark upon such a career—even if ladies did take employment, to work for money would be a social degradation, and to be an investigator would be hardly a step up from being a common actress, and yet... And yet Alexander was an honourable man. He strove for justice and the righting of wrongs, and even Mr. Darcy, with his noble relations and his great pride, deemed Alexander Lyons a friend. Consequently, if she were to help him once more in his investigations, it would not be so terrible a thing, would it?

"I am sorry to have disturbed your rest." Fanny's reply wrested her from her musings. "Pray, pardon me." The girl shuffled her feet as if intending to leave, but something in her eyes called to Mary's sympathy. There was something the girl seemed to want to say, something she could not discuss with her family. Once more, she felt that connection with her own younger self that was embodied in this put-upon cousin.

"Miss Price, come sit with me a moment." Fanny looked alarmed, pleased, and then relieved, the emotions passing over her face like moonbeams on a rippling pond, before she settled once more into her accustomed expression of complacency. The two moved to a low settee that had been pushed to flank the wall on the other side of the room. Once seated, Mary asked, "Is there something particular you wished to ask? I recognise that look on your face. It is one that has surely sat upon my own on too many occasions to recall." When Fanny said nothing but looked embarrassed, Mary added, "I, too, grew up in a house of busy and beautiful people, where I was the quiet one, more often neglected than recalled, and longing for a friend. Oh, my sisters were never unkind to me, but as the middle of five daughters, I was as often forgotten as not."

Thus, she proceeded to tell Fanny about growing up at Longbourn; about beautiful and sweet Jane who was the most admired young lady in Meryton; about witty and sparkling Elizabeth, who reminded her of Miss Crawford and who went on to make such a brilliant marriage with Mr. Darcy; about lively and spirited Lydia, who was next to Jane in classical beauty, and about Kitty, who lived in the light reflected off of Lydia.

"I was the middle one, the plain one, who never made trouble and who had to shout to be heard—"

"Oh! But you are not plain at all." Fanny was indignant. "Why, you have a lovely face. It is a quiet beauty, perhaps, but it is no less beautiful for it. And you carry yourself with such poise and confidence, I should never have imagined you to be anything other than the centre of everyone's attention."

Was it true? Had she really developed such a demeanour? "That must be," she spoke slowly as the notions turned about in her mind, "because I finally have somebody who places so much confidence in me." It seemed she had more to thank Alexander for than merely his friendship. She continued, "If you wish to open your heart to a sympathetic listener who will hold her tongue, my time is yours."

Fanny stared into the shadows for a moment, contemplating, before opening her mouth to speak.

"This house…" she faded away, then began again. "Oh, Miss Bennet, I know not how I feel, or why. I am not easy. This house is full of people whose moral conduct is lacking." She blushed a deep red and continued. "My cousin Mr. Bertram—that is, Tom, not Edmund—has brought this theatrical performance to our midst, and a most improper play it is too. There are displays of intimacy and unsanctified unions and all manner of questionable actions, and we are intended to portray them. They are a stain upon our own characters!" Her eyes were wide with pleading.

"Maria and Julia have been both attempting to attract Mr. Crawford's attention, and Maria being engaged to poor Mr. Rushworth, and Mr. Crawford has only been encouraging them, and has shown the most inappropriate attention to Maria, leaving Julia angry and filled with jealousy, and…." She stopped and turned white. "Oh no. You do not possibly think…? Could Maria have had some hand in this? I can hardly imagine it." The last words were almost a sob.

Mary took her hand. "No, I doubt it very much."

Fanny nodded and took a fortifying sniff. "Miss Crawford is little better, for she flirts incessantly with Edmund and never stops trying to have him forsake his chosen profession in the church, although it is what he most dearly desires. At every breath, she urges him to reconsider his choice and take up the law. She makes him forget who he is, and she takes pleasure in it. Why, Edmund had not wished any part of this dramatic production until she convinced him to play opposite her."

Mary blinked. Edmund was part of the theatricals? He had given every indication that he was apart from it, that he disapproved too strongly to take a role. He certainly had not mentioned his involvement to her. She wondered if Alexander knew, and if it would change how he approached this new case.

Fanny must have noticed her surprise, for she explained, "He is quite under Miss Crawford's spell, I fear. All of his protestations of the improper nature of it vanished with the application of her allurements. And poor Edmund..." She broke off again.

"You like him, do you not?"

Fanny nodded.

"Do you love him?"

She did not answer, but the tears that suddenly flooded her eyes told Mary the truth of the matter. This was a fix for poor Fanny Price indeed.

After a minute, Fanny dried her eyes and gathered the items she had come in search of, and exclaimed how much she would be chastised for taking too long at her duties. She wished, Mary considered, to be alone with her embarrassment. And now, with everybody in the house gone his or her separate way, Mary was alone with her thoughts and her notes, and there she sat, watching the clock's hands move ever so slowly, as the sun set and the sky darkened, wondering what Alexander would make of what she had learned that afternoon.

Chapter Eight

Things that Alexander Learns

Half-past six. Alexander's eyes grazed the clock on the mantel as he walked through the rehearsal room in search of Mary. He was in no fit state to be seen, covered with dust and mud and gore he did not want to identify, but he needed to see her, if only for a moment. He excused this urge as a wish to inform her of his safe return, to arrange a time later when they might relate what they had learned, to hear whether she had discovered anything. But he knew in his heart that it was a need to see her, to hear her voice, to be in her presence, that directed his feet.

He had not far to go.

"Alexander." She stood there alone. Had she been waiting for him? The thought made his heart beat faster. "I am so pleased to see you back. I..." Her eyes travelled up and down his filthy body.

"Oh, you are a mess!" He was about to take offence at her criticism of his person when she continued, "You must be exhausted beyond measure. We do need to talk, but I imagine you need a rest and a wash more. Shall I ask about sending someone to draw you a bath?"

This was his Mary. She observed his physical state only to determine his well-being. How much had changed since their first unfortunate meeting. If he were not so indescribably filthy and wretched, and if it were not entirely inappropriate, he would have pulled her into his arms for a long hug. Instead, he bowed to her, his eyes barely remaining open. "Thank you, Mary. Edmund has already made the request. I shall seek my room directly, now that I have seen you."

She nodded at him. She understood. "I, too, shall retire to my chamber for now. Maria has declared that we shall not dine in company tonight, but shall all have trays sent to our rooms. When you are ready, send a maid for me." She stepped forward and, with a feather touch, laid a hand upon his cheek—perhaps the only visible part of his body not encased in a layer of grime.

Before he lost control and pulled her into his embrace, he bowed again and retreated to repair his toilette.

It was only half an hour later when Alexander sent a maid to request Mary's company in the small withdrawing room that Edward had set aside for his use. He had braved the cool autumn night air and had had a stable boy douse him with two changes of clean water to remove the worst of the muck on his body before he returned to the house wrapped in a clean banyan and proceeded to his hot bath. Now, clad in clean trousers, shirt, waistcoat, and coat, he sat by the fire, finally warm once more.

"Alexander?" Mary knocked at the door and entered upon seeing him. Suddenly bereft of all energy, he did not rise to greet her, but sat still in his chair as he watched her cross the room. She did not take offence at his lack of manners, but instead she laid a gentle hand upon his shoulder, a chaste touch that meant so very much more to him. Then she pulled another chair to flank his, and asked in a low voice, "Would you care to tell me about it?"

He looked at her through eyelids that suddenly weighed a hundred pounds each. She had become so dear to him; she understood him, complemented him. He had rather grown to love her. How would he survive when she discovered what he had hidden from her and fled from him? He could not contemplate that now, and instead, with a heaviness of heart that had only something to do with the dead man, he allowed his eyes to close and his head to fall back onto the cushion of his chair as he replied to her.

"Mr. Edmund Bertram will join us in about half an hour. I wished for a few moments alone with you." He felt her hand alight upon his and give it a squeeze. He forced his eyes open.

"You have not eaten. Your hair is still wet," she remarked. "You can hardly stay awake. Let me call for some food and coffee…"

"Mrs. Grey has promised to bring us each a tray. I expect her at any moment. I shall be fine. It was, however, a most exhausting day." He whispered more than spoke the words and allowed his eyes to close once more. At that moment, a maid brought in the promised victuals, and he heard Mary move a low table to the space between their chairs and set up the impromptu meal. He forced his eyes to open once more and shifted his body upright in the chair so as to partake of the food.

"Vegetable stew without meat?" Mary's voice was full of surprise.

"It is as I requested it."

"Are you a Quaker that you limit yourself to vegetables?" Mary frowned. "But no, for I saw you enjoy the chicken at your friend's house in Northampton. Never mind, for it is hot and fragrant and will warm you more surely than the fire. Here, shall I put some cheese and bread on your plate as well?" She prepared a plate for him and poured him a glass of cider before seeing to her own food. They ate in silence for a few moments before Alexander succumbed to the need to speak.

"He was killed. I am almost certain of it." He had not intended to say the truth so bluntly, but the words would not be stayed.

She did not shy from the statement, but asked him what he had seen.

"It seemed, at first, to be an accident. Rushworth seems to have tried to jump a hedge of sorts at the edge of the scrubland, was thrown from his horse, and fell into a gully where he died from his head hitting a large and sharp rock. And that is what happened. I am certain of it. But the specifics of it bother me. We are meant to think, I believe, that he saw a stag or something in the field beyond and went after it, but when I went to see what markings were on the ground there, I saw not deer spoor, but horse prints. I have taken casts of them, which we will retrieve when they are dry. I expect there to be three individual horses involved, only one of which was Rushworth's. He was called over that hedge for some reason."

"Might they not have been friends, people he knew? He may have wished merely to greet them."

"Aye, that's my Mary, so considered and logical. It might have been, but why, then, did they leave him? Would they not have gone for help?"

"If he were dead," she spoke slowly, testing the idea in her head, "might they not have become frightened, not wishing to become implicated?"

"A very likely possibility indeed, and one I might consider if not for two other details." He described the two shrubs on either side of the hedge-like thicket, where the stems had been shorn of all twigs and foliage for the top two or so feet. "If something like a long rope were strung taut between those two plants, just high enough to catch a horse's hoof as it leapt, and then were quickly torn away, either by the horse's own motion or by some men pulling at it with great force, it might leave damage like that."

"If the horse caught its hoof, it might also have been killed!" Mary sounded horrified.

"Your heart is too kind. If these people were seeking to kill a man, they would likely have little care about the well-being of his horse."

She frowned, but said nothing, and so he continued.

"There was one more matter, the one which convinced me without reservation that Rushworth was deliberately killed. He fell, as I said, into a shallow gully and hit his head there upon a stone. The fall did not kill him. It may well have knocked him senseless, but I found the stone which matched perfectly with the hole in his head. It was covered with his blood and... and other matter." He could not describe for her what he had seen. She might be strong enough to hear it, but he could hardly look at his food and tell it. "Had he fallen, the stone would have been beneath his head, where he landed, or perhaps beside it, had his fall knocked it aside. But the injury that killed him was on the upward-facing part of his head and the stone positioned such that the only way it could lie like that is if somebody were to have smashed it down on him deliberately." Now Mary gasped with horror and his own stomach became unsettled.

"If I am being too fanciful, there is the final evidence that I found marks in the blood that coated the stone in the shape a man's hand would leave were he to have wielded that awful weapon. I am quite certain of it. Rushworth was murdered. Now I merely have to convince the coroner of this." In as few words as possible, he told her about Harris and his insistence upon finding the affair an accident.

Mary sat in silence as the import of the words settled upon her. Then, in a voice so low he hardly heard it, she asked, "But if it were indeed murder, who might have done it?"

"Doctor Tallis from the village came shortly after Harris departed. He had little to say about the hoof prints and the stripped stems, but concurred about the injury to Rushworth's head. He will support my claims at the inquest. Upon examining the body, he posited that Rushworth had been dead for a little over four hours. Dr. Tallis arrived shortly at about half past four from the village, which means the accident—or whatever it was—occurred shortly after noon."

"Where were the other hunters?"

"They claim they were all hunting together, going after some poor fox or two, but in the heat of the chase, one does not concentrate on one's companions. Anybody might have ridden off for a time and rejoined the group with a loud tally-ho, and nobody would know he had been gone. Rushworth was only a mile or so from where the others were hunting, a quick ride on a fast horse. I shall have to question each very carefully, but I do not believe I shall find any answers there. For if I am correct, there were two people who lured him over the hedge, and had two of the hunting party been gone at the same time, I should almost certainly have heard of it. No, I suspect we are looking for somebody from outside the household in this affair." He sighed deeply at the enormity of the task and lapsed once more into silence.

They had finished their dinners and were sitting quietly when Edmund arrived. Like Mary, he knocked at the door and entered at once. He glanced at the table between them and turned back to the door, where he called for someone to remove the trays and bring a plate of cheeses and pastries and some tea. His obligations as host discharged, he returned to the room and settled himself in his own chair. "Are you recovered from the difficult day? I believe we have much to discuss."

A maid came in to remove the dinner trays, and another trailed behind her with a tray of tea and sweets. The water must have been hot already, merely waiting for the order. Mary performed the duties of pouring out, and as she did so, Alexander explained to Edmund in a weary voice, "I have just now recounted to Miss Bennet what we discussed on our ride back; however, let me quickly apprise you of my findings from earlier in the day, before we move on to other matters."

He went on to explain that none of the toll keepers had seen Tom Bertram pass by. He was known to almost all, and the small painting that Edmund had lent him, with a fair likeness of the heir to Mansfield Park, had sparked no gasps of recognition. "It is possible he took a country lane or went cross country if he travelled on horseback, but it seems most unlikely that he has left the vicinity. If we find him, I believe it will be in Northampton." Edmund looked up in alarm at the words *"if* we find him," but he said nothing. There would be enough to say in the event that he was not found, or rather, not found alive.

Instead of allowing Edmund to dwell on that dire possibility, Alexander had more questions for him.

"You said Mr. Rushworth was called away from the hunt. What can you tell me of that?"

Edmund's eyes narrowed in thought. "It was at the start, whilst we were waiting for the chase to begin. The hounds were just now arrived but had not found the scent, and we were talking to the farmer about the den he had found. We were mounted and ready for the chase. A man rode up and called to Rushworth, saying he was wanted."

"What sort of a man? What did he say, if you can recall his words?"

Edmund paused again. "A rough sort of fellow, nothing to remark upon. Perhaps somebody from one of the villages beyond our immediate vicinity. Old and dirty clothing, an equally shabby horse. I may have seen him before, but I cannot swear that I have, for he looked like so many of his sort. I was paying more attention to the dogs and the gamekeeper than this man. He approached our group and rode up to Rushworth. I did not hear his words, but Rushworth called out that he was wanted somewhere and would find us later. Then he and the stranger rode off, and the dogs began to bark, and I quite forgot about it in the excitement of the hunt."

Alexander's pencil seemed to weigh more than ever it had as he struggled to make his notes. Edmund could tell him no more about Rushworth's departure, but perhaps he could provide some insight into the gentleman himself.

"What can you tell me about Rushworth himself that I do not know, that might shed some light on this awful event?"

Edmund sat back in his chair and steepled his fingers together, twitching them as he spoke. "He is... was one of our nearest neighbours. Sotherton is twelve miles distant by road, but much closer cross country, and our estates abut. He was not, perhaps, the most learned man of my acquaintance, nor the one with the best understanding. He was malleable and not particularly observant."

As Edmund spoke, Alexander saw Mary's eyebrows rise and he imagined she had something of import to tell him later. He turned his attention back to Edmund.

"Sotherton is an extremely prosperous estate. Due to its size and the quality of its land, it brings in over twelve thousand a year."

Alexander whistled. "That is a great fortune indeed! And your sister was to marry into that?"

Instead of looking proud, Edmund grimaced. "Our aunt Norris encouraged the match. It would have been an excellent triumph for Maria, had she liked the man. But she could not have respected him. I do not believe she expected love from a marriage, but there must be some meeting of minds for a union to be a happy one, and I had fears for her."

"Was she anxious to escape the union?"

"That is something I could not understand from her. She had every opportunity to cry off. Father is not yet returned, and he requested that they delay the marriage until such time as he was back at Mansfield Park. He would not compel her to proceed with an engagement were she not satisfied, nor has she made any comment or suggestion that she wished to reconsider her choice. Father did give his provisional approval by letter, but the settlement has not been signed. The engagement has not been announced in the London papers. It is therefore still not a legal matter and it would be a simple affair for either party to renege."

Alexander had pulled out his notebook as Edmund spoke, and he made his notes before asking, "Forgive the implication, but is your sister particularly attracted to the great wealth of the estate?"

Edmund gave a low chuckle, though one devoid of all mirth. "My sister loves everything fine and elegant, but she is in no danger of falling into poverty. Even when my own family's income was weakened by my brother's gambling and poor returns from the holdings in Antigua, we wanted for nothing. Maria would never lack for her little luxuries."

Mary asked the next question. "What happens to Sotherton now? I heard something about a brother…"

"Yes, Robert. He is James' younger brother. I believe he is about six and twenty. I have not seen him in several years. He is a far more intelligent man than James was, poor sod. I should not speak ill of the dead, but—"

"This is a murder investigation. Speak your mind. Save your genteel thoughts for later."

"Yes. Yes, of course. Robert is not, perhaps, the brightest man to have graced the halls of Oxford, but neither was he the dimmest. He can hold an idea in his head, and he reasons slowly but effectively. He is an efficient manager—indeed, he has been in Montreal in Lower Canada these last two years with the colonial government there—and is apparently a valued member of the bureau. He will, of course, have to be recalled to take up the estate. He will not be as easy a man to manage as was James. Father will have to find another proxy to carry out his wishes in Parliament." He chuckled at this last statement, but Alexander sat up in his chair.

"Explain, please."

Edmund seemed to understand the import of the question at once and straightened his shoulders. "The village at Sotherton has only a handful of permanent residents remaining, for most have gone to the larger towns. It is a pocket borough, a rotten borough, as it is called. Rushworth was a sitting member of Parliament, and he always listened to Father for his political direction. With Maria being his wife, Father's control would be stronger yet."

Beside him, Alexander saw Mary screw up her forehead. "A rotten borough?"

"Rotten because the populace that once comprised the constituency is in long-term decline and the riding is corrupt," Alexander explained.

Edmund picked up the thread. "There are no more than a handful of electors voting for a particular candidate for Parliament, and these can be swayed either by bribery, outright threat, or mere tradition. There is no political debate such as you find in larger constituencies, and as often as not, there is only one person standing for election, and so is assured of the seat. It is in the pocket, so to speak, of the holder of the estate."

"So Sotherton returns Rushworth to Parliament simply because there is no alternative?" Mary grasped the notion at once.

"Indeed it is so, Miss Bennet. And Mr. Rushworth was suggestible. He could be relied upon to vote however he was told by someone to whom he felt at all beholden."

"Such as a father-in-law?"

"So it is." Edmund sighed.

"What areas of policy, may I ask, are particularly dear to your father's heart that he might wish for such an advocate in the halls of power?" Alexander had a suspicion in mind, but wished to hear it from the man's own son.

Edmund did not disappoint him. He raked a hand through his hair and let out a heavy breath. "This is an area where my father and I disagreed most vigorously. It is a reflection of our stations in life as much as our personal convictions, I suppose. He is the baronet and holder of Mansfield Park and is concerned for the wealth and stability of the estate; I am for the church, and am concerned for the state of men's souls and the dignity of their being." Alexander clucked his understanding. Mary was frowning, but she seemed to have a notion as well as to the matter.

"It will come as little shock to you," Edmund continued, "that a considerable portion of our wealth comes from our holdings in Antigua. Sugar." Alexander nodded. He knew where this would lead. Edmund did not disappoint him. "These plantations are productive only because of the slaves who work them. I am ashamed to admit to my father being the owner of other men. The very thought of it repulses me, and yet, as you see, I am happy to live off the profits of it. It makes me a rather poor sort of man, does it not?"

There was little Alexander could say to that, and so he kept silent as Edmund continued. "This has been an issue long debated in Parliament as well as in our parlours and clubs, and I believe

Father wished for Rushworth to side against the abolitionists in Parliament.”

“And Robert Rushworth is his own man, has lived in an environment that does not rely on slavery for its prosperity, and where slavery is, if still legal, much more rare than in America and the West Indies. Thus, he is much more likely to be brought over to the side of the abolitionists and vote accordingly.”

The three looked at each other. Could this be a motive for murder? Would somebody be so vehement about ending the practice of slavery that he would kill another human being to further his aim? One man’s life in exchange for the lives and freedom of thousands? It bore consideration.

Mary cleared her throat. “I heard mention of two men looking for Mr. Rushworth...”

“Two men, you say?” Alexander recalled the two men Rollings mentioned the day before, who were seeking Tom Bertram. A pit opened up in his belly. Could Tom’s disappearance and Rushworth’s death be connected at all?

Chapter Nine

Back in the Fields

Shortly thereafter, the tea and pastries consumed along with the conversation, Edmund excused himself and rose to leave. He must be exhausted; Mary could see dark smudges below his eyes and the fine lines born of stress higher on his brow. He was two or three years younger than Alexander, but at this moment, he looked ten years older. He had, after all, been administering a large estate without assistance, been trying to manage his older brother's profligacies, and was now deeply concerned about his brother's wellbeing, if not his life. He must surely need some hours of sleep, if such would be granted to him.

Before Edmund could bow his goodnights, however, Mary had to ask one question.

"I had the honour of a conversation with Miss Price earlier this evening. She is quiet, but she sees much and she feels deeply." She waited to see how Edmund would respond.

"Indeed she does," he said warmly. "She is, at times, the one glimmer of calm sanity in a house I feel is going mad. As much as my aunt tries to force her into the shadows, she is the centre that grounds us and keeps us together. If only my aunt and parents would see her worth." His eyes were now bright and his manner animated. "She has been much affected by the recent upset here. She seems placid, but in her heart, I believe there is much happening."

As he left the room, Mary reflected that he was not untouched by her, no matter that he might not recognise his own affection. She was convinced more by his manner and expression than by his words, but they told her a story. Whether this affection would blossom into something more intimate or remain as a sort of bland familial regard was to be seen; however, Fanny was not entirely without hope.

Alexander had a different set of thoughts in mind. "You learned about those two men seeking Rushworth, and I suspect you learned something about Miss Price. What else did you discover as you sat here? Let me tell you about my investigations yesterday in Northampton, and then you may return the favour."

He told her then about Tom's room at the inn, about the note he found, about Rollings at the tavern, and about the two men who had been asking after him, both on that night six weeks before and only two days ago when Tom vanished.

"I sent an express to London, to my associates there. I hope very much to have some sort of response tomorrow."

In exchange, she then brought out her notebook and recounted what she had overheard to Alexander. She told him once more of the two men who were seeking Rushworth, and of Henry

Crawford's callous joke that Maria was now relieved of the obligation of marrying a man she could not like.

"Edmund does not think she wished to be rid of him," Alexander muttered, "but perhaps she felt the need to act without the embarrassment of a broken engagement."

"But murder, Alexander? Would she resort to that, when a mere word would suffice? And even had she wished it, how would she have done it? She would surely need assistance."

"Might Julia have been her accomplice? There were two other sets of hoof prints, after all. We must inquire as to their whereabouts at about noon today."

"There is another possibility." Mary chewed her lip. "Mr. Crawford is not indifferent to Maria, nor she to him. Mr. Rushworth must have been blind not to notice their flirtation—"

"Which, from what Edmund has told us, he might have been…"

"Might he have threatened Mr. Crawford? Might this have been Mr. Crawford's response?"

"Or," Alexander mused, "might this have been an unprovoked attack on the part of Mr. Crawford in order to break by force the engagement that Maria would not break by words?"

"How horrible!" And yet she could not refute the thought.

They stared at each other for a moment in the flickering firelight. The weather had been pleasant this day, but it was now nearing nine o'clock at night and the air was growing cool, even in the comfortable and well-appointed modern room they had for their use. Alexander shivered in his chair, and once again Mary saw his exhaustion written on his body.

"You should retire," she laid a hand upon his. "There is little more you can learn tonight and tomorrow will be a long day, I am certain of it." He nodded, but made no effort to rise from his chair.

"Alexander…" she dared.

He raised his eyes to meet hers.

"Will you join me at church tomorrow? It is the Lord's Day, and I am certain there is no meeting of... of your community in the vicinity."

"Mary..." His voice threatened a warning.

"You might find the service beneficial and restful."

"Mary, do not do this."

"Is it that you do not believe at all? Perhaps Doctor Grant, the parson..."

He leapt from his chair, every glimmer of exhaustion gone from his manner. He shot her a tight bow and left the room with scarcely a goodnight.

Alexander rose long before the sun. Despite his exhaustion upon falling into bed last night, he had slept ill. No matter that it was his bread and butter, murder was a bad business and one to which he hoped never to grow accustomed. He could not put away the images of a man's broken body as he might his ledgers of account at the end of a day. They stayed with him and tormented his sleep. In the darkness of his room, he saw with vivid clarity the smash of stone upon the man's head, the glint of white bone through broken skin, the sickly grey slime of brain that lay exposed to his sight. Despite the faint floral scent on the clean sheets of his bed, he smelled the metallic tang of blood as it seeped into the spongy ground, almost masked by the riper odour of human waste and rotting foliage. He never slept well whilst he was investigating a case.

He had spoken of this to Mary once and she had replied that this was an indication of the goodness of his soul, that such a pure person could not tolerate evil with equanimity. Perhaps she was correct. But this was yet another cause of his poor rest. This had been the source of too much animosity between them, and no matter the depths and sincerity of her personal devotion, he would not and could not accede to her wishes for him to accept her church and her version of God. They had had this argument before, and seemed to move past it, only to return to the same troubles again and again. He had not wished to leave her so discourteously the previous evening, but to rehearse that same debate again would have been both pointless and damaging.

And yet, knowing that she was distressed took its toll on his own peace of mind, and the hours between blowing out the lamp and the first sounds of the servants were long and restless.

It was no hardship, therefore, to leave his bed. There would be no more rest for him, and there was work to be done. He dressed in simple riding attire and put together a satchel of materials he might need for the day, including an extra notebook and a small selection of pencils. Then he crept to the kitchens for a quick cup of coffee and some provisions before finding the back door and the path to the stables.

By the time the sun's fingers began to caress the sleeping earth with their rosy touch, Alexander and two grooms were mounting their horses. He had asked Edmund the previous day if he might expect such assistance, and Edmund had provided him with the names of two men who might be of particular use to him. "Both good, sensible men," the young gentleman had asserted. "They are intelligent and take direction, but will speak up if they have something they feel needs saying." With such an endorsement, Alexander expected to be very pleased, and he was.

Nat was the younger of the two, close enough to Alexander's own age to make little difference. He was stocky and very fair, and with hands calloused from hours of hard work. He greeted Alexander with due deference and seemed more than pleased at the request to ride with him for this task. "Make a nice change from mucking the stables, it will. Normally I tend to Miss Fanny's mare, and keep the carriages and farm equipment in good condition. I haven't much book learning, but I'm good with my hands and understand machines."

John was older by about a decade, and he was a complete surprise to Alexander. Where Nat was so blond and pale as to be nearly as white as an albino, John was as dark as the water-soaked earth. He was tall and solid, with black hair and eyes, and his English, whilst perfect—perhaps better than Nat's—was tinged with the strains of some other land. The palms of his hands, dark pink against the deep mud-brown of his skin, were almost as much a surprise to Alexander as was the presence of a Black man in a baronet's staff of stable hands. Should circumstances allow, he hoped to learn more of this man as they worked today. But for now, their main intent was on their task.

"I wish to return to the site where Rushworth died." He eyed both men.

"I know it well, sir." Nat spoke without asking permission, which pleased Alexander. He was no toff who commanded men to his will. He was a working man himself and preferred colleagues to servants. "I helped bring his remains back to th' ice house yesterday. I know where to go."

They rode quickly in the cool morning air, and soon reached the place where the thickets shielded the gully, opening into the vista of the field across the small ditch. The three men dismounted and moved towards the gully itself. Without Rushworth's broken body sprawled across the rocky floor, the sight was peaceful, pleasant even, but even now in the watery light from the early sun, Alexander could see where the ground was darker, where Rushworth's blood had stained the earth. His shiver had little to do with the cool air.

"There, in the field," he gestured, "I set some plaster to dry. I hope the impressions will be clear enough to show me what I need to see." He had set tarpaulins over the plaster to protect the samples in the event of rain, which now made locating the casts a simple job. The three men found the place where the gully was easier to cross and made their way to the field. Alexander uncovered the first of the casts and lifted it from the ground. "Good. It is dry." He had marked the top side with the letter A, which matched the location in the sketch he had made in his notebook. This would allow him to identify which sample had been found where. He replaced the cast and asked his assistants to take a second set of measurements between the casts. This they did with the lengths of rope they had brought, and as they called the numbers, Alexander confirmed the figures in his book. He could confidently recreate the scene now, placing each cast exactly in relationship to the others, should he need to re-examine his evidence.

Now he knelt by the first cast. He turned it over carefully and blew as much of the loose dirt as possible from the impression. A smile stole over his face.

"Good news?" That was John's deep voice.

"Aye! Come, see. This captured the shape of the hoof and shoe exactly. See the nail in the shoe there—how it is not quite in line with the others—and there, where the shoe seems to have been worn? Two horses, eight hooves. If I am correct, we will have enough with these casts to show beyond a doubt that there were two horses here, and that set there," he pointed a way yonder, "will be different still. But those will match with Rushworth's mount, I am certain of it."

Nat smiled in understanding. "Very clever, Mr. Lyons!" He gave a grin of comprehension. "You'll be wanting these laid out then, will you?"

Alexander assented and quickly made a second sketch of the area, complete with the measurements, which he passed along to

Nat. "If Mr. Bertram has no other need for your services, I would be most appreciative of your work in recreating this scene."

The blond man grinned. "I know exactly what to do."

"Before we part ways," Alexander stayed the eager young groom, "I have another task for us. It might be a fruitless search, for I've no reason to expect to find it, but if we do not look, we certainly shall not find. I'm looking for a rope, about ten or twelve feet long, possibly tossed into a bush or a pile of leaves, possibly hidden."

"A rope long enough to span that gap?" John looked over the gulley to the thicket in the space between trees. Ah yes, Edmund had chosen well. These men might be mere labourers, their work confined to the stables, but there was nothing inferior about their thinking.

"Just so." He nodded. "Let us take no more than half an hour to search, for whoever tied it may as easily have taken it with him; but on the chance that he did not, I would be pleased to have it in my hands.

The search began. Each man chose a different direction, and they worked in silence for several minutes. John walked upstream from the thicket, Nat downstream, and Alexander searched in the shrubs along the path down which they had come. As he had explained, he had no real hope of finding the rope, nor would its discovery change the direction of his investigations. But having the rope itself on hand, especially if there were evidence of knots at the same interval as the two stripped treelets on either side of the gap, would make his case to the coroner that much easier. Harris was a lazy man, he mused, and one who wanted the easiest answer, but he would hopefully not be one to dismiss clear evidence.

He poked through rough and grabbing branches, kicked aside piles of leaves, and scratched himself on more twigs than he could count before he heard John call from a short distance away.

There, flung up into a tree, where its fibres seemed almost to blend with the drying wood of the branches and the crisp leaves that still clung tight, was a length of rope. John gave Nat a hoist, and the younger man scaled enough of the tree to grab the tail. Within moments, the three had the rope on the ground. "Is this it?" John asked.

"We shall see. Take that end to where the stem is stripped of its branches, and I shall take this end to the other side." One knot was still in place; on the other side, the kinks remained in the rope. It measured exactly.

"Good work, my friends. If need be, you will be my witnesses in front of the inquiry? Very good. This should convince Mr. Harris that there has been foul business here."

Soon the party split into two; Nat returned to the manor with six of the casts in his bags; he would return for the rest immediately and would then proceed to recreate the scene according to the plan Alexander had drawn. Alexander and John were to head towards Sotherton across the fields. John knew the way and offered his services, and Alexander looked forward to conversation with the dark man. He looped the rope into a coil and stowed it in one of his own saddle bags, and they began the gallop across the empty fields.

Although by the roads that could accommodate a curricle or a phaeton, it was a distance of twelve miles between Mansfield Park and Sotherton, across the fields it was only eight. Since the gully and thicket were already two miles past the house in the direction of Sotherton, the remaining distance was short enough to allow the horses to run. It was, therefore, not long before the riders crested a hill and the back of the great house at Sotherton Court came into view.

Where Mansfield Park was modern and elegant, Sotherton harkened back to much older times. The building, from this distance at least, looked to be Elizabethan in its origins. It was a large, regular brick building, and very grand looking. Only its situation in the expansive park was to its detriment, for rather than crowning a rise of land, it sat low in the dell between a cluster of hills, which must make it unfavourable for improvements and would surely limit the prospects. Nevertheless, it was an impressive building, suitable to an estate that earned its master twelve thousand pounds a year.

The two slowed their horses to a trot as they crossed the final fields to the stables. At this gentler pace, Alexander was able to converse with his companion. "Am I impertinent to ask where you are from? You do not sound like you are native to these parts."

The Black man chortled. "Neither, my friend, do you!"

Alexander threw his head back in an answering roar of laughter. "Very true. I was born and raised in a small village near Glasgow. My father was the local doctor." He waited for John to respond, which he did in short time.

"I don't remember much of my family. I was born on the island of Antigua. My parents were slaves. Perhaps they still are; I have had no news of them." There was no bitterness in his voice, but there was a tinge of sadness. "The late Sir Thomas—the present master's father, that is—was visiting his plantation there and decided I would be a fitting gift for his wife. I was seven years of age, small and by all accounts bright and of suitably pleasant features, and upon his return to England he ordered that I be prepared to accompany him, like a piece of furniture or a piece of art. If my parents objected, their voices were not heard. I served as Lady Bertram's personal attendant for a time, bringing trays of tea from the kitchens and entertaining her friends almost as an exotic pet. Eventually I grew too tall to be considered fashionable, and was given a place in the stables."

Alexander grimaced. "I was curious. I did not want to ask. And now?" He both needed and dreaded the answer. No matter John's legal standing at present, the fact of his past and his arrival in England was deeply troubling. Alexander was uncomfortable being deferred to by servants. For him, the notion that one man might claim ownership over another and might take a child away from his parents as a toy was nothing short of abhorrent. How could one man hold such sovereignty over another's entire being, depriving him of the fundamental value of humanity, of control over his own body? Being an owner of men must surely destroy a soul.

He stifled a bitter laugh. Mary was concerned to the point of distress about the state of Alexander's immortal soul, but she happily attended church with a family that lived off the unwilling sweat and pain of others, and seemingly without a thought.

Heedless of this series of thoughts, John answered Alexander's question. "When I arrived on English soil, I became free, as is the law here. This I learned later, when I began to ask questions. But I was a child with no family or friends and was equally dependent upon the Bertrams as if I were their slave. I could set out and try to make my way, but I have a home and a position here. It is all I have known, so far as I can recall. I ought to be most grateful. I can read and write, and I am paid according to my position, just like any other groom. I am far better off here than I would have been had I remained with my kind in the West Indies. And yet..."

His voice trailed off. He did not need to finish the thought. He was a man without a people, torn from his homeland and his family at the whim of others. No matter his present circumstances, the cruelty of the situation must never be far from his mind. They were never far from Alexander's. He suddenly felt a deep kinship with this dark and intelligent man, and wished he might one day work with him again.

By now, the stables were well within sight, and by the time they slowed their horses and dismounted, three stable hands were present to tend to the animals. The family were likely at church, but these men were on hand for such events as this unexpected visit.

"John." One of the men scowled and all but spat the name. John was clearly known here, and not universally liked. From the look of resigned acceptance on the Black man's face, it was not an uncommon reaction to his presence, and Alexander bristled again at the unfairness of it all.

Alexander ignored the sour expression—it seemed to be only one of the stable hands after all—and quickly explained his mission. "I am most dreadfully sorry about your master," he bowed his head. "I hope to do everything I can to find out what happened. To that end, I must request some help." The sour man who seemed to hate John for no reason scuttled back into the stables and the atmosphere lightened, despite the solemnity of the occasion.

Mr. Rushworth's horse had indeed returned the previous day, shortly after one o'clock, without its rider. The staff had been most concerned, and when the message arrived from Mansfield Park later that evening, their worst fears had been confirmed. Mrs. Rushworth, the dead man's mother, had been given a draught to help her sleep, and the solicitor from Northampton had been summoned.

Alexander would inquire into the internal management of Sotherton Court later; for now, he needed to confirm his evidence that Rushworth was deliberately killed. "May I examine his horse?" He asked the man whose stance indicated a level of authority over the others. "I shall do him no harm, but I need to see his legs. I may require someone to hold him."

This request was granted, for there could be no harm in it after all. Alexander and John were led into the stables, to a large stall where a majestic grey snorted at the strangers before him. When the beast was calmed and held steady, Alexander lowered himself to his knees. "This abrasion," he pointed to a raw patch on one leg just above the fetlock, "is it new?" It looked raw and was scabbing over as fresh wounds do.

"It is, I reckon," the stable master said as he narrowed his eyes. "'Twasn't there when he set out with the master, God rest 'is soul. Came back with it, 'e did. Must have caught it on sompin' as 'e was out."

"A rope, perhaps, whilst leaping a hedge?"

"Now's you mention it, perhaps." The eyes narrowed further.

Asking permission, Alexander reached into his satchel and withdrew the rope John had found in the tree. Without touching the injured animal, he held the rope up the wound.

The stable master let out a grunt. "Fits right, don't it?" And to Alexander's eyes, it did. Perfectly. Then, with the man's permission, he rubbed a great deal of his pencil lead on the creature's one hoof and coaxed the animal to stand on a sheet of paper, giving him an impression of the underside of the hoof to compare with the casts back at Mansfield Park. There was little doubt in Alexander's mind that this, too, would be a match.

Alexander and John thanked the grooms from Rushworth's stables for their assistance, and procured enough hearty agreements to testify willingly if called before the inquiry as to leave him satisfied on that account. Before they departed, however, Alexander had one last question about the two men who had been asking after Tom Bertram and, presumably, the late James Rushworth.

By now, more of the stable hands were back at their stations and several of the men had seen this pair. One fellow, short and wiry with squinty eyes, admitted to seeing two strangers on the lane that ran beside some of the fields. Another, large and sandy, had encountered the pair in the local village when he was at the smithy.

"A fine pair of nobs, they were," he chewed his lip. "Nothing to remember 'em by, but dressed all fine and fancy. From London, by the sounds of them."

"No, they wasn't!" the first man spoke up. "One was large enough to warrant his own parish, and the two of 'em looked more akin to us than to the nobs. Just plain folk in plain garb, I tell you."

"You can't see your nose, Joe," came the retort, but Joe was insistent.

"Didn't hear 'em talk, and mebbe my eyes aren't the best, but I can see a man the size of a house, and that was one right such man. I pitied his poor horse to carry 'im, though the beast was big enough too."

The argument went back and forth for a time, with no clear conclusion. Perhaps the same men had traded their fine city clothing for rougher country wear, more suited to the fields. Perhaps one man's idea of a giant was another's of a man of slightly greater-than-normal girth. Alexander jotted down some lines in his notebook before asking Hal, the second man, "Did you speak to these men? You clearly heard them in conversation with somebody."

"I did indeed!" Hal straightened up and stood tall and proud. "They asked if I knew of the master of Sotherton, and I said that yes, I did. Then they asked if he was at home, and I said he wasn't, and they asked when he might return. I said I had no right idea, and they asked directions to the house and I gave it, and then they tossed me a coin."

Alexander made his notes. "You spoke to them for a moment, then. Can you recall at all what they looked like? It would mean a great deal."

Hal preened again. "I did talk to 'em for a time. Lemme see. Not young, nor old, and fairly average looking. Nothing much comes to mind about 'em, nothing too special for good or ill. One was about my colour, I suppose," he ran a hand though his dust-caked sandy hair. "The other was darker, maybe a touch of grey at the edges."

"Yer going crazy, Hal. The dark one was like an ox."

"Nonsense, Joe! There was nothing big about 'em at all."

"Yer—"

Alexander cut them both off. "Were the two gentlemen mounted?" He asked Hal. Joe, he knew, had seen the men riding.

Horses seemed to be more distinct in their individuality than men to the grooms, and both men launched into detailed descriptions of the beasts they had seen. It became clear very quickly that there were, if not two sets of men, then two sets of horses.

"It seems," Alexander considered, "that Mr. Rushworth was being sought by two sets of people. Most interesting indeed."

Chapter Ten

A Surprise at Tea

Mary, too, had risen early, but rather than dressing to scour the fields and woods for hints about Rushworth's demise, she had dressed for church. Only Edmund, Fanny, and Mrs. Norris were gathered in the morning room: Edmund and Fanny were both of a pious disposition, which would make them well-suited should Edmund ever leave off his doting admiration of Miss Crawford. This pleased Mary, for it accorded perfectly with her own sense of inner devotion. Mrs. Norris, on the other hand, seemed eager to attend Sunday services only in order to comment afterwards about how Doctor Grant failed to live up to the standards set by her own late husband, the former incumbent of the living.

Mary had not slept soundly and was tired and out of sorts as they slid into the Bertrams' reserved box just moments before the service began. She settled her heart upon finding peace in the familiar words of the prayers, and sang quietly with the congregation when they came to tunes she knew, casting away her cares with the notes to the hymns. It was a pleasant service, neither too quick nor too slow. Doctor Grant might be given to some indolence, with a passion for food and drink, but mild gluttony and sloth did not make him any less of a fine speaker, and Mary strongly suspected the well-chosen words of his sermon were, indeed, his own.

After the closing hymn, the small party filed out of the church, at last to greet neighbours and acquaintances from the village. The feeling of discontent that had weighed Mary's shoulders before the service now threatened to settle there once again. All around her, the hum of conversation was not about Doctor Grant's fine words, but on Mr. Rushworth's unnatural death, and with every new voice that added to the chorus, her spirits became lower.

"Did you hear..." one voice began. "—in the icehouse! Awaiting the inquiry—" another added. The sorry tale had spread quickly, and speculation was rife even as facts were thin.

Mrs. Grant invited the party from Mansfield Park in for refreshments, but Edmund looked as tired as Mary felt, and the invitation was refused with every evidence of good grace and breeding. However, an invitation for the Grants to join the residents of Mansfield Park later that day was offered in exchange, and accepted with pleasure, and the two groups parted ways for the nonce.

The house, when they entered it, looked devoid of its inhabitants. Only the quiet and efficient staff of servants, glimpsed momentarily before disappearing through some disguised doorway or into another room, prevented it from seeming entirely abandoned. Baddeley, the butler, answered Edmund's questioning glance.

"Mr. Lyons was the first out, long before seven o'clock, according to Cook. He was garbed in clothing suitable for a ride, and left in the direction of the stables. He has not returned." He expressed neither approbation nor disapproval at the suggestion of riding on the Lord's Day. He, after all, was at his duties, as were many of the servants. It was not his place, so it seemed, to comment upon another doing likewise. "Miss Bertram and Miss Julia requested trays be sent to their rooms, and have asked not to be disturbed. Mr. Yates and the other gentlemen came down for coffee and are, I believe, in the rehearsal room." He did not mention Lady Bertram. Mary suspected that her presence before mid-afternoon would be more remarkable than her customary absence.

Edmund's face betrayed a grimace at the mention of his sisters. Fanny remained quiet, but her eyes narrowed with disdain, a sentiment which Mary echoed. Had Maria shown any suggestion of distress at the death of her betrothed, Mary might have felt great sympathy for the lady and her wish not to be in company. Instead, she felt only vexation and disapproval of a woman who cared so little for her dead intended that she could not even bother herself to go to church and pray for his soul.

Edmund began to lead the ladies to the back parlour that opened onto the expansive lawns, but Baddeley called him aside. "Begging your pardon, Mr. Bertram, but Cook and Mr. Barnaby have both requested a word." He executed a respectful bow.

"Cannot my mother…? Oh, never mind. I shall see them directly. Excuse me, Fanny, Aunt, Miss Bennet." He took his leave most politely and hastened towards his duties. Mrs. Norris was less polite in taking her own leave and scurried up the stairs to her rooms, seeing no one of suitable interest to keep her busy, and leaving Mary and Fanny in each other's company once more.

Fanny invited Mary to join her in the parlour but did not request tea. Mary could see the discomfort in the girl's face, but imagined that Fanny was not accustomed to requesting anything in this house, not even a drink for a guest. She took the comfortable seat by the window which Fanny offered her, and watched as her hostess glanced first at one seat, then another, and then another yet, before choosing one in which to sit. Of course, Fanny must never have her choice of chairs, being always commanded to leave the "good" seats for the family or company and being required to be at her aunts' sides to fetch and carry and execute whatever duties were required of her.

Mary picked up the book that was sitting on the small round table at her side, but before she could examine the cover, Fanny opened her mouth to speak. "My cousins... that is, Maria... I dread to consider what you must think," she spat out at last. "You must imagine her quite devoid of every ounce of feeling that is suitable for a lady. Poor Mr. Rushworth, so recently dead he is almost still breathing, and Maria behaving as if nothing were at all the matter. She will put on mourning, of course, because she believes it reflects well on her, but it will all be for appearances and nothing else."

"She did not care for him, did she?" Mary knew the answer, but wished to hear Fanny's response.

"I do not know!" she exclaimed. "She was so pleased, at first, to receive his addresses. Aunt Norris claims the engagement was her own doing, but Mr. Rushworth had been often in the area in his dealings with Uncle or my cousin Tom after Uncle left for the Indies, and we all could see he admired Maria. Indeed, what man would not? She is lovely and accomplished and wealthy." Mary nodded but said nothing, not wishing to break Fanny's thread of speech.

"When he came to Mansfield when there were no matters of business to discuss, we all knew he was hoping to court Maria, and when he offered for her, she seemed more than pleased. This was a match settled upon solely by the couple; it was not arranged for her to accept or refuse."

"When did her sentiments change?" Mary breathed the question.

"It was when *they* arrived." There was no need to explain. *They* were clearly the Crawfords. "He seemed determined to flirt with her, no matter that she was engaged. I even heard him once, commenting to his sister that it was more pleasant to flirt with an engaged lady because she was satisfied with herself and therefore more easy to be pleased. I recall his words, for they so alarmed me. 'An engaged woman is always more agreeable than a disengaged. Her cares are over and she feels that she may exert all her powers of pleasing without suspicion.' It was most improper, Miss Bennet. Can he really have thought that no harm could be done?"

Fanny turned her gaze to the lawns beyond the window. "It is not seemly for me to speak of this. I ought to be better. Forgive me, Miss Bennet." The conversation seemed to be over.

Mary feigned a yawn and sought an excuse to leave her young companion to the solitude she clearly desired. "I beg your pardon, Miss Price. I seem to be fatigued. I hope you will not think ill of me if I retire to my room for a rest." Fanny exhaled in relief, and Mary made her escape, suddenly desperate to be alone as well.

The yawn might have been feigned, but Mary's exhaustion was not. When she had fallen asleep, she hardly knew. She scarcely recalled lying on her bed, but the knock at her door woke her from what was assuredly a deep sleep. She croaked some unintelligible words, and Alexander's voice came back through the closed door. "Sorry to wake you, Mary. I did not know you were asleep. I have just now come back and I have some information you might wish to hear."

She made a somewhat more coherent reply, to which her friend called, "Shall we meet in the room Mr. Bertram appointed to us in a half an hour? Bring your shawl or coat. We shall head out to the stables as well."

The stables? This was intriguing enough that further thoughts of sleep vanished, as did any lingering ill feelings from Alexander's rude departure the previous evening. She pulled herself up to sitting, and then to her feet, before walking to the basin to splash enough water onto her face to wake her completely.

As promised, Alexander was waiting in the room Edmund had given over to their use. To her delight, he had procured the tray of tea and sustenance that Fanny had felt unequal to ordering earlier. The thought of a nice tea, along with that much-needed rest, brightened her spirits somewhat, and she gazed with pleasure upon the tray. He must have caught her appreciative gaze, for he explained, "I was not certain whether you had eaten. With so many of the family keeping to their rooms and the gentlemen keeping to the billiards room, which is where I found them, I imagined there was no set meal. Edmund explained how he was called away as you arrived, else he would have ensured that you were fed."

"Yes." She eyed the selection of breads and cheeses. "Miss Price and I talked for a few short minutes, but quickly parted ways. Thank you." She chose a slice of bread and poured a cup of tea, which she passed to Alexander before preparing her own. "I am sorry. I was rude last night. I ought to know…" She turned bright eyes on him. "Why do we always find ourselves arguing over the same thing? Every time we seem to find a satisfactory conclusion, but then we…" She blinked. "I start again. Why cannot I not accept your answers?" She swallowed, trying to hold back tears. This was not the time to be missish.

To her surprise, rather than counter words with words. Alexander rose from his chair and stepped towards her, pulling her into his arms and hard against his chest. She stiffened at the unexpected contact and this most alarming breach of propriety, but then allowed herself to relax and melt into his embrace.

"Och, Mhairi," his brogue was as thick as ever she had heard it. "We are friends, are we not? Friends have their disagreements, and do not allow those disagreements to damage their friendship. We do have to have a talk about this, I agree. But can we wait? Can we first conclude our investigations here, before we engage in that conversation? Then if you wish to part from me, I will not put up an objection. But later. Will you allow me that?"

Whatever could he mean? Did he believe that what he had to tell her was so dire that she would cease her association with him? What could be that terrible to recount? He was no murderer, no roue or gamer. He had not pursued his career in law, but she was certain he was no thief or other sort of dishonest man. And whilst their current position—she enfolded in his arms in a private space—was hardly one that would escape the scrutiny of a gossip's eye, he had never pressed his attentions upon her, had never encouraged a degree of intimacy with which she was uncomfortable. He was a gentleman in every way but by birth, and she could imagine no matter he could have to tell her that would cause her to flee from him.

She nodded; he surely felt her head move against his chest, for he squeezed her to him more tightly for just a moment before kissing the crown of her head gently and letting her go. The release was both a relief and a loss. They were friends; she wished to be a great deal more, and knew—or thought she knew—that he did likewise. She admired him greatly and loved him as a friend, and was more than halfway to loving him in other ways that were new to her young heart. If only his circumstances were different, she might allow herself to love him completely. But she was a gentleman's daughter and he a working man of unspoken background and firmly in the middle class with no prospects of moving upward and out of that sphere. Unless he could find himself a fortune and abandon his business, or unless she were prepared to lower herself in the eyes of society, they could be nothing but friends. Friends, therefore, it would have to be, for she could not imagine giving him up completely.

Now he guided her back to her chair, ensured she had a plate of bread and cheese at hand, and began the account of his morning.

"Then it was definitely murder? The rope, being exactly the length of the gap and the knots matching the two stems exactly, as well as matching the injury on Mr. Rushworth's horse? And the hoof mark matched as well?" She had no doubts, but needed to hear the confirmation.

"I am certain of it. And do not forget the rock, which was surely used by one of the riders to bash the poor man's head, if the fall from his horse hadn't done enough damage to him. I believe even the coroner will have to agree now. But come!" He leapt to his feet. "Nat, the groom I mentioned, has set out the casts exactly as they were found. Let us see what they have to tell us."

The young groom bowed shyly upon being presented to Mary and led the way to the small paddock behind the stables where he had set up his simulation. Alexander looked very pleased and heaped praise upon the towheaded man. "Excellently done! My thanks indeed. I shall surely let Mr. Bertram know what a treasure he has in you. Very good." Nat showed Mary the different casts and explained how Alexander had encoded them so as to be able to form this replica of the field. Nat could not read well, he explained to Mary, but he knew his numbers and his letters well enough to perform this task.

"Here is the front hoof of one of the beasts, from what we can see." He pointed out slight irregularities on the different shoes, the better to distinguish one from another and to assert without reservation that there were two horses waiting in the field across from the thicket which Rushworth had tried to leap, as well as the tracks, some distance further, of Rushworth's own horse. "See how deep this one is? That is where the horse landed after his jump, now without a rider. And there, you see the back hooves. He must have been scared and set off straight for home." He further explained how these casts matched the impression Alexander had taken at Sotherton earlier, and by their depth and distance apart, suggested that the animal was running.

The prints from the other horses were less eloquent, however. Other than the small marks that told one shoe from another, however, there were no identifying markings that might point to a specific smith or farrier. Who these two mounted strangers were remained unknown.

Alexander thanked Nat, and then asked Mary's leave to introduce John to her, which she granted gladly. He had spoken well of the groom in his account of the morning, and Mary was pleased to meet the person who had so impressed her friend.

The groom seemed surprised to be introduced to Mary. Had Alexander not apprised him of his plans? He bowed low and kept his eyes diverted, which behaviour Mary did not even see at home at Longbourn, except from the very lowest of servants. Mrs. Hill certainly met Papa's gaze with her own frank assessment, and Mama—although raised to the gentry through her marriage— insisted her servants look at her when being spoken to.

Alexander cast a quick glance towards her as he saw John's deference. In an instant, he seemed to come to a decision.

"I have some lemonade and cakes from the house. If your master can spare you for a moment, we would enjoy your company as we take refreshments." He patted the bag slung over his shoulder. Had he brought the treats along for just such a purpose?

No matter. John seemed at first taken aback, then leery, and then pleased. "I shan't tell a soul. I can claim I needed to discuss some matter about the case with you. Where can we go where we will have some privacy?"

John led them to a clearing behind the stables, where a set of stones formed a sort of bench, and there they enjoyed some fruit breads and the contents of a flask of lemonade, poured into three small tin cups. The conversation was light and quite unrelated to any matters touching upon poor Rushworth, just three friends enjoying a mid-day snack. John was intelligent and witty and he could read, a result of his years as Lady Bertram's page. Edmund gave him old copies of the newspapers that came to Mansfield Park, and for a man whose life was spent in the stables, he was remarkably well informed. The company and food revived Mary's spirits all the more until she felt almost her usual placid self.

"You have taken to him as a friend," she commented as they wandered back to the house. "Is he not your inferior?"

"You mean as a Black man, a former slave?" Alexander's regard was not friendly.

Mary started. "No! That was not my meaning at all. I meant as a stable hand. You are an educated man, the son of a doctor and a lawyer in your own right, whereas John is lucky to be able to read. And yet you did not let your differences in rank prevent you from treating him as your equal."

The stern gaze eased. "He is my equal. He is interesting and worth keeping company with. I hope I shall never fall into the sin of treating my fellow men according to some circumstances over which they have no control. Heaven knows, I have been the victim of such displays often enough myself. I shall not do that to another."

"Alexander?" What did he mean by that? But he said not another word on the subject and turned back to Nat's display of horse hoof casts and knotted rope, leaving Mary to ponder what sort of stories there were in her friend's past that he would have been subject to such ill-considered behaviour.

They had no sooner returned to the house when men's voices were heard, and the honourable Mr. Yates strode out of the billiards room. He greeted both Mary and Alexander with the grace of his station and asked after their health.

"The day has been fine, sir, and most informative." Alexander returned the bow. "If you do not mind, I have some questions I would put to you about Mr. Bertram—Tom Bertram, that is. Despite this most unfortunate incident with Mr. Rushworth, I am still concerned with locating your friend. You surely know him the best. I hoped you might have some insights into where he might be."

Yates' face went white for a moment. This was unexpected, for he had seemed quite undisturbed—or at least, no less disturbed than might be considered normal—by Rushworth's death. Nor had he expressed any indications of worry when he spoke to Mary and Alexander upon their first arrival at the house. Mary glanced towards Alexander, whose raised brows suggested he was similarly surprised. Yates foundered for words for a moment before collecting himself. "Yes, yes of course. Definitely want to find my friend. Cannot imagine where he might be... well, if we may speak in confidence, sir?" His eyes settled on Mary.

"Miss Bennet is completely trustworthy, sir," Alexander replied. "She is made of sterner stuff than most men, and will divulge none of your secrets. You may consider her my secretary."

"A woman secretary!" the nobleman's son snickered. "How drole. Yes, indeed, a secretary. Ha ha!" He tittered for a moment before Alexander's stony face damped his mirth. The titters quieted and his face grew astonished, then serious. Restored to his accustomed demeanour, he held out an arm in a dramatic effect. "I see. Lead on."

Mary had just closed the door when Mr. Yates began his account. He refused a chair, but paced around the perimeter of the room as he spoke. "I ought to have told you," he began. "When Tom returned.... No." He pulled at his lip again. "It begins before that. Three years ago, nearly four now, before Tom went with his father to see to affairs in the Indies, we were at my family's estate in Devon, with a party of others from our school days. We had been drinking and, well, there was an accident. The details are unimportant. I fell from the church roof and broke my leg."

Mary's back stiffened as she sat. What under heaven had these young men been doing on the church roof? How much drink had they consumed? She swallowed her retort and let Mr. Yates continue.

"It was a simple break and it healed perfectly, as you see," he gestured to his unimpaired and easy gait, "but for a while, the pain was considerable. Our physician recommended a tincture of opium, taken very sparingly, until the worst of the agony subsided. Whilst I recovered, most of the party took themselves off to their homes or to those of their friends, but Tom Bertram stayed with me. I was bed-bound for a time and he read to me and cheated me out of a great deal of money at cards and generally kept my spirits up until the physician allowed me to walk again. I had long since forgotten the opium, and so did not notice when the bottle disappeared.

"It transpired that Tom had taken it. His mother, Lady Bertram, has long since used a mild tincture of laudanum for her nerves, and he was eager to try it when he could not sleep. I believe what Doctor DeQuincy gave to me was far stronger than what he had seen his mother add to her cordial. I am afraid he became rather more obsessed with it than might be healthy. He claimed it helped him sleep, but at times, he would retire to his rooms far earlier than the rest of the company."

Alexander clucked and nodded his head. "My father was a physician as well, and he spoke to us often of the benefits and dangers of opium tincture. A small amount can cure pain, but a larger amount taken regularly can lead to a bodily reliance, a desperate need for it. I have seen some of his patients, how the substance made them suffer. I pray I will never need recourse to take it myself."

Yates stopped pacing and found a chair. "I had not seen him partake of the drug since his return and whilst we have been in company, but I cannot say he has not done it. He may have become more adept at limiting his consumption to times when he was not expected in company; I know not. But now I have to wonder if his disappearance has aught to do with this."

"Thank you for your candid account, Mr. Yates." Alexander regarded him with a sober gaze. "Do you have any notion where Mr. Bertram might have gone? Was he seeking a new source for his habit?"

The gentleman shook his head. "I cannot say. But..." he seemed lost in thought for a moment. "But some short time ago, he did ask me if I had heard of the new Chinese fashion for smoking opium, rather than eating it."

Mary was confused by this comment; this was part of a world she knew nothing about. She knew, of course, about the dangers of laudanum use and how one might come to need more and more of the tincture and become most distressed in its absence, but to smoke it? How was that even possible? Alexander seemed to know a little more, for he nodded, his brows low over his brown eyes. She would ask him later.

A tap at the door interrupted her thoughts. Edmund's voice filtered through the heavy wood. "Miss Bennet, Mr. Lyons? Are you in there?" At Alexander's response, he opened the door and stepped through. "Ah, Mr. Yates. Excellent! My mother and sisters are downstairs and we await the Grants and the Crawfords for tea. Would you care to join us?" Mr. Yates had concluded his sad tale. There would be little more to learn from him.

He led them through the grand house to a comfortable room Mary had not seen before at the front of the house. It was not excessive in size, and if it lacked the comfort of the lovely back parlour, it atoned for this lack in a particular beauty of style Mary knew she could never match. The three Bertram ladies, mother and daughters, were enthroned in three elegant chairs that set their uncommon looks off to the best advantage. Mrs. Norris sat across the low table from them, accompanied on one side by the visitors Mr. Maddox and Mr. Oliver and the Grants, and on the other by Henry and Mary Crawford.

Maria Bertram was dressed in mourning, her choice of clothing seeming to have been selected for its ability to accentuate her beauty. With a bitter pang of contempt, Mary thought that a better show of honest loss and devotion would be to eschew such social occasions as this tea party. But Maria's aim was clearly not to mourn but to impress, and from the look of admiration on Henry Crawford's face, she was achieving some measure of success.

"Ah Edmund. You have returned. And with your friends. How lovely." Lady Bertram's soft voice and vague gestures brought back to mind Yates' comments about the habitual use of laudanum in this house. Mary wondered, briefly, if such habits were learned young, from watching as much as from partaking, and if a tendency to such habits might be inherited along with a particular physiognomy or colour of hair.

"Mother," Edmund bowed, and all suitable greetings were made as the newcomers were settled in their chairs around the central table.

"Where is that maid?" Mrs. Norris flustered. "I requested tea nearly ten minutes ago. Surely Cook ought to have known to have hot water at the ready. I really must—"

A burst of activity outside the window called everybody's attention, and a cloud of dust arose from the dry driveway. Mrs. Norris leapt from her seat to rush to the window before any of the men could achieve their feet, and she snorted.

"Some sort of rider, and not very well dressed. Really, he ought to know to go around to the stables at the back. Coming up the main drive seems quite unsuitable for one like that. What? Now he is at the front doors? I hope Baddeley puts him to rights. He has no business being seen in the front of the house. The kitchen is too good for him!"

But rather than being turned from the house as Baddeley surely ought to have done, the rider was permitted entrance, for he arrived at the salon doors within seconds of this pronouncement.

"Mr. Bertram?" he asked through the hard breaths of exertion. "Mr. Edmund Bertram?" Baddeley stood behind him with a frown of disapproval at this most improper interruption, but he remained silent. "I've just come from Bedford. Mr. Newton sent me here with all speed to give you this message." He belatedly held out a folded piece of paper, which Edmund took and opened. But before he could read the contents, the rider continued. "They found a body. Nothing too unusual of it for he was floating in the river, and they find 'em like that once in a while, and especially near the new moon when it's dark and people misstep. But they found this on his finger." He reached into a pocket and drew out an object. "Says TFB on it, and with your family coat of arms. Mr. Newton thinks it's your brother's signet ring."

Chapter Eleven

Shaken and Stirred

Edmund's face went white and his jaw slack, whilst his sisters turned to each other with pretty little moues, murmuring "What? No! It cannot be." at each other. Mrs. Norris looked more angry than upset, for surely this had upset some great plan of hers, and Lady Bertram, the man's mother, called out, "Edmund? What is this? I do not understand. What has happened?"

As for the others in the room, Alexander quickly schooled his own reaction enough to take note of their expressions. Yates looked about to swoon in his chair, and Maddox, Oliver and Crawford all wore the usual expressions of shock. Mrs. and Doctor Grant gaped at each other in shocked disbelief. Miss Crawford's expression, however, Alexander could not identify so quickly. Was hers a look of horror? Of resignation? Her lips quivered and he was unsure whether she was about to laugh or cry. Her brother looked over at her in alarm and took her hand, so marked was the change in her demeanour. Alexander was concerned she might be ill.

Likewise, Mary's face was unreadable, so quickly did emotions pass across it. Of all the people in the room, she seemed one of the most profoundly affected, more so than Tom Bertram's own kin, and she had not known him at all, had seen him only once, and that only in passing. Had she expected such a sad outcome? Surely they all had, for when a man vanishes so completely, there is often no other explanation than that he has left this life. He knew that, as much as he held hope and was working as though the man were alive and needed rescuing, even he had despaired of seeing Tom Bertram alive again.

Alexander turned his attention now to Bertram's family and friends as they heard the dire news and reached the inevitable conclusion. He stood back, all the better to watch their faces and their bodies, to gauge their reactions, and to listen.

After an initial beat of deafening silence, a great din erupted. "It cannot be." "I saw him just three days ago!" "How terrible." "What will Sir Thomas do?" The cries of alarm seemed genuine and unrehearsed. Surely nobody in this room had expected the report that the rider had brought of the body in the river. Had anybody expected any other news? That was something he would need to determine in due course. In the middle of the chaos, a young maid wheeled a treat-laden trolley into the room and stood, transfixed at the doorway.

Eventually Edmund raised his voice. "Please!" The chatter ceased at once.

Edmund moved to the window to examine the ring, which he had accepted from the rider. "It is undoubtedly Tom's signet ring. There, on the back, is the jeweller's mark, which I know, for he makes many of our new items. And there," he pointed to something on the side of the signet, "is the dent he made when he fell from the table while celebrating his majority." The hum swelled like the cresting waves of the ocean, a disquieting crescendo and diminuendo better suited to a concert hall than a group at tea.

"But," Edmund screwed up his brow and the noise ceased, "Tom has not worn this ring in years. He used it... Pardon me, Mother, Aunt, but I must explain. He used the seal once too often to promise payment for debts he should not have incurred, and after one such incident, Father announced broadly that he would no longer honour letters sealed with this stamp. Every merchant and innkeeper in Northamptonshire was made aware of this. Through them, it transpired, every gaming house and other place that... that might accept his credit learned it as well. Tom stopped wearing it then. It may have been stolen. He may have sold it..." His voice trailed off and silence flooded the room once more.

Alexander decided it was time to speak. He rose from his chair. "Begging your pardon," he addressed the rider. "Can you tell me more of where you found this unfortunate soul, and when? I will need to see him; will somebody accompany me to identify him?"

"We found 'im in the River Ouse near Bedford last night. Looked like 'e'd been floating a while. Not a pretty sight. Sorry, ma'ams."

"Why are we only told now?" Edmund's voice was breathy and he rubbed his palms compulsively on his trousers. "Bedford is little more than an hour away for a man on a fast horse. And yet you have waited nearly a day."

"We 'ad no notion it was important to you, sir," the rider explained. "Not till we found the ring. It was so caked in mud, we could not see it for anything more than a piece of dirt, till it was cleaned. And since it's a different county, the first people to see it didn't know it was important."

Edmund still looked agitated, but a shift in his stance suggested he accepted the rider's explanation. "Very well. Bedford, you say?"

"Just this side of it, sir. No more than ten miles, I'm guessing, from this place."

"Then I must be off at once. This man may not be Tom, but I must see." He cast his eyes down to his fine Sunday clothing. The waistcoat alone must have cost enough to feed a village for a week, Alexander thought bitterly; how many men would his father buy and sell in his precious sugar islands for that same cost? "I shall change at once. Baddeley, please request my horse be made ready. Mr. Lyons' as well."

"Very good, sir."

The room lapsed once more into a horrified silence. It seemed, to Alexander, to last for an age, but it could not have been more than a second or two before a new voice sounded from the doorway. It was a man's voice, cultured and rich, and one that Alexander had heard before.

"Your horse, Edmund? Wherever are you going? You have company, and it is most impolite to abandon them."

Heads swivelled and gasps of disbelief replaced the cries of dismay from moments before.

For there, leaning against the door frame, and looking very much alive, was the man who only moments ago had been given up for dead. Could it be a ghost? No, of course not. Alexander was a man of reason and science, and no ghost would wear such strong cologne. It must be, therefore, Tom Bertram himself who now strolled into the room as if nothing at all were amiss.

"Tom!" Lady Bertram cried. "Where have you been?"

From the corner of his eye, Alexander saw Mary Crawford blanch as her mouth moved without sound, but almost at once his attention moved to Julia, who had risen at Tom's entry and now collapsed to the ground in a dead faint.

By the time Julia had been tended to and roused with some of Mrs. Norris' salts (which, Alexander noted, seemed never to have been previously used), it was deemed too late for the ride to Bedford. At this time of year, the sun dropped early into the horizon, and the moon was a mere sliver, not casting nearly enough light for a safe return.

"I must still go to see this man." Edmund worried at the sides of his trousers. "I feel an obligation, somehow, to him."

"Surely not." Henry Crawford left his sister's side at the words. "Your brother is returned in good health and there is no need. All is well once more."

"All is well?" Never had Alexander heard so much anger from the younger Bertram. "Our friend Rushworth has died and now another is dead with Tom's ring upon his finger. All is certainly not well. Can there be some connection between the two events?"

Murmurs filled the room again, before Edmund squared his jaw and repeated. "I feel an obligation. Lyons? What think you? I can at least get there before full dark."

Alexander tempered his desire.

"There can be little learned tonight," he coaxed, "and after the shock of your brother's presumed death and return, your mother and sisters surely need you here, with them. Perhaps our messenger might have more to offer us before he starts back for Bedford. If you still wish it, I will accompany you tomorrow. There might well be something to learn, but it can wait until morning."

With obvious reluctance, Edmund agreed, and Alexander approached the messenger.

"Before we allow you to take some rest and nourishment in the kitchens and whilst your horse rests, have you any more to tell us?"

Alexander's calm tones brought a nod to the rider's head. "Who found the body? Where is it now? How was he found?"

The rider cleared his throat. "I know only what I was told, but Mr. Newton—he's the coroner in that part—said he was summoned about half-past nine o'clock last night. Some men walking home from the tavern saw something in the water from the light of their lanterns."

"The men who found him…?"

"Farmers from the estate. Mr. Newton knows them; so do I. All good, honest men. I'd swear on it."

"And the dead man? Nobody knew him?"

The man shook his head. "It was not an easy matter to see. He was… not pleasant to look upon."

He seemed about to take his leave, but stopped halfway through a turn. "One matter, though, if you please, sirs. It happened just now, about two or three miles down the road, when I come off the road from Bedford to ask directions at the inn—the White Gryphon?"

"Down at Yardley?" Edmund asked.

"Aye, I believe that was so." He shuffled his feet. "'Twas another fellow there, heard me mention Mansfield Park and come over to listen. When I had my directions, he asked my business and I told him, and he then asked me if I had seen or heard of two strangers also heading this way."

He paused again and Alexander encouraged him to continue. "Two strangers, eh? What about them?"

"He saw I was in a hurry, so didn't talk long, but just wondered if I'd seen them about, what they had been doing, who they had been looking for. Said they was dangerous sorts and not to be trusted, that we shouldn't tell them what they was wanting to know."

"Did he say what these men looked like?"

"One looked nothing unusual, he said, but the other was very large, both tall and broad. Might be a bit unsteady on horseback, since they was sailors and more accustomed to sailing than riding."

"Indeed!" This was interesting news. The stable hands at Sotherton had spoken of such a pair, one man as large as a titan. But they had been seeking Rushworth, had they not? Were they looking for Tom Bertram as well? What sort of men had business with both Rushworth and Bertram? For every question answered, another two arose in its place. "And the man asking after them? What about him?"

The rider smiled. "Polite sort of man, sounded like he was from somewhere south, but with something smarter in his talk than a regular tar. Like a gent's son sent to sea."

"And his appearance?"

"Tall, like you lot, fair hair and red skin, but that's from the sea, I reckon. Looks a lot like the girl on yonder chair." For the first time, Alexander turned and noticed Fanny Price sitting in the distant corner of the room, shrouded in shadow and as silent as one. He felt a wash of shame at having failed to notice her before this very instant.

For her part, Fanny gasped and rose from her chair. "Did he…" she began, then fell silent, afraid to be heard.

"Speak, Fanny, please." Edmund crossed the room and took her hand.

She allowed her eyes to swallow the sight of it, then in a stronger voice asked, "Did he have a small scar just above his lip?"

"That he did."

"William!"

There was little more information to be gleaned from the rider. He was only the chap chosen to convey the message and knew very little else. He was sent, with all due thanks, to the kitchens for some sustenance, before starting back for Bedford.

As the door closed behind him, the room dissolved once more into pockets of excited conversation. Alexander hardly knew where to begin. He needed to hear from Tom Bertram about his whereabouts these past several days, but also wondered about Fanny's exclamation. Upon hearing of William's presence in the vicinity, she had broken into a wide smile, but had said not another word. From her joy and the description the rider had given, he must be her brother. Alexander strolled to where Mary stood near the forgotten tea trolley.

"What make you of all this?"

She blew out a puff of air that set the stray strands of hair escaping her coif to swaying. "I hardly know what to think. First Tom Bertram is missing, then he is dead, and then he is alive, and now some person named William is seeking the same men we are. Or is he?"

Alexander shrugged. "This William…?"

"Her brother?"

"I can think of nothing else. You have achieved some manner of rapport with her. Would you see what you can discover?"

Mary turned a brilliant smile upon him and his heart beat a little faster. "I would enjoy nothing more." She widened her smile for a moment, and then glided across the room to where Fanny Price sat alone in the shadows.

Alexander now turned his attention to the group gathered around the newly resurrected Tom Bertram. His appearance had been met with that incredulity that so often begets spontaneous exclamation. The gathering, in turns silent with surprise and bursting with amazement, turned its entire attention upon him. How often is it, after all, that a man, just now declared dead, walks into the room of his own apparent mourners?

His mother was the first to move. With a speed and agility Alexander had never yet seen from her, she flew to his side and held both his hands in her own. "Wherever have you been, Tom? We had all quite given up hope. You are well, are you not? Yes, yes, of course you are. But you are so thin. Perhaps there's a tray of something to eat. Fanny? Where is Fanny? She can help you."

But Julia had recovered and had already moved from her chair to prepare the suggested plate of food, with Yates at her heels in case she required assistance or felt faint once more.

Mrs. Norris looked rather more cross than relieved. Alexander could not figure her out; she had seemed quite put out by her nephew's presumed demise, but was now even more disgruntled by his miraculous return. "Really, Tom!" she chastised him. "It was very unkind of you to make us all think you were dead. What were you thinking?"

Now it was Tom's turn to look amazed. "Dead? What made you imagine that? I have not been dead a day of my life. Ah, thank you, Julia." He took the plate but did not eat.

"Come, sit, and we shall explain all," Edmund insinuated himself at his brother's side. He led Tom to one of the sofas and sat down beside him. "When you did not return to your rooms on Thursday last, Barnaby became alarmed. We spent two days and more searching for you, and only now, this man you saw when you entered had come to tell us of a body found near Bedford, wearing your signet ring. You must understand what we all thought."

"By gum! What a thing, eh what?" He lolled his head back onto the cushions of the sofa. "What a fix indeed. But as you can see, I am quite well." He gestured down the length of his body with theatrical movements. Of course. He was almost as much a thespian manqué as was his friend Yates.

"But where have you been?" Mrs. Norris' voice cut through the chatter.

Tom's eyes flicked aside for a brief moment and for a second, he did not speak. Was he avoiding some confession? "I was with friends," he replied at last. "I may have overindulged and took advantage of their offer of hospitality."

"In Northampton?" Edmund clenched his jaw. "We searched every inn and tavern and rooming house we could imagine, and discovered some we knew nothing of. Nobody had seen you at all."

"No, no, not there. Out of the town a way. Along the river. With friends… acquaintances." He added nothing more, but to Alexander, his eyes betrayed much.

Alexander now had the opportunity to observe this prodigal son more carefully. Unlike the first time Alexander had seen him, Tom Bertram was not so in his cups that he could not stand. His speech was precise and unslurred, and his face freshly washed. But there was still something of the reprobate about the gentleman that Alexander needed to examine. He did look thin, and his clothes hung unnaturally upon him as if he had recently lost weight and had not yet taken his clothing to the tailor to be altered. His hands twitched when they lay in his lap, and although he toyed with the food on his plate, he ate nothing.

Was it his breathing that bothered Alexander? As a doctor's son, who had assisted at many a bedside, such things came to his attention. It was scarcely noticeable to one who was not making a survey of his physical condition, but Tom's breaths came shorter and shallower than they ought, and his pupils in his eyes were tight and constricted. He kept shifting around as if uncomfortable in his skin with a sort of nervous energy that Alexander knew he had seen before. He recalled Mr. Yates' confession from earlier and sighed. It did indeed seem that Tom Bertram was an opium eater.

The others were still talking, however, and Alexander put aside his reflections for the moment to listen to what was being said.

"How long have you been here?" Julia asked, as Lady Bertram asked with uncharacteristic interest, "When did you arrive?"

Tom sprawled against the cushions. "Oh, a while ago. Perhaps an hour or two. Nobody was here; or rather, I heard voices but decided not to follow them. Po... my friend drove me to the end of the drive past the gardens and I walked in through the little wood there. I came in by the side door closest to the stairs to my chambers. I imagine nobody saw me either, and I wished for a rest, and so I lay down to sleep. Barnaby discovered me there and woke me and shaved me and dressed me, and here I am." Suddenly the actor was back, all charm and elegant movements and conceit.

He reclined back in his seat and allowed the others to gush over him for a moment, a king upon his throne, being adored by his subjects. Everybody had questions, some of which he answered and some of which he ignored, and he clearly relished the attention.

Alexander had other questions he wished to pose to Tom Bertram. He wished to know about these "friends" who had taken the inebriated man in. Had they supplied him with the opium that he surely had been taking? And why had he been with them for so long a time?

He wished to ask about the man—or men—to whom he had owed those debts six weeks earlier, when first Alexander had seen him falling down drunk in the Meldolas' house. He wished to ask if that person was still seeking him, or whether the debt had been repaid.

And more pressing, he wished to ask if Tom knew anything about the two men who had been asking after him in Northampton and in the village, the gentlemen rather than the two rougher men. Were they the ones to whom he owed money? If so, was it from wagers lost, or purchases unpaid? Or did it perhaps have to do with this unfortunate custom of taking opium that he seemed to have acquired? These first two men seemed to be gentlemen from London and were unlikely to be the sort to resort to violence themselves. Men of substance, however, had often been known to employ others to deal with some less gentlemanlike business. Could that be the connection with the other two men, the ones with rougher speech and dress, who had been seeking word of him in the villages closer to Bedfordshire and in the fields outside of Mansfield?

Hopefully, the messages Alexander had sent to his colleagues in Town would have long since arrived, and responses would be arriving soon. His associates worked quickly and well, and with luck, he would have some answers on the morrow.

He turned his attention back to Tom Bertram. The man was clearly pleased to see his friends Maddox and Oliver at Mansfield Park and asked after their journeys. "The ride was pleasant enough," Maddox answered, "but imagine our surprise and distress when we arrived to find you missing. It really was quite a to-do. And then the hunt...." He recoiled from the thought.

"Heavens, yes. That was dreadful." Oliver supplied. "Simply awful."

Both friends seemed to believe that Tom knew of what they spoke, but Alexander suspected that Bertram had no notion of what had occurred during his absence. Before anybody could supply him with detail, however, he abruptly changed the subject.

"Well, we all are here now, which is most excellent. I am anxious to be rehearsing this play and performing it as well. Now we have a full cast and an audience, or has Julia not decided to resume her role? Must we still convince Fanny to take her part? You will do it, will you not, Julia?" He talked on with sudden animation, oblivious to the agitation and alarmed looks passing between those around him.

He prattled on about the sets and the script and rehearsing those last small details that make a performance worthwhile, and then he spoke of the room they had commandeered for their space, and the great curtain Mrs. Norris had procured for them from the town, brushing off every attempt to interrupt him and deliver the dire news. Not once did he ask about the sudden hush that had grown about him, or the alarmed looks in everybody's eyes, until he said, "And Rushworth, I do hope you have learned your lines by now. What ho?" he spun his head around to examine the whole room and seemed to notice Alexander for the first time. "Who is that? And where is Rushworth? He ought surely to be here, for we have to perform our play."

"Tom," Edmund reached out to still his brother's arm. "This is something we have been trying to tell you. It happened during the hunt."

"That awful hunt," Henry Crawford whispered from his seat across the table.

"What about the hunt?" Tom screwed up his brow. "By gum. I missed the hunt. Bad luck, eh what? Did you catch the foxes?"

"There was an accident. Rushworth was in an accident. There can be no play. He was thrown from his horse and was killed. He is dead, Tom."

Chapter Twelve

The Show Must Go On

Mary poured two cups of tea from the abandoned tea tray and carried them across the room to where Fanny sat. She placed them on the small round table at Fanny's side and settled herself into the empty chair she found there.

"I hope the tea is as you like it."

Fanny blinked in surprise. Did nobody ever take the time to make her a cup of tea, or to ask about her preferences? "Yes. It will be excellent, I am certain. Thank you." The look she offered to Mary was all the thanks she needed. This poor girl was all but a slave in this house, her position in many ways not so different from that of the groom John. She was here upon their sufferance, subject to their whims, treated as a servant, and despite the ties of blood, never allowed to be one of the family. Mary would never consider Fanny's poor treatment as equivalent to the untold horrors of slavery, but the mentality of a family who could claim ownership over other humans and command the bodies and souls of others to their will was reflected in the lack of concern they took—all but one—in the genuine wellbeing of their poor cousin.

Mary arranged the chair cushion to her liking and then took up her own cup of tea. "Is William your brother? You seemed pleased to hear of him."

Fanny's face lit up again. "Yes. He is my older brother, and dearer to me than anybody in the world, although I have not seen him in too many years. He is a sailor in the Navy, and we correspond as much as his duties allow. He is a midshipman and wishes to improve himself further in the ranks."

Now that the gates had been opened, Fanny spoke freely about her own family in Portsmouth. She had mentioned them before, but finally allowed herself the breath to introduce them to her companion, one by one.

She spoke again of her mother, who was sister to both Mrs. Norris and Lady Bertram, and who had married so far beneath her, to disoblige her family. She spoke of her father, then a proud and strong officer in the Navy, so handsome in his uniform, but now injured and on half-pay, drinking away most of what little income he had. She spoke of her siblings—nine now, some of whom she had never seen or barely recalled—and especially of Susan, only one year younger than her, and of William, the older brother she so adored.

"He went to sea when he was eleven years of age, about the time I was invited here to live with my cousins. Until that time, we were inseparable. He was everything a brother ought to be! Have you brothers, Miss Bennet?"

Mary smiled. "No indeed! I have not as many siblings as you, but I am the middle of five, and all daughters. My poor father did not know how to manage us, or at least until my older sisters married."

"Then you know of the bond between siblings, that unbreakable link." Her eyes were mild and assured.

"I am afraid that it has only been recently that my sisters and I have developed such friendships. The older two, Jane and Elizabeth, were always in each other's confidence, and the younger two, Catherine and Lydia, were the silly children of the family. I was alone in the middle, often solitary, as if I were the only child."

Fanny's eyes misted over. "Yes. I am sorry for that. It is much as I felt once I arrived here. After the noise and activity and love of my home at Portsmouth, no matter how little we had or how many of us were in such a small house, arriving at Mansfield Park was like being cast away on one of the isles William would write of. I was so very, very lonely. Whatever would I have done without Edmund, and without William's letters? It was Edmund who showed me where to find pen and paper. That first act of kindness still lives in my heart."

She lapsed into memory, and Mary allowed her a moment of reflection before asking, "Tell me more of William. What might he be doing in Bedfordshire? It is a great distance from any port."

"I know not!" Fanny leaned forward and clasped her hands together. "He wrote nothing of it in his most recent letter, which I received only last week. His ship had just put in at Southampton, and he wrote of his joy at seeing our parents and brothers and sisters once more, and of his regret at my being so very far away. Before he left for the Indies, Sir Thomas once did suggest inviting William for a visit, but nothing came of it."

"I wonder, then, at the man not being William at all." Mary's suggestion met with disapproval on her companion's face.

"No, that cannot be! For we were always said to favour each other exceedingly, and had I been older and a boy, people would have imagined us to be twins. William does send drawings of himself at times in his letters, for one of his shipmates is skilled at the pencil, and my cousins all agree that we still look very much alike."

"And what of the scar on his lip?"

At that memory, Fanny laughed. "It was not such a joke then, but one of our antics as children involved jumping from the sea wall down to the beach below. It was not a great leap, but it seemed very high to us then. William was about to take his jump when Susan—she is our next younger sister, as I have said—came running to find us and warn us that Mother insisted we not play at our game. Of course, that announcement alarmed William just as he was flying from the wall, and he landed poorly and scratched his face on a rock. We had to think of a grand story to tell Mother, for she would have been most upset to hear that we were, indeed, leaping from the wall."

She stared into the images occasioned by the recollection. "William told Mother that he had been hit by a stone whilst protecting me from a ruffian who wished to steal my shoes. Mother was so proud of him he never told her the truth, and he wore the scar with pride."

Mary could not help but smile at the mirth this story conjured up. She could well replace the specific names and places with ones from her own youth and provide similar stories. Perhaps her childhood had not been so bereft of amusement. "And now?"

"And now he works hard for his captain and hopes daily for a promotion, which he is unlikely to get. He has passed his midshipman exams, but we have not the influence or the connections with those who are in a position to aid in his advancement. But you wished to know why he might be in Bedfordshire, and that I still cannot answer. He had three weeks' leave from his ship; perhaps he wished to come and visit me even without an invitation. Although he knows my direction, and he is in the wrong county."

As Fanny lapsed once more into silence, Mary heard Tom Bertram's voice boom from the gathering at the other end of the room. "No, I will not have it! We must do the play."

"He cannot mean it!" Fanny sounded horrified.

Edmund must have said something similar, for Tom complained again, "It is not indeed the same thing. At Ecclesford, we were forced to discontinue our plans because of the death of our host's relation. But she was a close relative and such duties must be done. But Rushworth, whilst a neighbour, holds no such power over us; we can mourn him and still proceed with our performance."

"But what of Maria?" Edmund now asked in a loud enough voice for Mary to hear. "Surely you have some care for her feelings. She was engaged to be married to the man."

Tom turned to his sister. "Are you so distracted that you cannot continue? Has his death left so great a hole in your soul that you cannot fill it with the words from our chosen play? No, you can see, Edmund, by the look on her face, that she is keen to proceed."

From where she sat, Mary thought that Maria Bertram's eye roved more quickly to Henry Crawford than was seemly, but she schooled her fancies; it was too far across the room, really, to tell with certainty where the lady looked.

"Furthermore," Edmund remonstrated, "even if I were to accept your arguments, you forget that we have no actor for Mr. Rushworth's role. Who do you propose to play the count?"

Tom looked up with a smile. "Why, we have Oliver and Maddox here. They came to watch, but surely one can act as well."

Two voices of absolute refusal sounded in the room.

"Well, if that is not to be, then what about this fellow right here?" And he leapt to his feet and pointed directly at Alexander.

Edmund also rose to his feet and made the introductions, presenting Mr. Lyons of London to Mr. Bertram of Mansfield Park. "We engaged Mr. Lyons to help in our search when you disappeared the way you did," the younger brother explained after all the social niceties had been concluded. "We were most seriously worried, Tom! Could you not have sent a note or a messenger? We thought you were dead."

"Bah!" He sneered. "Balderdash."

"It was not nonsense, when nobody had heard of or seen you in days, neither had anybody seen you leave the area. And what of this poor dead man? How did he have your signet ring?"

Tom snorted. "I lost that ring months ago—nay, longer, much longer, before Father dragged me across the ocean on that wretched ship. It was no good as a signet any longer, for Father made certain no one would take credit with it, and so when it went missing, I thought nothing of it. Must have been some tramp who found it and took a fancy to it."

Alexander cleared his throat. "Pardon me, but even without its value as your personal seal, it must still have considerable value as a piece of jewellery. It is gold, I assume?"

Edmund handed the ring to Alexander, who now carried it to the same window Edmund had used earlier to make his own examination.

"Yes, gold, and a lot of it, too. Even at a poor price, this would keep a tramp in food and drink for a very long time."

"Well, whoever he was, it matters little now. But we have an actor for our play, I shan't be put off again. We must do the play, and Mr. Lyons shall take Rushworth's part. It is only two-and-forty lines, after all! Come, sir, say you will do it. We are quite depending upon you for all our hopes. Do not be so cruel that you would deny us the opportunity to complete what we have been working so hard to achieve."

Alexander raised his head and his eyes met Mary's. Whatever was he thinking? Was he asking for her permission? She could think of a hundred reasons to refuse the request. He was not a guest in this house, but rather a servant of sorts, and he had his obligations to meet. Furthermore, reading out the lines to a play in the quiet company of one's family was one thing, all very proper and within the bounds of propriety, but to act out, in full costume and—heaven forbid—cosmetics, to engage in the physical actions of the characters as they fought and embraced and caressed each other, was another.

Acting was a profession, a task done for money; and actresses were only one step removed from (she gasped to think of the word) prostitutes, and sometimes not even that one step. It was unthinkable that a baronet's children would engage in such a scheme.

And yet, what might Alexander learn in such intimate conversations as the loosened strictures of the rehearsal room might allow? The desperate need to find Tom Bertram was gone, but if one of these people knew anything of the death of James Rushworth, agreeing to act might well be worth his while. She chewed her bottom lip and gave a slight nod, which he echoed.

"Very well, then, Mr. Bertram. I agree. I shall gladly take up the role our sadly lost friend has been forced by fate to abandon."

The remainder of the gathering for tea was consumed with talk of Tom's miraculous reappearance, the sad demise of Mr. Rushworth, and, of course, the play. There was nothing new to be learned about the first two subjects, other than that the company would gladly repeat the same conversations again and again, and with the same morbid pleasure as the first time. The matter of the play soon became the primary topic of conversation, and Tom himself promised to run Alexander through his part.

"But not on a Sunday, please!" Fanny finally raised her voice. "I am unhappy enough with the performance, and especially so in the wake of poor Mr. Rushworth's death. But to rehearse on the Lord's Day, to befoul a holy day with so profane an entertainment, cannot be good. Please, I implore you."

Her cousins gaped at her as if she had never spoken so passionately or asked anything of them ever before. This, Mary considered, might well have been the case.

"Really, Fanny!" Tom rolled his eyes. "Surely you will not spoil our fun yet again. You are not even in the play."

But the young woman held her head high and insisted, and with a longing glance towards the Crawfords, who were looking rather uncomfortable, Edmund stepped in to reinforce her requests.

A woman's voice now joined the chorus as Mary Kate Crawford spoke from her position on the sofa where she was sitting. "I admit, I am feeling somewhat fatigued." These were the first words Mary had heard the lady utter since that shocking moment when Tom had entered. It was unlike her to be so quiet and her face was still quite white; it must speak strongly of the profound disturbance she felt at the troubling events of the evening. "I, too, should be relieved to delay our rehearsal until tomorrow."

And thus it was decided. Shortly thereafter, the Crawfords and Grants excused themselves from the party, and the group broke up. Tom took himself off with Oliver, Maddox, and Yates. The Bertram sisters and Fanny went up to their respective rooms, and Mrs. Norris and Lady Bertram left for the lovely back parlour, "for I never did have my cup of tea." Once again, Mary was left in the company of Edmund and Alexander.

"I can hardly rehearse his play if I am off to Bedford in the morning to take a look at this poor dead man they found." Alexander watched Tom's elegantly clad back disappear through the door as he followed his friends. "There is also the matter of Mr. Harris' inquest at the village tavern, which I am bound to attend. I have information which I am certain will convince even him that this was no mere accident.

"I admit to some interest in this play, however, not for the sake of the theatricals themselves, but for what I might discover. And yet I have a task to complete. I shall, of course, return your bank draught, since Mr. Bertram has returned without my assistance and in perfect health."

Edmund demurred. "No. That is unnecessary. I engaged you to look for him, not to find him. I am exceedingly grateful that he is back, and you took enough trouble in the searching you did undertake. Keep it, and help us find who killed Rushworth. That one lies heavily on my mind at the moment. Might this poor dead man in Bedford lead to a solution?"

Alexander turned his hands palm-up. "I cannot say. But it is an avenue worth following, especially if Mr. Price was in those parts."

"My conscience demands it."

Alexander nodded. "Just so." He shuffled his feet. "And the play?"

Edmund walked over to the tea tray. The tea itself had surely cooled too much to drink, but there remained platters of biscuits and little tarts and small thin sandwiches all arranged so beautifully. "Miss Bennet, what may I prepare for you? I recommend the lemon tarts, unless you prefer savoury..."

Mary grinned. Lemon was a favourite of hers. "That will do admirably, sir. Thank you." He placed two of the tarts on a plate, and then added a round pale biscuit that smelled of lavender, and handed it to her. After performing similar duties for Alexander and himself, he led them to the now-empty chairs at the table and sat down.

"The play should afford little difficulty. I imagine you will wish to depart for Bedford shortly after dawn—"

"—if not before," Alexander corrected. "The ride is about an hour; the inquest at noon. If I depart early, I shall be able to return in time to be a witness for the inquest."

"Yes. Yes, of course. And if my brother opens his eyes before the clock strikes eleven, I will be most surprised. After he wallows in his bed and takes a leisurely breakfast and spends his hour dressing, we will have more than enough time for both obligations. I will join you to Bedford, if you have no objection. Perhaps we can also stop at the White Gryphon and learn something about these two mysterious men, and the reports of my cousin William. Miss Bennet, do you ride?"

Mary flushed. It was an unexpected delight and honour to be thought of, to be included.

"Alas, my skills are not such that I can ride ten or more miles, and then turn around and ride back. I would slow you down far too much."

"I have a smart little curricle I would be pleased to take for a drive. It will seat three, if we are clever about it. What say you?" He posed his question to both guests, and to Mary's joy, Alexander smiled.

"That would suit very well."

"I shall request it be made ready for departure at dawn, and will have Cook prepare a basket for us."

"And I shall settle myself somewhere with the play, and learn my lines. I have two-and-forty of them, I believe. Mary, can I count on your help?"

The trio set off for Bedfordshire as the sun rose. The morning was clear but chilly, and the curricle was open to the air. There had been some discussion about seating, for there was a small box at the back, which Alexander had offered to take, but eventually common sense won out over propriety. Three people seated in close quarters would help to keep each other warm. Even with her extra stockings and warmest coat, and the blanket wrapped about her shoulders and down over her legs, Mary was glad for the warmth and gentle pressure of Alexander's body against her side.

They arrived at the village where the body had been discovered at about eight o'clock, an hour or so after they departed. They had eaten the biscuits and cheese in the basket on the journey, but were thankful for cups of steaming tea and coffee offered by the proprietress at the small inn. The village was situated at a point along the Great Ouse where the river bent sharply in its course, allowing such flotsam as a dead man to be caught in the osiers that decorated its shores. It was about five miles from Bedford proper and saw very little traffic by road. The inn itself was a low stone building with diamond pane windows and an upper storey nestled under a steep and heavy thatched roof. The inn, called the Cock, had neither an air of dissipation nor the markings of prosperity. It seemed to do no great amount of business, but enough to keep the building in good repair and the proprietress well fed and in excellent spirits.

For her part, Mrs. Goodwin seemed delighted to have any guests at all, even if all they desired was something hot to drink and the promise of an order of stew later, and served them happily. Likewise, she seemed not at all upset to have the coroner sleeping in one of her two guest rooms above, or the deceased keeping company with the blocks of ice in the ice house attached by a long passage to the cellars below, under the shade of the thick woods that surrounded the village. It was all custom for her inn, and she would entertain the neighbours with her tales for weeks to come.

She was as generous with her speech as with her hospitality, and as they warmed their bones with the hot drinks by a crackling fire, the three heard everything they had ever wished to know about the hamlet.

"'Twas Davey Miller—he's the miller here, right suits his name—that found him, floating at the bend, half caught in the twigs. Reckon he had some shiny buttons on his coat, and that's what the torch light fell upon. Glinted different than water, is what Davey said. Will and Jacob—they have the farm yonder—were with him, and they pulled him out of the water. Brought him right here, and sent for the coroner from Bedford, who came straight away. Didn't think much of it, of course, since things happen and things that float in the water get caught at that bend all the time, but when they began to clean him up and found the ring, then the coroner, he thought he might have heard something about it, and sent back to Bedford for more news, and that's when he thought to send Davey's son Jake out to you folks to tell the news."

And on she spoke, painting a rather precise picture of the excitement that had suffused the village over the last day and a half. At the conclusion of her recitation, Mary felt that if Davey Miller or one of the farmers were to walk into the inn at that moment, she should know him exactly, from his features and temperament to what he best preferred for dinner on a Sunday evening.

She was saved from such a meeting with the unlucky men who had discovered the body, however, by heavy footsteps on the staircase leading to the guest rooms above. Within moments, a new face appeared at the door to the public room, where she and her friends were now finally warm.

"Ah, Mr. Newton, sir." Mrs. Goodwin leapt from her chair and found him a seat at the table around which they sat. "Here is some hot tea for you, sir, unless you would prefer coffee, and I shall prepare you some porridge at once, unless you would prefer bread and cheese and cold meats today. But first, you will be wanting to know these kind people here, come all the way from Northamptonshire to meet with you. If I may make the introductions?" She posed her question to Edmund, who granted this request, and they now became known to each other.

Mr. Newton was a large man both in height and width, although his girth seemed to owe as much to brawn as to fat. He was somewhere between fifty and sixty years old, with a bald pate, silver whiskers, and a ruddy complexion. His eyes shone with good humour, but as soon as he had finished the last morsel in his bowl, his manner became one of business.

"To the ice house, then! I would very much like to have this matter dealt with, so I may return to my family. Very good. Gentlemen." He stood and regarded Mary with something like suspicion. She was very much aware that his invitation to the gentlemen did not include her.

"Mary?" Alexander's voice asked her what she wished. She was no stranger to ugly and violent death, and had seen more such bodies than a gently bred young woman of twenty summers ought ever to have seen. She knew that her mettle was up to the ordeal, but whilst she would like to know what might be learned from the corpse, she had no desire to see it herself. If Alexander had offered his hand and led the way, she would follow, of course, but given the choice...

"Miss Bennet is welcome to accompany the gentlemen, but I am not often in new company and would be pleased to entertain her here should she wish to remain." Mrs. Goodwin shuffled around the room again and tested the teapot to see how much more water she would need to refill it.

"I shall remain, thank you," Mary rose and curtseyed to the men. Then, when Edmund and Mr. Newton were turning towards the door, she grabbed Alexander's hand and leaned in to whisper in his ear, "Thank you."

He responded with a squeeze to her hand and followed the others out of the room.

For a few minutes, she and Mrs. Goodwin talked of general matters. She heard about the lady's daughter, now married and living in Bedford with her husband who owned a small dry goods store there, and of the new grandchild who was six months and as chubby and cheerful as ever a babe should be. She heard about the harvest that was just brought in, and of Mrs. Jones' new tablecloth, and of the trouble that the vicar was having keeping the boys in school when they wished to be playing outside.

When Mrs. Goodwin paused to refill the plate of bread and cheese, Mary took the opportunity to ask, "Are things... people... often found in the river?"

The woman settled into her chair. She seemed to have a story to tell and wished to relish the telling. "Here, dear. Have another biscuit. Things, we often find. Old pieces of carriage or clothing, or other such rubbish that falls in upstream and no one cares enough to rescue. Sometimes pieces of old barges or things that fall off them. We don't have a lot of visitors in these parts, but there are some who travel on barges along the river or folks fishing a bit far from home. We get our chub and perch from the river, and sometimes buy off the fishers on their boats when our men are out at harvest. There are some fine fish in the river, excellent for eating, and very good in pastry."

Mary kept her eyes wide open and hoped she looked interested. Hopefully Mrs. Goodwin would tell her more about what was found and where it might have come from, rather than divulge her family's secret receipt for baked fish. Her wishes were granted.

"Once we found a barrel complete with some milled wheat still in it, and not even damp, so well sealed it was. That one even had the miller's name on it, from Felmersham upstream. Sometimes we even find things from as far as Milton Keynes, but most of them get trapped in bends and eddies long before they find these poor shores."

"But no other, er, deceased people?"

The innkeeper shook her head. "Not for many years, not here. Sometimes we think we see things floating by, but not many end up in the trees where the river bends. Don't reckon he's been from anywhere too close, though, since I could not recognise him, at least from what I could see of his face. Wonder where he's from. Olney, p'rhaps, or there's a water mill at Odell. Or maybe one of the bigger towns? I hope there is someone to mourn him."

The conversation at this point was brought to a halt by the return of the men from the ice house. Their faces were grim and Edmund looked rather grey. Even Alexander, who was accustomed to facing the deceased, looked more than a little ill at ease. Mary silently chastised herself for being grateful not to have seen the deceased.

"The doctor left his report with Mr. Newton. Poor fellow must have been dead some time. It is hard to tell exactly how long, for he has been in the water, which has warm and cold currents... Forgive me, Mrs. Goodwin." Alexander had begun to speak to Mary before recalling the other lady in the room.

"No, not at all. One does not get to be my age out in the country without seeing a sad thing or two. I saw the poor fellow when they brought him in. I'll be pleased enough to have him out of the ice house. When is the inquest, Mr. Newton?"

"Tomorrow at eleven. We shall use the back private salon if we can have enough chairs. You might want to put on some stew for food afterwards, and have enough ale for the men. That should earn you enough pennies to compensate for your unwanted guest in the ice house."

There was little else to be said. Edmund returned his brother's signet ring to the coroner, who would now take charge of it until such time as it was deemed to have played no role in the man's death, and arrangements were made to convey the news of the outcome of the inquest as quickly as possible to Mansfield.

If there was any connection between this poor man's demise and that of Mr. Rushworth, Alexander said not a word. His gaze, however, suggested he had something to say to Mary that he did not wish to utter at the moment. He would tell her soon enough; when they were investigating a matter, they had no secrets between then. With a start, Mary realised that they were engaged on this matter as a pair, no matter that only Alexander was the official investigating agent. In her mind, as she believed it was in his, they were partners.

It was soon time to depart. Alexander and Edmund refused offers of food, their faces still somewhat green from their venture to the ice house. "Er, thank you, Mrs. Goodwin, but we have more to do this morning, and we must be back in Northamptonshire by noon."

Before long, the three were in the curricle once more. Mary related Mrs. Goodwin's tales of goods from upriver finding their resting place at the crook where the river bent, and she listed the places the innkeeper had mentioned.

"Olney, Odell, and Felmersham, and even Milton Keynes, eh?" Edmund grimaced. "I know those places, and there must be hundreds more. Hopefully Mr. Newton will put out notices, in case some person knows of an acquaintance who has gone missing." He paused for a moment, holding the ribbons loosely in a hand. "I am relieved to have seen him, no matter how unpleasant it was. I, at least, will be able to pray for his soul, even if he has no others. I had to do this one service for him, especially if his death had anything to do with my family."

He lapsed into silence, but Mary thought she heard Alexander mutter, "Amen."

It was only half-past nine in the morning; their first visit had gone quickly, and Alexander looked pleased, although his face was still pale from his examination of the body.

"Was it so horrible?" Mary asked as their road took them through mud-brown fields and half bare woods. Their next stop was the White Gryphon at Yardley Hastings, and as early as it might be, Mary thought that an ale might do both men some good. Their custom also might encourage the proprietor to speak more freely.

Alexander gave a narrow nod. "Aye. He was pretty bad. I read through the doctor's report, which he made upon being called to examine the body on Saturday when it was found. The man was not drowned. He was dead before ending up in the river. The state of... his condition made it less than easy to see without an examination, but his head was smashed in by a large blunt object."

"Like a rock?"

"Aye, just so, Mary. Like a rock."

Chapter Thirteen

Tales of a Traveller

Alexander looked about in interest as the curricle approached their next destination. Yardley Hastings was a larger and busier village than the collection of cottages they had just now left, being situated along the Bedford Road. Likewise, the White Gryphon was larger and busier than the Cock, although it, too, was made of stone and sported a thatched roof. Inside, the public rooms were quiet, most of last night's guests having already started their day's journeys and tonight's still far away, but there were one to two folk still sitting at their tables, either taking a late tea and bread, or an early ale.

Alexander offered to see to the horses and the curricle, allowing Edmund to step inside to request a short interview with Mr. Watts, whom he knew somewhat. Yardley Hastings was not the primary town that supplied the day-to-day needs of Mansfield

Park, but it was close enough that the residents of one were not strangers to the residents of the other. Mary accompanied Edmund.

Alexander quickly found a groom to take care of the vehicle and horses, and stepped inside just in time to see Mr. Watts greet Edmund with the deference due his status. The speculative eye he cast upon Mary, however, was less honourable. Alexander could almost hear the innkeeper wondering what a young woman was doing with a single man in an inn, with no visible chaperone. To his credit, Edmund's back stiffened as he noted the innkeeper's curious interest in the young woman. "Miss Bennet," the gentleman acted to forestall any rumours, "allow me to present to you Mr. Watts, who runs this fine establishment. He has excellent pies and lemon tarts. Watts, this is Miss Bennet, a guest at Mansfield Park and the associate of... ah, here he is now. My friend, Mr. Lyons."

Ignoring the look of disappointment that flashed through the innkeeper's eyes, Alexander strode forward with a great grin and a hand outstretched for shaking. "Pleasure to make your acquaintance, Mr. Watts. Fine place you have here."

"A Scotsman! Mr. Bertram, I didn't know you had friends like that." His eyes narrowed.

Alexander stifled a snicker. Was he to be insulted by such a comment? Surely an innkeeper was accustomed to travellers from all across the isle of Britain, and likely some from abroad at times as well. If he were to be painted with such a brush, he would make the most of it. He found his heartiest brogue and gave a good-natured laugh.

"It's early in the day yet, but we've had a busy morning so far, and I, for one, am dry and dusty from the road. An ale for me, sir, and one for my friend, and a pot of tea and some cake—or did you mention lemon tarts?—for Miss Bennet, if she so wishes." He looked around. He was not hungry, not after seeing that awful sight in the ice house, but the coins from some custom would likely loosen the man's tongue. "And some bread and cheese to wash down the ale, if you have." He noted Watt's smile. "And perhaps, sir, you might sit with us a time."

"We have some questions, Watts, which you might have answers for," Edmund explained quickly. "Nothing to do with you or your inn, of course! I've never heard of any trouble here. We are merely asking after some who might have passed through recently. I know what a keen eye you have, and how well you recall what you've seen."

His flattery seemed to smooth feathers before they grew ruffled. "Very well, sir. Let me call for the food and drink, and then I am at your service."

He did as promised, and within moments was leading the group to a comfortable gathering of chairs around a low table at the far side of the room. The space was separated from the main area and afforded some privacy for conversation, but still allowed Watts to survey his domain, in the event he was needed.

"This will do very well indeed, Watts. I thank you." Edmund was oozing aristocratic charm, and Mary was looking amused. "We were wondering if you happen to have seen a young man of about my years who was looking for two other men. Fair hair, skin roughened and reddened by the sea. The man is my cousin, on leave from his naval posting, and we hoped to have had word of him before now."

Alexander smiled at the slight distortion of the facts; nothing Edmund had said was untrue, but his redirection of the import of his question would surely elicit information more quickly than something that hinted of trouble.

Watts leaned back in his chair and held up a finger, cautioning silence. At that moment, a young maid arrived with a heavy tray carrying three pints of yeasty ale, a large platter of breads and cheeses, a teapot and cup, and a plate of biscuits and lemon tarts. Watts thanked her and waited for her to return to the other side of the room before speaking.

"Yes, now that you mention it, I might just have done. Let me think..." He made a great show of his pensive recollections, likely hoping that the display of such effort would result in a few coins, or at least another round of ale. "'Twas several days ago, if I recall. Andrew and Simon—they're my sons—were out at the edge of the fields where they meet the woods with their friend, the smith's boy. Not boys anymore, I suppose, but all grown now. Anyway, they saw this fellow set for sleeping rough. He wasn't ready to heed them at first, but the night was chilly, and they made him come back with them for a hot meal.

"Of course, Mrs. Watts took one look at him and sent him upstairs to one of the empty rooms. Just a small one, mind you, not one of the good ones. The inn is a business, of course, and how I feed my family, but if the rooms are empty, having a soul sleeping in one at my invitation won't harm me now, will it? And my wife has too much of a soft heart for handsome young men. He paid happily enough for the food, but Mrs. Watts would not hear of taking a penny for the bed that was empty, anyway."

Alexander saw Mary smile at this guileless expression of generosity. Watts himself could well have argued against his wife or taken the coin, but his heart was clearly as big as his wife's, despite his crusty manner. He might seem rough and stern, with a distrust of strangers and an eye to his profit, but he was, by this deed, as good a man that walked the earth. Alexander resolved to come back for an ale or a meal once this case was resolved, in one way or another.

Instead of embarrassing the man with reference to his kindness, he asked instead, "What can you tell me, from your own knowledge then, of this young man?"

"He was polite, as the boys said. He sat with us as we took our dinner as a family, at my oldest's invitation. Told me a bit about his own folk, back in Portsmouth I think, with a pa on half-pay and a ma caring for a houseful of children. Imagine my amazement when he told me his sister lived nearby, and imagine again when I learned she was Miss Price! Should have known by his face, mind, for they're two peas in a pod, but I didn't think to wonder. 'Why, I know her,' I told him, and he seemed as surprised as me. Then, after telling and answering my questions, he asked some of his own."

Alexander sat forward. He longed to take out his notebook to record what the innkeeper said, but knew that nothing would stop the man's tale as quickly as that. Instead, he asked some casual question about Mr. Price's query and hoped that Mary would recall every word, as she so often managed to do.

"He wanted to know if there had been two men in the area asking questions about Mr. Tom Bertram. Seemed mighty odd to me, but then my Simon recalled that he had seen such a pair just a day or two before asking exactly that. Said they had a message for him. Simon didn't like the look of them and said he never saw your brother, Mr. Bertram.

"When, exactly, did all of this occur?" Alexander leaned forward, elbows on the table.

"Young Price was here Friday night, then stayed again on his own coin the next night. The men were asking about Mr. Tom the day before that, maybe one day earlier, too."

Wednesday or Thursday last—exactly when Tom Bertram had disappeared. This was a most strange coincidence.

"Did he say anything of interest about the men?"

"He only asked if I had seen them. One mostly normal, one very large, and both likely poor riders if they were on horseback. I think he was hoping to find them and stop them from undertaking some awful task."

"Did he say how he knew them?"

"That he did, but it wasn't much of a story. They are not from his ship, but one meets men from other ships when you're in dock, and these two had a bad history, from what he said. If they were asked to do some ill deed, they would not be shy."

Mary settled herself on the seat of the curricle for the final short drive back to Mansfield Park. The morning had been long and her bones ached from the bumps and jostles that twenty and more miles in a light vehicle will produce, but she had rather liked sitting so close to Alexander on the bench as the horses raced along the country roads. It would not do to be too proximate to Edmund Bertram, after all, and so she had pressed up almost against Alexander's side, and he had seemed not to mind at all. Indeed, he had shifted his arm to the back of the bench to allow her to slide even closer to him, although he had been most gentlemanly about not enforcing contact when it was not necessary.

She really ought to be horrified at the idea of driving about the country almost sitting in a man's lap! Whatever would Doctor Fordyce have to say about this? It was not seemly, and certainly not modest. And yet it had felt so natural and right that it could not be a moral lapse, could it? After all, they had not been secluded, and Edmund had been right there the entire time. But with his eyes on the roads and the horses, would he even have known had she sidled just a hair closer to Alexander's side, and had he allowed his extended arm to slip down from the back of the bench to secure her shoulders?

That part of her mind she tried to ignore wondered whether they might take another ride, just the two of them, before returning to Hertfordshire.

All too soon, they were back at the park. Edmund drove the curricle to the stables and coach house at the back of the main building, there to be tended by the servants. John was on duty, and he accepted the reins from Edmund as he leapt down from the high bench.

"A useful morning, Mr. Bertram?" he asked. Edmund nodded. "And a good morning to you, Mr. Lyons, Miss Bennet. Mr. Lyons, sir, will you be wanting my testimony at the inquest? We have a half an hour before Mr. Harris begins."

Mary liked John and his clear good sense and direct manner. Alexander turned to her, but spoke loudly enough for John to hear. "Miss Bennet, pray excuse me. This good man reminds me of my appointment. Hopefully we can convince the coroner of the story the evidence tells." He bowed to her. Then to John, he added, "Allow me five minutes to gather my notes from my room, and I will join you here. I presume you have Mr. Bertram's permission to attend the inquest, at my request?" John and Edmund both answered in the affirmative. "Then we can walk to the village together and still be early."

Alexander then held out his elbow to escort Mary into the house, even if he must depart thence almost at once.

Mary both appreciated and resented not being invited—or welcomed, even—to the inquest. She was eager to know what the various participants would say and wished to see Alexander present his evidence. His training as a lawyer would surely equip him exceedingly well for such a task, even if he did not practice the law as his profession, and his years of experience as an investigator would allow him to know what evidence was the most meaningful and which would be most likely to convince a magistrate, coroner, or judge, of its import.

At the same time, the members of the coroner's jury who sat to pass initial judgement on the nature of the death would have to observe the body, and that was a task she was pleased to forego. She felt a pang of pity for the poor people called upon to look at the man found near Bedford. If the sight of him turned Alexander green, she imagined a few less hardened men becoming quite ill. Mr. Rushworth, at least, had rested in an ice house these past two days rather than a river, and would not be quite so... unsettling to look upon.

Regardless of her wishes and desires, an inquest was not a place for a woman unless she had particular information to impart, and so she must sit at Mansfield Park and wait. In truth, despite all the tea and cakes she had consumed over the course of the morning, she was dry from the dust of the road and would not refuse a glass of lemonade.

Whilst Tom Bertram was still, according to Baddeley, in his chambers, the other gentlemen in residence at Mansfield Park were expected at the inquest, and consequently had risen, breakfasted, and departed. "I am relieved for that," Alexander whispered when Edmund excused himself, "for I would prefer not to be classed with them by appearing at the inquest all in a gaggle. Let me instead be seen as a working man rather than a useless sort like them. The jurors will be men from the village and the farms; they will believe me better if I am seen with a sensible servant like John than a puffed-up crew who live only for the next entertainment." He gave her hand a squeeze. "I shall report on the inquest directly upon my return." Then he ran for the stairs to retrieve his notes.

The hours dragged by. Maria and Julia had decided once again to keep to their rooms, and there was no visit from the Crawfords this day, since Henry was required at the inquest and with Edmund there as well, there was little incentive for Mary Kate Crawford to visit the ladies. Lady Bertram was in the parlour, alternately working at some useless piece of embroidery, talking to her pugs, and nodding off to sleep, and Mrs. Norris had found some vital task that only Fanny could discharge, thereby occupying the girl for the next several hours.

Mary, therefore, took herself up to her room, where she could rest and read in welcome silence until the inquest was over and the men returned to the house.

When, exactly, she had drifted into a light sleep she could not say, but a noise from the drive below her window roused her, and she moved to the bright window to see what was happening. There seemed to be little reason for concern, but a private messenger had drawn up his horse and was handing a package to one of the grooms. There was an exchange of words, and the messenger left his horse with the groom and was pointed towards the kitchen door, presumably to take some refreshment whilst his mount rested and was given food and water. Could these be the replies to Alexander's queries to his associates in London?

Mary glanced at the small clock on the mantel. It was half-past two. How long would the inquest last? Would Mr. Harris take heed of Alexander's words, or would he insist upon a verdict of accidental death? A coroner ought to be impartial and take note only of the evidence presented to him, but too many men sought easy answers, and from all she had heard, Mr. Harris seemed to be one of these.

The half-written letters on her writing table held no interest for her, and instead of writing to Lizzy or Jane, she straightened her dress and checked her hair before leaving her attic room for the sunny back parlour. Perhaps, once there, she might see the men on their return from the inquest in the village beyond the lawns.

The parlour was as empty now as it had been when she returned to the house, but a bright sunbeam caressed a comfortable chair and sang its siren song, begging her to take a seat there. The chair was perfectly situated for a good prospect onto the lawns, and within minutes she saw shadows moving through the trees that backed the property, quickly to become the shapes of the men.

Her eyes picked out the tall lanky shape of Edmund Bertram, the solid stride of Alexander, the forms and outlines of Yates, Oliver, Maddox, and...

Who was that with them? As they neared, she counted among their number a man she had not seen before. In the clear afternoon sun, his hair shone almost golden, and he walked with the rolling gait of a man accustomed to the deck of a ship. There could only be one such person to be returning from the inquest in the company of such others.

Her supposition was proven correct a few minutes later when the group entered the parlour. This newcomer was, indeed, William Price, Fanny's beloved older brother. Looking at him, Mary realised how strong the resemblance between siblings was. If Fanny had suddenly added several inches to her height and taken on the physiognomy of a man, this is exactly how she would appear.

"The pleasure is mine, Mr. Price," she recited upon an introduction.

"And mine, Miss Bennet." His voice was pleasant and rich, with the echoes of both a gently bred mother and the tars of Portsmouth. "Have you been long in this neighbourhood? My cousin Edmund has told me that you are visiting from Hertfordshire."

"A mere few days, sir, on my journey homeward from visiting my sister in the north. I might ask the same of yourself, for the very last time I saw her, your sister made no mention of your planned visit."

He blushed a warm pink under his sun-darkened skin. "I had... that is, I had not expected to make this journey, and had no time to write to her. Any letter would have arrived after me if I had done so."

"What, then, brings you to this part of Northamptonshire? It seems about as far as a man may be from the ocean and still remain in England."

Once again, his face reddened. He was pleasant company, but a terrible liar. This spoke well of his character to Mary. "I had business... matters I needed to attend to..."

"You may speak frankly to the lady." Edmund sidled up to the two chairs where Mary and William Price were conversing. The room was now crowded and noisy enough that their conversation was private. The men had requested ale and sandwiches, which had been carried in on a trolley, and the room buzzed with the noise of their chatter. "Miss Bennet is in the confidence of Mr. Lyons, and has offered her own insight into his endeavours on more than one occasion." How very tactful that sounded.

"A lady investigator?" William sounded amazed.

"No, not that. I have no occupation. I merely apply my mind to Mr. Lyon's problems, and at times, discover that I have information that might be useful to him." She looked about the room. "Where is Alexander, Mr. Bertram? I thought I saw him come in with you, yet he is not here."

"There was a package of letters from London. He asked me to inform you that he will join us as soon as he has seen what is enclosed therein."

A movement behind her caught her attention, and she turned to see Alexander's smiling face. "Nay, I am here, Mary, although shortly I must go and tend to my correspondence. That package did indeed contain replies to the queries I asked of my associates in London. Perhaps, if these gentlemen can suffer along without you,

you might assist me with my notes? Your handwriting is far easier to read than my own sad efforts." His eyes spoke his true meaning, but his request for her scribal skills made the invitation to join him somewhat less improper.

Edmund bowed. "We shall, of course, be less happy for Miss Bennet's absence, but I understand your need for her assistance."

Mr. Price echoed his cousin's bow and sentiments. "I shall enjoy a longer conversation later, Miss Bennet. Until then. I must now find my dear sister, whom I so dearly wish to see."

She curtseyed as William made for the door, and she followed Alexander to the room set aside for his purpose. "What think you of William Price?" His voice was mild, but his eyes shone with curiosity.

She said nothing until the door to the room was firmly latched. "We can speak of him later. I am more eager to know of the outcome of the inquest. What was the verdict? And whence came William Price? How can he have been in the vicinity and not call upon his cousins, for a roof and hot meal if nothing else?"

"You are all full of questions, Miss Mary." he teased. "No, do not get missish. I would have you no other way. Here, let us sit and I shall tell all."

She sat upon the small settee along the wall, and he sat beside her, almost close enough to touch. She was pleased to be warm and on the soft cushions, but she wished, almost, to be back on the hard cold bench of the curricle, pressed against his side. As if reading her mind, he shifted a hair closer, their knees inches apart.

"How quickly they have accepted this arrangement." His eyes were on the door, which was closed and latched but not locked. "Were this to be Maria or Julia, or even Fanny, alone with a man, Edmund should never allow it. And yet, here we are, alone in a private space, with the full knowledge of everybody of import in the household, and it seems to trouble not one of them. I imagine they see me so much as a servant that they cannot imagine anything might happen other than strict matters of business." His words were cool, but his eyes remained bright and fixed upon her.

"Perhaps they have already assigned to me the role of a fallen woman, so far down the road of perdition that I am beyond saving." She teased him, knowing as well as he did that she had for so long been the voice of moral rectitude within her family; indeed, she still was.

Now he turned more serious. "Nay, that cannot be. A woman's virtue is painted as much by her acquaintances as by her behaviour. You would never be allowed in the Miss Bertrams' company were there to be the slightest stain on your character. 'Tis best they see me as an underling."

Mary was silent for a moment. Responses both serious and arch flew through her thoughts and she knew not how to respond. Was this some sort of declaration? Did he like her? She rather thought he did, but was he now suggesting they distance themselves from each other? That could not be, for Alexander had sat beside her in an otherwise empty room, had moved closer to her, had his eyes fixed upon her.

She decided on a quip. "It is a good thing, then, that we are not courting." She hoped her smile would belie her words.

"Indeed not! For then, we should never be alone. If we were courting," he said lightly, "I might look about and if your father had his eyes averted, I might dare to take your hand."

"But he is not here," she returned, "and there is nobody to tell. I might extend my hand thus," she did as she spoke, "and you might take it at your will."

"Thus?" He smiled an impudent grin as he nestled her hand in his. "Perhaps I shall keep hold of it, in case you choose to run away."

"A veritable danger," she giggled, "but you seem to be avoiding my question. What happened at the inquest? Perhaps I ought to grab your hand and hold you still until you have told me what transpired."

"Very well. You are too clever for me by half." He laughed with her, but did not relinquish her hand. "The inquest progressed as I expected," his voice grew more serious as he gave his account. "Mr. Harris had little desire to return a verdict of anything other than accidental death in the course of a misjudged leap over a hedge, but he had to give me leave to present all I had discovered. With the promise—or perhaps threat—of witnesses, and in front of those three-and-twenty jurors who had seen the injury of Mr. Rushworth's poor head, he had little option but to instruct them to call as they found it. The outcome was murder by person or persons unknown."

"You do not seem pleased." She felt his warm hand grow tense as she held it.

"I am never pleased when a person is dead at the hands of another. But," he sighed, "I am satisfied that he will have justice."

"Is the magistrate a competent man? What of his bailiffs? Is there a local constable?"

"That is the other matter, Mary. The magistrate, once he learned of what we have been doing here, deferred to Edmund Bertram, and he has officially engaged my services to discover Mr. Rushworth's killer. I know not how long I shall have to remain here at Mansfield Park."

Chapter Fourteen

Unexpected Company

Alexander tore his eyes from Mary's and glanced down at his hand, holding and being held by hers. As he had explained the outcome of the inquest and his continuing employment, she had begun, ever so gently, to rub her thumb back and forth over his. Whether she acted by design or by instinct, or whether she even knew what her hand was doing, he knew not, but the motion was soothing and pleasant and he did not mention it for fear that she might stop it.

"Will you travel on to Hertfordshire alone? I can request that Mr. Bertram send a groom or footman to accompany you and your maid. Perhaps John... he is most trustworthy, I believe..."

The soft motion of her thumb across his hand ceased. "Do you wish for me to go?"

"No! Not that! But I must remain, and you surely need to return to your family in Hertfordshire."

She shook her head and sighed as if about to reprimand a naughty child. "My brother Darcy requested that you accompany me home. It would be most remiss of you not to fulfil your obligation. And since you must stay, then it stands that I must as well." She met his eyes. "Furthermore, who will help you to solve this case if I am not here to tell you what your evidence means?" After a moment of serious silence, she burst out into a trickle of laughter and her head inclined towards his. It took every ounce of his self-regulation not to pull her into his arms and kiss her.

Then she looked up at him and stopped laughing. She leaned forward the slightest bit more and, for a second, he thought *she* might kiss *him*. How hard it was to resist that pull. He had too much still to tell her before he could commit his heart—or rather, before he could confess his heart. He felt his heart had committed itself long ago without his permission.

This would not do. If he allowed himself that momentary lapse, he would have no chance of escape. He must, rather, steel himself for her eventual rejection and for the life that would inevitably stretch on without her. She would never deign to continue their friendship once she knew his secret. But still, as unwise as it might be, he could not give her up quite yet, in whatever form she would have him. If it was to be this strange relationship, more than friendship but less than acknowledged lovers, he would be satisfied. Instead of accepting her lips, therefore, he pulled her forward that small degree more and planted his kiss on the top of her head.

"Come," his voice was rough to his ears, "let us see what my friends have sent up. That package of letters awaits."

She looked as disconcerted as he felt as she pulled back from him and nodded. Her face was flushed and her eyes darted everywhere in the room, refusing to alight on him. Ah, what a pair they were. He forced a smile to his face as he rose from the settee and opened the curtains wide so they might have ample light by which to read. She was still sitting on the settee; what was she thinking? What thoughts were rushing through that remarkable brain of hers? He longed to know every one of them. But even had they not this chasm between them, she could never accept him. He could not ask her to abandon her class and step down from the gentry into the unwashed arms of the working class, to ally herself forever with a man who had no true footing in her world, as out of place as his copper hair and broad Scots accent marked him to be.

He busied himself at the table, sorting through the pile of notes and letters, and soon was relieved to hear Mary's quiet approach. At his invitation, she took a chair and turned her eyes to the letters. He settled himself beside her, excusing his choice to himself as having excellent light, and he surveyed his correspondence.

"Shall we begin here?" He reached for the largest pile and took a missive from the top. This was a simple half sheet, folded once and sealed, but it was from one of his best sources of information in Town. Before opening it, he found the stack of paper Edmund had given him and he passed several sheets to Mary. "Let us set a sheet for each of my questions. We may copy the relevant information into my notebook once it is all organised."

He broke the seal, scanned the note, and wrote at the top of his sheet of paper, *Rushworth*. As he set up the page, Mary reached for the note as well, and he passed it to her to read. In this matter, at least, he had no secrets from her.

"Mr. Rushworth has been in Town of late?" She asked after a moment. "No one had said anything of that, but I suppose it is not unexpected. He would be meeting his lawyer about the settlement for Maria, of course, and perhaps seeing to his house in Town, and ordering wedding clothes and gifts for her."

Alexander scanned the next note in the pile; it bore the same handwriting as the first. He cracked the seal. "It seems there is more. This is also from Bowes. James Rushworth was not that often in London, but he did visit frequently enough, and more to the point, he spent lavishly enough that he was remembered. Bowes does good work, and he had discovered that on some of Rushworth's recent visits to the city, he was seen in company with two gentlemen whose names he has not yet discovered. Because he is relying on people's recollections, this is not a firm account of Rushworth's activities, but it appears he was taken as a guest to some of the clubs frequented by the younger set and the Whigs, and one of his contacts recounts him disappearing, with two men, into a gaming hell, from which he did not emerge for several hours. Whether money was won, lost, or changed hands at all, he cannot tell."

Mary had begun to scratch notes on the paper before her, and Alexander did likewise. His page now read:

Rushworth

Two men—same ones as were seen in Northampton?

Gambling—same men? Any outstanding debts? To whom?

When he glanced over, he saw something similar on Mary's page. Good girl. She had the makings of a natural investigator.

Now she took and opened another missive. "This is concerning Mr. Yates. It tells us little we do not know: his parentage, the number of people between him and the barony, which is three at this point, should you wish to know, his annual income, his favourite seat at the opera, and his favourite—oh my—his favourite singer at the opera. It appears Miss Julia might not be the only light in the honourable Mr. John Yates' eyes. He visits Town regularly to have clothing made and to attend performances. His associates are the usual set of first circle dandies, but with no particular stain on anybody's name, and he is not a known gambler or over-indulger of spirits."

Alexander wrote his notes. "Not much of a suspect then, is he? Furthermore, I can think of no particular reason he might wish to see Rushworth dead. If Tom were the intended victim, he could more easily have done the deed during their stay at Ecclesford or on the road than here, at Tom Bertram's own estate. Still, one never knows what secrets men may hide."

The next notes contained similarly uninformative information about Messers Oliver and Maddox. Both were gentlemen with holdings in Northamptonshire and comfortable, though not excessive income, and both were known in Town, although with no particular vices that anybody knew of.

"What is this?" The next letter he opened was from one of his trusted colleagues. "Here is something interesting, Mary! Listen. Fuller has been inquiring about these two men from the descriptions and direction I had from Mr. Rollings at the tavern in Northampton. He has done his work and done it well. It seems these two gentlemen, who had not before given their names, are Robert Wilberforce and Arlen Ottley.

"Wilberforce?" Mary's eyes opened wide, her pen hovering above the notepaper.

"Just so. He is, by Fuller's account, the young nephew of William Wilberforce..."

"The abolitionist!"

"The very same. I wonder if this has anything to do with our friend John in the stables, or the Bertrams' holdings in Antigua. It is no secret that the plantations only earn such profits because of the unpaid labour of the slaves who work them."

This was an interesting piece of news indeed. Alexander would have to think hard on what it might mean, for the Bertrams, for Rushworth, and for his entire investigation. That the abolitionists might wish to speak with Tom Bertram and convince him of the evil of his family's possessions was almost a given; but what of Rushworth? Would he, as the chosen representative of a pocket borough, and one beholden in some ways to the Bertrams, also be subject to the efforts of these men? If they wished for his support—or more likely, wished for him not to support his future father-in-law—they might well come calling.

However, they could well have been the men with him in London; then why seek him out here? And further, could they be at all involved in his death? It hardly seemed likely. Thus far, to Alexander's knowledge, the men and women of the abolitionist movement had never resorted to threats or violence. They chose, rather, to try to sway people to their cause with words and argument, augmented by the voices of those few men who, having once been taken into slavery, had escaped to tell of their ordeals. Perhaps John might lend his voice to this chorus.

Mary, as usual, put voice to his thoughts. "Would these men go so far in their schemes as to cause harm to a slaveholder? I have not heard of such a thing, for it seems so contrary to their stated aims. They are incensed by the cruelty inflicted upon other men; can they really justify violence in their efforts to protest violence?"

Alexander shook his head. "It is not, I believe, generally one of their tactics. For as you say, to cause harm in the attempt to prevent harm is contradictory at best and the exercise of pride to an awful degree at worst. But zealous men are not always wise. We shall have to consider the possibility.

"Here is another." He picked up a note from one of his smaller piles. The handwriting on this one was rough, the letters crudely drawn, as if the output of a man who had taught himself to read and write as an adult. Which, it transpired, he had. Ned—which was the only name by which Alexander knew this particular man—had been born in the slums and had attended no school but that of life, and yet had turned his remarkable intellect to improving himself, trading odd jobs for merchants and craftsmen for the rudiments of an education and a scrap to eat. He was a hard worker and extremely capable, and in another sort of world, would have gone on to great success at some career or another. As it was, he was still very much connected to London's seediest underworld, and one of Alexander's chosen informers when some matter required such knowledge. He now paid Ned in good coin for his work, although at times the two would sit before a fire and discuss Plutarch or Machiavelli or some other component heretofore missing from Ned's spotty education.

In this note, however, Ned had proven his worth and would be compensated accordingly. "He brings us some interesting news," Alexander murmured. Mary lifted her head and regarded him with interest, but said nothing, waiting for him to continue. In a few words, he told her about Ned, and then recounted the contents of the brief note.

"There are rumours—as there always are—about some of the more powerful people in Town, be their power social, political or military. I had sent Ned an accounting of the people of interest here, and he, in turn, tuned up his ear when one of those names fell upon his hearing. It seems there is an Admiral Crawford who was overheard engaging two of his less gentlemanlike sailors for some extra duties. It was Ned himself who happened across this transaction, in circumstances he did not relate. I suspect it involved a rather unseemly tavern at some strange hour of the morning. Ned can seem to be fast asleep whilst instead he is wide awake and misses nothing.

"To continue, he heard Crawford engage these two rough tars for some whispered task that he did not hear, 'as a favour upon request.' The men were to ride directly to Northamptonshire and were to work out then how best to discharge their duty."

There was nothing flirtatious left in Mary's regard. "What is this? He engaged two men to perform some evil here? But how can that be? What possible reason…?" She wrinkled her brow in confusion.

"Henry Crawford. Do you think?"

Mary was silent for a moment. "It would fit with what we have seen. Maria is betrothed to Rushworth, but prefers Henry, and he is similarly taken with her. He will not step in to disrupt the engagement by normal means, for he might need Sir Thomas' blessing if he is to have Maria's dowry. However, if Rushworth were to be removed in some other fashion, he could be the man on hand to help Miss Bertram through her sorrow and then conveniently step in to marry her as soon as propriety allows."

This matched his own thinking. "I believe we may need to have another conversation with Mr. Crawford. But, perhaps, not yet."

"Indeed?" Mary's brows rose upon her forehead.

"Let them not know that I have this information yet. I wonder how the rehearsal this evening will play out. Henry and Maria have several scenes together; I would like to observe them. Perhaps you might act as my eyes when I am otherwise engaged in my own scenes. I come in three times, and have two-and-forty speeches, after all. That is something, is it not?" He smiled, but he did not feel so mirthful.

"And in the morning we shall interview Mr. Crawford?"

"Him, aye, and the others."

There was another silence as both lapsed into thought. At length, Mary's voice intruded into his musings. "And what of William Price? How did he come upon you all at the inquest?"

"This is another tale. The inquest had just begun, and the jurors just returned from viewing the body, when the door at the back of the room opened and he slipped in. I would not have taken any particular note of this, for he was far from the only man to do so, but for his particular resemblance to Miss Fanny Price. He took his seat with the other observers, and afterwards came and made himself known to his cousin Edmund and the rest of us. He explained that he had taken a room at the White Gryphon, but opted to delay his business when he heard of the unfortunate incident and the inquest. Edmund, of course, insisted he remove to the house and sent a boy with a cart to retrieve his belongings and pay for his entire planned stay at the inn."

"How very odd. Did he say why he had chosen not to make himself known earlier to his family?"

"He offered only the excuse that he did not wish to intrude and make demands when he was in the area on a serious matter."

"And did he say what that matter was?"

Alexander shook his head. "He did not. But I have been wondering what the connection might be between William and these two rough sailors, for a connection there must be."

Mary chewed her bottom lip, as she often did when she was deep in thought. "Yes, so I see. For William is a sailor with the Royal Navy, and these two men were sent here by an Admiral, who just happens to be the uncle of the closest neighbours, and we are here, about as far from the sea as one might get in this country."

Alexander ran a hand through his hair and let out a puff of air. "I believe we have just begun this investigation."

Despite his self-indulgent ways, it seemed that when Tom Bertram decided to act, he did so with a particular intensity, and nothing was allowed to deter him from his aims. Thus, when at last he had risen and eaten and joined his friends and family downstairs, he naturally became the leader of the group and the sole arbiter of what they might do next. And what he decided they must do without delay was to rehearse their play.

There came a knock at the door: Mr. Lyons' presence was required in the rehearsal room at once; there would be trays of food if he had not yet taken his meal. Miss Bennet was welcome to observe. This was no request, but a command, and one which Alexander did not mind obeying, for he felt he might well discover something. "The play's the thing," he mumbled as he and Mary set about organising the piles of messages and locking them in the desk drawer that Edmund had allotted for this purpose.

He walked with Mary to the rehearsal space, then ran up to his chamber to collect the book of the play he had been using to learn his lines. When he returned, the room was full, the company gathered in groups of two or three, going over their lines and gestures and arguing over who should stand where so as best to be seen by the non-existent audience.

The Crawford siblings had returned to the house during the time that Alexander and Mary had been examining the messages in the study. Henry was standing with Yates and Tom Bertram, discussing some arrangement of the furniture for one scene, whilst Maria stood to the side, listening carefully to the conversation. On the other side of the room, Edmund stood with Miss Crawford, their play books open in their hands, but their eyes never dropping to the words they held. She seemed to have recovered well from the shock the previous afternoon, and she looked very well with bright eyes and rosy cheeks. Alexander caught snatches of their conversation, which seemed to wander indistinctly around the topic of the play, though veering off in a variety of directions before being reined in to return to the nature of their scenes.

Tom now looked up from the pile of properties on the table before him to regard the two new arrivals in the room. "Ah, Mr. Lyons and Miss Bennet! Lyons, if you have no objection, I thought we might take some time to rehearse your lines, for you are new to this performance. Who is in your first scene? Let us read through it first, you and Yates and I, and then call in the others." He began to arrange affairs to this end, leaving Alexander quite certain that whether he had an objection or not, it would matter not to the heir to Mansfield Park.

At a glance, Mary nodded at him and settled herself upon a chair not so close to Edmund and Miss Crawford as to intrude upon their conversation, but near enough to overhear anything above a whisper. He felt a rush of pride at how well she was attuned to what he needed to know. It would be of equal, or perhaps more, value to overhear what transpired between Maria and Henry Crawford, but that would be less easy to arrange without the conceit being apparent to all.

Without preamble, Tom set the introduction to the scene. Alexander had spent a while at his lines the previous evening, and the combination of his diligence and his skills of recollection now allowed him to recite his speeches with some success and confidence. He had a naturally good memory, and this had been honed during his years studying the law and with the demands of his profession. As he presented his lines, he saw Tom Bertram's eyes widen in admiration and a smile grow over Yates' aristocratic face.

"I say, Bertram, what a pleasant change this is. He has learned his part perfectly, and even puts some meaning into what he says. If only we had known before of Mr. Lyons' abilities, we might have got rid of Rushworth ourselves."

He let out a chortle of laughter, then stopped short as the realisation of what he had just said fell upon him. His smile melted into a look of mortification, and he mumbled a litany of abject apologies. Alexander watched carefully and believed them to be most sincere; but what was that strange look that now stole across

Tom Bertram's face? Surely the man did not kill his friend merely to acquire a better actor.

Quickly satisfied that Alexander had learned his lines to some degree of competence, Tom called over the other actors for his first scene. Alexander was playing Count Cassel against Mr. Yates as Baron Wildenhaim and Mary Crawford as his daughter Amelia, with Edmund entering later in the scene. Here, the count was to be wooing Amelia, although she strongly preferred Edmund's character, Anhalt.

The interplay between Miss Crawford and Edmund Bertram, even in the context of the script, was of great interest to Alexander, who hoped he would recall his lines whilst his attention was upon the two would-be lovers.

Tom read the lines of the servant.

"Mr. Anhalt begs leave—"
Yates, as the baron responded:
"Tell him to come in.—I shall be ready in a moment."
Now Alexander replied with his own line:
"Who is Mr. Anhalt?"
Miss Crawford, as Amelia, added,
"Oh, a very good man."

Her line was written with the direction to speak with warmth, but the glance the young woman cast at Edmund went beyond the scope of the play. Trying to keep his attention on both the text and the actors, Alexander spoke his next line.

Count: "A good man." In Italy, that means a religious man; in France, it means a cheerful man; in Spain, it means a wise man; and in England, it means a rich man.—Which good of all these is Mr. Anhalt?
Amelia: A good man in every country, except England.

Count. And give me the English good man, before that of any other nation.

Baron: And of what nation would you prefer your good woman to be, Count?

Count: Of Germany. [bowing to Amelia.]

Amelia: In compliment to me?

Count: In justice to my own judgement.

Baron: Certainly. For have we not an instance of one German woman, who possesses every virtue that ornaments the whole sex; whether as a woman of illustrious rank, or in the more exalted character of a wife, and mother?

Now came the part where Edmund entered the scene as the young clergyman, Anhalt.

Anhalt: I come by your command, Baron—

Baron: Quick, Count.—Get your elegant gun.—I pass your apartments, and will soon call for you.

Count: I fly.—Beautiful Amelia, it is a sacrifice I make to your father, that I leave for a few hours his amiable daughter.

Here Alexander's character made his exit, but the scene continued, wherein the baron expressed his dissatisfaction with the count as a beau for his daughter, and his concerns that she could never love him as a wife ought to do. To gauge Amelia's thoughts on the matter, the baron then bade Anhalt to find her and explain to her the duties of a wife and of a mother, and ask if she thought she could fulfil them as the wife of Count Cassel. Being in love with her himself—and knowing those feelings to be reciprocated—Anhalt found himself in a quandary. Alexander listened with keen interest as Edmund pronounced those final lines in the scene.

This commission of the Baron's in respect to his daughter, I am—[looks about]—If I should meet her now, I cannot—I must recover myself first, and then prepare.—A walk in the fields, and a fervent prayer—After these, I trust, I shall return, as a man whose views are solely placed on a future world; all hopes in this, with fortitude resigned.

It was a fine thing, Alexander considered, that Edmund's chosen career was in the Church and not on the stage. He had a fine voice and enunciated well, and would do well for reading sermons, but he had not the mannerisms and sensibilities of an actor. He declared his words, but did not feel them. His eyes did not stray to where Miss Crawford stood, immediately off the scene, nor did his breath catch as he proposed, in this dramatic persona, to lead his beloved to the arms of another. That he admired and liked Miss Crawford, there could be little doubt. But whilst a few lines of a play were hardly telling of a man's deepest sentiments, Alexander felt quite certain that Miss Crawford had no real piece of Edmund's heart.

The rehearsal progressed for some great length of time until the sun began to caress the horizon. As the actors began to complain of fatigue, Mrs. Grey appeared with two maids in tow, each wheeling in a trolley laden with food and drink for the actors in lieu of the dinner they would not be taking. Tom was determined and a surprisingly insistent taskmaster.

"Now, Miss Crawford and Mr. Lyons, let us begin again from your entrances, when Anhalt speaks," he gestured to Edmund. "Yates, will you provide the cue?"

The action had only just begun when the door to the room was thrown open, and Julia, appearing at it with a face all aghast, exclaimed, "Tom, Tom, we must stop at once. My father is come! He is in the hall at this very moment!"

Chapter Fifteen

A New Suspect?

At Julia's words, all action ceased, all gestures seemed frozen in stone, all hearts stopped their life-giving beats. The return of Sir Thomas from Antigua, it appeared, put an end to the performance of *Lovers' Vows*, a feat that the mere death of the host's relative at Ecclestone could not quite accomplish.

From her vantage point on the chair by the wall, Mary observed the shock that stole over the room. How is the consternation of the party to be described? To most, it was a moment of absolute horror. Sir Thomas in the house! All felt the instantaneous conviction. Not a hope of mistake was harboured anywhere. Julia's looks were evidence of the fact that made it indisputable; and after the first starts and exclamations, not a word was spoken for half a minute: each with an altered countenance was looking at some other, and almost each was feeling it as a stroke most unwelcome, most ill–timed, most appalling.

By the looks upon their faces, Mr. Yates seemed to consider it only as a vexatious interruption for the evening, and Edmund might have imagined it a blessing; but every other heart was sinking under some degree of self-condemnation or undefined alarm, every other heart was suggesting, "What will become of us? What is to be done now?"

But most striking to Mary's eyes was the stage where, in and amongst the actions frozen in time, Henry Crawford was listening with a look of devotion to Maria's Agatha. They stood there, as if turned to stone by the Medusa of Sir Thomas' return, unmoving and unflinching, as the sudden surprise permeated every inch of the room. Even as the shock of the *paterfamilias'* unexpected restoration to his family home melted into various senses of horror and shame, Henry Crawford retained Maria's hand in his, a moment of such peculiar proof and importance, that convinced Mary of some particular attachment between them.

And then, as quickly as if somebody had snuffed a candle, the frozen tableaux dissolved into a chaos of noise and aimless action, the need to move, say, or do something overcoming the shock of this interruption. Edmund and Tom cast looks of gloom and horror at each other, which might have been suitable for Frenchmen facing the guillotine, and walked together from the room with strides best matched to a funeral march.

"We had better put this room back to order." Maria's small voice settled through the sense of disaster, and she began tugging at small tables and chairs in order to return them to their habitual places. This must be, Mary thought bitterly, the first physical labour of any sort she had performed in her life.

The others joined in the efforts, the need to be doing something overcoming the degradation of such menial tasks, and another silence settled over the room, this one sullen and thick, rather than the shocked and brittle spell which had transfixed them all so short a time before.

Alexander pulled a rug to a darker spot on the wooden floor, which it covered exactly, and then carried a light settee to where it seemed to sit along one long edge. He placed it carefully on the floor and then moved to Mary's side.

"It seems our plans, such that they were, must be changed. I have always hoped to conclude this investigation as quickly as possible, but with Sir Thomas back in the area..."

"A hasty conclusion is all the more necessary," she finished his thought.

"His appearance on the day of the inquest is..." he paused to think of the word he wanted, "...interesting. First, Tom vanishes, then Rushworth dies, then Tom strolls in as if he had been down at the local pub for an ale. William Price appears as if by some magician's trick, and then Sir Thomas returns. It might well be coincidence, but I am not satisfied. I believe I must ask some people a few questions."

"In the stables?"

He smiled at her. "Just so, Mary. I need to know who brought Sir Thomas home, and when, exactly, he returned to England. Will you be well here as this little bit of play acting turns into a drama of real life?"

She allowed her hand to brush his arm. "Of course. I always am."

He found her hand and gave it a squeeze, and disappeared out the closest door.

Mary stood by the wall near the screen that she had hidden behind before. Now it was artfully placed to best direct the heat from the fireplace, which itself protruded a few feet into the room. In the dimming light of early evening, the once-bright room was now a patchwork of shadows and she was about to make for her chamber when she heard voices. Out of instinct, she stepped backwards into the lee of the hearth and held her breath.

"That was a damned close thing," one voice breathed, just above a whisper. That was Maddox, and he sounded quite close. Had not everybody retired for the night, now that Sir Thomas had returned?

The sound of shuffling feet answered her question. Maddox and his companion had left with the others, but were now returned. From the sound of their steps and voices, they were standing just inside the doorway. Hopefully, they would not enter the room any further. Mary pressed herself further into the small alcove beside the mantel and hoped she would not be seen.

"Too close." That was Oliver. There was a moment of silence and Mary wondered if they had left again on silent feet until Oliver continued. "It was not a moment too soon. Even a week later, and matters would have been quite different. Terribly different."

"He certainly cannot do it now," Maddox whispered in reply. "It would have ruined you."

There came a noise in return that Mary took as agreement. Then Oliver added, "It quite saved me."

"Shall we both be off for home tomorrow? I cannot think Sir Thomas will want us haunting this place."

"It will do. But there is that blasted inquest. Are we still needed?"

More silence. Then Maddox replied, "We were not told to remain, and they came to a verdict. Thank heavens they only asked about the hunt. Not a word about that other chap. And if anybody had mentioned... Well, you know. It is all done now, and there will be no more bother from it. I must find my man to pack my trunks. Perhaps a drink later?"

Mary just barely heard this invitation as the two men left the room, the sound of their feet all but silent on the polished floors.

What had they been talking about? She committed the conversation to memory, a skill that had earned her a great many disapproving sneers from her sisters in their youth, and poked her head around the door. The halls were empty.

As she crept up to her room, she wondered what Alexander would make of this overheard conversation, and if it had anything to do with Mr. Rushworth's death.

Alexander crept out the back door by the kitchens. The entire household was in an uproar over the unexpected return of its master after so long away, and he thus escaped quite unseen by any creature other than the cat who kept the mice at bay. It was not quite dark in the back enclosure behind the house. The sun had long since dipped below the horizon and the streaks of oranges and reds that cry the closing of the day had faded, leaving the sky a deep luminous blue. This light was his favourite of all the times of day, and it would last mere minutes. He stood in the yard, halfway from the estate house to coach house, marvelling at the beauty that the Creator, blessed be He, had deigned to grant His mortal children.

"Lovely, is it not?"

Alexander was startled from his reveries. "John. I did not expect to find myself in company. Aye, that such colours should exist."

There was a moment of reverent silence. Then the groom asked, "What brings you outside in the dark?"

"The house is in an uproar and I wished to be anywhere but in the midst of the storm. But I do have other designs as well. Some information, perhaps. About Sir Thomas. You know he is just now returned." This was a statement rather than a question. Nobody in the household could be ignorant of this fact.

John nodded, a dim movement in the thickening dark.

"How did he arrive? By coach, I imagine. Surely he did not ride?"

"No, not he. He keeps a horse for his pleasure, but does not ride to cover distance. It was a hired coach, carrying him, his valet, a servant, and some small pieces of luggage. Crabbs, the servant, says the rest of the trunks follow by cart.

"And the driver? Were there others? Outriders?"

"A driver and his lad. They left the horses here to be looked after, and went to the tavern in the village. Mrs. Grey offered them food, but they only took a drink and a piece of bread before leaving; said Sir Thomas had paid for a room for them for the night, them not wanting to bed down in the hay."

That, of course, was little removed from John's own spartan accommodations. The great cruelty of the matter crashed down upon Alexander's shoulders once more.

"I, too, feel the desire for a drink and some food at the pub, and I believe I must take a room as well. With the return of Sir Thomas and the arrival of his nephew William, there is little extra room for a working investigator in the guest chambers. And so, with Mr. Edmund Bertram's coin, it is the tavern for me. Perhaps we can go there, you and I, for a drink and a chat away from the confines of the house, and try to find these two and draw them into conversation." John looked distinctly uncomfortable at this suggestion. "I, of course, shall pay your way, with Mr. Edmund's coin. Why the concern? Are you not welcome at the tavern?"

"No, 'tis not that. If I am needed..."

"I shall tell them that I required your assistance in my investigation. Will you join me? I would enjoy the company if nothing else."

"Very well, then. Thank you."

The two soon crossed through the field that lay to the side of the elegant lawn behind the house and achieved the village tavern. It was a neat building of moderate size with a handful of guestrooms above, which he had not seen, and a comfortable private salon, which he had. It also served decent ale, as he knew from the quick drink he had taken after the inquest earlier in the day.

Sounds of men talking and laughing seeped through the heavy stone walls and the light from the candles and lamps poured through surprisingly clean windows. The night was pleasant and the heavy oaken door stood slightly ajar, welcoming new arrivals. Alexander gave a grin as he opened the door to allow John to enter first. "They are awaiting us. Let us see if there is a seat or two available."

The tavern was almost full. It had been a good harvest and men were now at leisure with some coin in their pockets. Somebody near the fireplace started a line from a popular song, the words to which Alexander hoped Mary would never hear. Perhaps the local version was more suitable for ladies' ears. One or two others joined in, confirming the prevalence of the ribald lyrics, but after a sad attempt at the refrain, the singers turned sour notes into yeasty ale and chose to drink rather than sing.

John nudged him in the side and gestured with his head to a table at the far end of the room, where two men sat in comfortable silence. One was on the older side of forty, with a weathered complexion and a bald patch in his wiry black hair. The other looked about five-and-twenty years younger, his hair still thick on his head. He did not resemble the older man in any tangible manner, but it would come as no surprise to find the two were father and son.

In the full room, there were no empty tables, which suited Alexander well. He slid through the crowd, careful of a wet or sticky floor, and shuffled about as he neared the pair in the corner. John made his own way through the beery throng. After making a suitable show of looking for a seat he knew did not exist, he turned to the two men. "Mind if we take a seat? Next beer is on my purse."

Whether or not the two had planned to be friendly or not, the offer of a free mug of ale was enough to bring friendly smiles to their faces. Alexander gestured to the serving girl, who came over to see what the newcomers wanted. As she made for the kitchens to prepare their order of drink and food, Alexander sat and made the introductions.

"Yer the one from 'is nibs' stable." The older man's working-class London accent sounded out of place in the midst of the Northampton countryside.

"I am. The name is John."

"Pete Tench. This 'ere is my sister's lad, Robbie Gane. Good company, and helps drive when I'm tuckered."

"Alexander Lyons. Pleasure." Alexander held out his hand in a friendly gesture, and his new companions shook it. At that moment, the serving girl swung their way with a tray, atop of which stood four glasses of deep amber ale and a platter which proved to hold some crispy rolls, cheese, and pickled vegetables. She served the men, accepted Alexander's coin, and left them to converse.

If the men were friendly before, seeing the proof of Alexander's offer made them more gregarious still. Alexander imagined they were friendly men even when paying for their own drink, but this was a penny well spent.

"Not from these parts?" Tench chuckled.

Ah, this line again. How many times Alexander had heard it, he could not say. "Indeed not," he returned a wider grin. "I am really from London." The looks on the two drivers' faces were amusement enough to make the old comment worth suffering once more. "I work there now. From near Glasgow in my youth. But London is home. Same as you, I imagine."

"That we are, eh, Robbie?" Robbie grinned and took a deep drink from his cup.

"Is that where you have driven from now?"

"Indeed we did. Nigh on seventy miles, at that."

"I enjoy London." Alexander kept his voice light. "It is very different from the village where I lived in Scotland, but one never lacks something to do. Have you been there all your lives?"

Both men smiled. "Born there, and me da' and 'is before 'im, and back for generations."

"Me ma too," Robbie spoke for the first time. "Seen a lot of England with this coach, we 'ave, but London is me best place."

"You must have travelled widely," Alexander added when the men grew quiet. "Is this your own coach, or do you drive for another?"

"Not ours! Mr. Croydon's. I cannot afford the rig and the 'orses. But I've been at this for many a year, and they've no complaints with me, nor will I give 'em any. I'm no toff, but I'm an honest man, not afraid to work for my living. Like the driving too, except when the weather turns nasty. But this ride has been good."

"Good," Robbie echoed.

"Does he have a great many coaches for hire?"

Tench and his nephew looked at each other. "Seven or eight, I think. I always get this one. I never drove Sir Thomas before, 'cause he has his own, but he come from overseas now, and didn't want to wait the time to send for his own and have it come for him. Least, that's what his servant told us when he was sitting up top with us."

They drank a bit more and made a healthy dent in the tray of food before them.

Alexander engaged in some meaningless conversation and solicited John's contributions about the local area, waiting for the two men to be quite at their ease before he posed the questions he really wished to ask.

"I imagine Sir Thomas hired you, then, through this, Mr. Croydon. I wonder how he heard of you. When I travel, it seems I am either in the hire of some wealthy client, or I travel on the mail coach. I've never had cause to find for myself a private carriage to take me where I need to be."

"Don't rightly know." Tench nibbled on a piece of cheese. "We were called by Mr. Croyden, given our direction, and told where to meet the gent. I imagine his valet did the arranging for him. I think it's one of those things valets are just supposed to know."

Alexander pondered his own ale for a moment. "He had just arrived from a long sea journey, then. I heard he was in the New World, in the islands."

"That's where I'm from," John added. "Came to England as a child." He did not add the rest of his sad story.

"Must be. Mr. Croyden said something about sending a cart to the docks for 'is trunks, but we were sent to get him at his club near St. James. Him, his valet, and the servant."

"The cart hasn't arrived yet," John yawned into his beer, as if the matter were of very little importance. Alexander stifled a smile. The man was intelligent and knew what he needed to learn. "It can't have been on the road very long. Your team of horses must travel quickly."

"That they can!" Tench boasted. "Ten miles an hour when we have good weather and dry roads. Have to change the horses often, but Sir Thomas didn't spare the pennies, wanted to keep up the pace. Told us we needed to get to Milton Keynes the first day, and that's fifty miles and more if it's an inch." He raised his tankard to his lips but did not drink.

"He was in a hurry, then? That's a good distance to travel. You must have left early yesterday. I am surprised the baronet travels on a Sunday."

"Some likes to worship and some likes to get home, I'm thinking. Funny thing, though." Tench paused and contemplated the pickled turnip in his hand as if it held the answer to the mysteries of the universe.

"What is that?" Alexander now allowed every bit of his curiosity to show.

"Me sister—that is Robbie's ma—sells pies down at the docks. She's a respectable woman, don't you think elsewise, but she needs to make a coin too."

Alexander and John concurred with great vigour. "Of course. I would never imagine otherwise."

"Well, she knows what ships come in and when, and she was sayin' about the sugar shipment come in from the islands because of all the men there to unload the sugar, and they bought out her pies that day. That weren't just yesterday, but were a week ago tomorrow. I was thinking it funny that Sir Thomas was in such a hurry to get here from London, when he was sitting in town for four days beforehand, doing a lot of nothing."

The two coachmen had no more information on the subject of Sir Thomas and his delayed but hasty flight from London to Mansfield. Alexander allowed the conversation to drift to other matters for a while before declaring that he, too, must find the landlord to seek a room. He bid his new friends a good evening, expressed a hope of seeing them on the morrow before their departure, and thanked them for sharing their table. Then, with John at his side, he did as he had said and asked after a room. He was offered one of the two remaining rooms, which he took and paid for with Edmund's coin.

He insisted on accompanying John back to the house. "I must retrieve my belongings," he explained, "and must see both to Miss Bennet's welfare and secure interviews with Maddox and Oliver, with whom I have not yet spoken at length." The evening was cool but pleasant, and he was not sorry for the short walk. "Perhaps, when I speak with Miss Bennet, you will join us, for you may have something to add. Is there a room near your quarters where we might sit and talk for a short time?"

The head groom's small office, so it transpired, was empty, and the man gave his permission for its use. Alexander found Mary and spirited her out of the house and to the stables, where John had lit a brazier for warmth and kindled a bright lantern.

"I heard something," Mary murmured as they crept through the back door to the stable yard. "Oliver and Maddox were talking."

"Just the men I was hoping to beard in their den. What did they say?"

She quickly recounted what little she had heard, and Alexander let out a low whistle. "I must wonder what this was about. It does sound rather dire, but so do many innocent matters when heard out of their context. Still, if they are so relieved, there must be something afoot."

In a moment, they were in the small office, seated around a low and rough table. Alexander withdrew his notepad as he and John recounted to Mary what they had learned from the two drivers.

"Why would he have spent four days in London without sending word, and then have raced home at such great speed?" Mary chewed her lip.

"He might have had matters of business there. After so long away, I imagine he had need to speak to his lawyer and banker."

"But why not send a message to his family? Surely they would have wished to be prepared for his return."

"Could he have wanted to surprise them?" Alexander toyed with the idea, teasing it like a cat after a mouse. "Might he have wished to see the state of the household as it was, and not as they wished him to see it?"

"Or," John interrupted, "might he have wished for us all to believe he had only now arrived? A note would tell the family that he was in England some days ago. A sudden arrival, and so late in the day, suggests that he traded his ship for a carriage and hardly stepped foot on the ground in between. Without any other word, they would easily believe him to have sailed in only yesterday morning."

Alexander stared at Mary, and she at him, before they both turned their eyes to John.

"That," Alexander whispered, "raises an entirely new set of questions."

Chapter Sixteen

More Questions

Alexander led Mary back to the house, through the kitchens, and back to the parlour where the guests had now gathered. Edmund was there, as were his sisters. Tom was not.

"Ah, Lyons," Edmund's voice was grim. "I need a word."

Mary gave him a quick nod and with a quick touch to her arm, he left her to the mercy of the others. "Mr. Bertram, how may I be of assistance? Is this about our residence here at Mansfield Park?"

The flush of shame that overtook Edmund's normally fair face answered for him.

"Never worry about that. I have already taken a room tonight at the tavern, and I have just now sent a message to my friends in Northampton, requesting them to open their home once more to Miss Bennet. For this evening, perhaps she might stay with Doctor and Mrs. Grant. She has sent her maid to pack her belongings already."

Edmund's flush deepened, but his stance relaxed. "Very well. I thank you. I shall, of course, include the cost of that in my accounts for your services. My father is... not happy with a house full of company. After his lengthy sea journey, he has expressed a wish to be only with his family, whom he has not seen in nearly two years. Yates, of course, must stay at least until tomorrow, but Maddox and Oliver..." He looked over to where these two young gentlemen were sitting with his sisters.

"I inquired at the tavern. There is a room still available, and I suggested to the landlord that he might have custom for it this evening. It is too late in the evening for them to return to their homes, but they will not be sleeping out in the cold."

Edmund relaxed further. "Good, then. Let us go and inform these men of their change of residence for the evening. They will not be pleased."

As it was discussed, so it transpired. The two men were not quite delighted with the polite request to relocate to the tavern's rooms for the evening, but neither were they surprised, and both had already instructed their valets to begin packing. They repaired to their rooms with fairly good grace to prepare, and Edmund promised whatever assistance he could from the staff. Likewise, Miss Maria Bertram was prevailed upon to ask Mrs. Grant for a room for Mary Bennet for the night, until such time as the carriage could be arranged to transport her and her belongings back to the Meldolas' house in Northampton. That message to the Grants was sent at once, and a reply returned within twenty minutes, assuring Miss Bennet of her welcome at the parsonage.

Shortly, a cart was on its way to the village with the various belongings of the four ousted guests whilst they and the Crawfords walked the short distance through the cool night air. Alexander left

Mary with Miss Crawford, promising to come by in the morning to see her settled at the Meldolas. Then he followed Oliver and Maddox to the tavern, where the landlord had indeed prepared the rooms for them.

"Join me for a drink?" Alexander invited them into the private parlour at the back where the inquest had taken place. "I have much still to discover about Rushworth's death, and you may be able to help me. I would be pleased to provide the ale if you would agree to provide some answers to my questions."

The two friends exchanged worried glances before Oliver nodded. "Very well. My dealings with Rushworth were not all entirely amicable, but I have no guilt to hide. I shall talk." Was this to do with what Mary had overheard? Alexander would not disclose what he knew, but would listen most carefully to what the men told him.

"It had better be good ale." Maddox growled, but his eyes smiled where his lips did not.

Soon they were settled in the parlour. Alexander inquired again after the stranger who had appeared at the start of the hunt to draw Rushworth away, but neither had anything to add to Edmund's statement earlier. He was unknown to all and unremarkable, rode up to Rushworth, and rode off again without drawing much additional attention, such was the excitement and chaos in the prelude to the chase. Alexander had not expected to hear otherwise, but the question must be asked. Now he would move on to the questions Mary's report had engendered.

"Tell me about James Rushworth himself," he continued. He had his notebook in front of him, but his pencil lay on the table and his hands were wrapped around another mug of the ale. He had to drink slowly. It would be fine to let some of the beer loosen other lips, but he needed his mind to remain clear, and he had consumed some earlier whilst speaking to the carriage drivers.

The two men exchanged another worried glance, which Alexander pretended not to notice. Then Oliver turned towards Maddox and shook his head. "Very well," he sighed. "This is hardly a great secret. I did not know the man very well, for all that we were neighbours of a sort. His estate lies in an odd shape and follows the stream around a bit. Where it bends, his land abuts my own."

"I take it this is important." Alexander put down his beer and picked up the pencil.

Oliver nodded as he exhaled again. "It is. He has, of late, talked much about improving his estate, or rather, the main prospect from the house, by means of a landscape specialist. He is… was a man much given to whims and quirks of fashion, but not to deep or rational thought." He stared at Alexander as if daring him to take issue with his words that spoke ill of the dead. Alexander met his gaze with equanimity.

"I am not here to pass judgement on your feelings, gentlemen. Speak freely with me. I care only for information concerning his death. Everything unrelated to this will be forgotten."

Assuaged, Oliver sniffed and continued. "He had once seen a drawing of a house fronted by a grand pond, created by swelling a natural stream into greater importance. He wished for the same for Sotherton, although the lie of his estate does not lend itself to that at all."

"No," Alexander nodded. "I have seen the house, and it lies at a low point. Such a pond would surely drown the house."

Maddox let out a bark of laughter, and Oliver scowled at him. "He thought to dig a pond behind a levee of some sort, and wished to divert and dam the stream to fill it, but this is the stream that also runs through my land. My farmers rely on the water for their crops and for their livestock. His whims of fashion would greatly injure my farmers and my estate."

"Then his demise must be a great relief to you." What had Mary recited to him? *Not a moment too soon?* He peered at Oliver through narrow eyes, his pencil hovering above the paper.

"I... that is... It was not..." Oliver gasped meaningless words as his face went white.

The pencil now scratched over the notepad, and Oliver looked down at it in alarm. He hunched forward, hands on the table before him. "I did not kill him! I hoped to have some time to sit with him that evening, after the hunt when he was in good spirits and amenable, and talk to him about it. Maybe see if we could discover some other means of beautifying the prospect. He also wished to chop down the avenue of oaks leading down the drive, which would be a great loss, and to which Miss Price objected as strenuously as she can—which is not very much, I confess—but she did not harm him about the oaks, and I did not over the stream. I swear it!" The man was in a panic, but something in his desperate words rang true.

"Be easy, Mr. Oliver. Thank you for telling me of this dispute, but I do not suspect you of killing him over it. It is, as you say, something I could easily have learned through other means. You do not seem so foolish as to take such a step without expecting to be found out."

Oliver leaned back in his chair and released a long breath. "I would rather have you discover this from me. I am prepared to answer any more questions you may have."

"Thank you. I shall. In the meantime, however, I would like to hear your thoughts, Mr. Maddox. What was your relationship with Mr. Rushworth?"

A flash of anger crossed his face and disappeared just as quickly. "The man was a fool. There, I have said it. We were often in company, although not of my choice; it is unavoidable in this neighbourhood, unless one is pleased to refuse all invitations like my friend Oliver here does. Rushworth was a bore, with not one intelligent or interesting thought in his head, and could be led as easily as a farmer leads an ox by the ring through its nose. He was in Sir Thomas Bertram's pocket, and a marriage to Maria would only make him all the more subservient to the man."

"You do not like the Bertrams?"

"As people, I like them well enough. We have our differences. I have a reasonable estate that I farm, like Oliver here, but I also derive much of my income from investments. The Bertrams have only a small amount of arable land; most of their wealth derives from blood."

"Blood?"

"The blood of the poor souls who are forced to work themselves to death growing the sugar on those islands." Like John's long-lost parents. Alexander wondered if Maddox knew about him.

"You side with the abolitionists?"

"You do not?"

Alexander let out a bitter laugh. "I cannot abide even being attended to by a paid servant without discomfort. The thought of men and women, children too, forced into servitude without even meagre compensation is repulsive."

"And yet you accepted their hospitality well enough." The voice was accusatory.

"As did you. And I was paid to be there."

Maddox released a peal of laughter. "Touché, my friend, touché. Yes, I have lent my support and my contributions to the abolitionists. I have donated from my bank accounts, I have offered them my home on their journeys through this country, and I have given them the names of people to whom they ought to speak, whether friend to solicit their support, or foe to try to sway their sentiments."

"It was you, then, who sent Wilberforce and Ottley after Tom Bertram."

"You know of them, I see. So I did. Can you blame me? He was seldom at home, but often frequented the pubs and gaming halls in Northampton. I thought that if removed from the house built on the proceeds of slavery, he might be more amenable to persuasion."

Alexander scratched in his notebook again. "Did they find success?"

Maddox shrugged and pursed his lip. "I do not know. But I do know that Tom is a venal man. He has few principles or morals, and lives for the horses and parties and wagering. I do not see him listening to two men with sad tales and a plea to relinquish his wealth for the betterment of humanity." He paused and thought for a moment. "His brother Edmund, on the other hand, is a different sort of creature. He would be sympathetic to the plight of the slaves who toil to support his brother's habits. Indeed, Edmund has already suffered for Tom's excesses when he lost the living here."

Alexander ceased his writing and looked directly at Maddox. "You have, you must know, just provided yourself with an excellent motive for murder. By getting rid of Tom, you leave Edmund as the heir to the baronetcy."

Maddox levelled his eyes at his interrogator. "Perhaps, but it is not Tom who has died."

"No, that is true. But neither am I convinced that Mr. Rushworth was the intended victim of this crime. The killers might very well have intended to murder Tom Bertram."

Alexander rose early in the morning. His note to his friends had been answered with an unqualified welcome for Miss Bennet to rejoin them at their house in Northampton. He would have to remain at the tavern until his investigation was concluded, however; he rather wished he were returning to the Meldolas' home as well.

He arrived at the parsonage as Mrs. Grant's servants were setting out the breakfast dishes, and the lady invited him to join them. Doctor Grant was an epicure, and even his morning eggs were exceptional in taste and texture. Afterwards, whilst they strolled along the village lanes as they awaited the carriage for Mary, Alexander took the time to acquaint her with what he had learned from the two gentlemen the previous evening.

She listened with interest, not speaking until he had concluded his recitation.

"Then we have three possible suspects: Oliver, who wished for Rushworth to desist in his improvement schemes, Maddox, who would prefer Edmund as heir and baronet because of his presumed sympathy for the abolitionists, and Sir Thomas himself, for no reason we know as yet, but who was in England for several days before he made himself known to his family."

"You have considered that as well?" Alexander asked.

"Of course. Having arrived on Tuesday last, he would have had ample time to hire the two men, send them up to Northamptonshire to dispatch Mr. Rushworth to his eternal reward, and then travel north as if he had only arrived and could not possibly be involved in any such business. Having spent a great deal of time on a ship, he might have befriended the captain, who, in turn, might have given him the name of Admiral Crawford. The relationship with his neighbours might be quite coincidental. It all fits rather too well."

"Might he have been involved with Tom's disappearance as well? The coincidence is too great to ignore."

Mary shrugged. "He was in London, surely. He could not have travelled the seventy miles here, done whatever it was he had planned, travelled another seventy back, and still have been in London to return again."

Alexander considered this. "If he had been prepared to spend his entire week in a carriage, running some poor horses to the bone, it is possible, but rather unlikely. Still, I shall send messages to some of the likely posting inns to inquire about whether he passed through and changed horses."

"Did you learn any more of William Price?" Mary asked after a moment.

"No. I inquired of both Maddox and Oliver, but both swore they had never seen the man before, nor even heard of him. Considering Price is their friend's cousin and his sister has been living at Mansfield Park for ten years, this might seem unusual, but it seems our Mr. Tom Bertram rarely thinks of others and even more rarely speaks of them, unless they are somehow of benefit to him. His cousin William has been out of sight and out of mind for all of his life. I believed both when they professed complete ignorance."

"Then we are no further ahead." She sighed, and Alexander sighed with her. This mystery was proving far too perplexing, with too many poor suspects, too few good ones, inadequate clues, and uncertainty as to the intended victim of the crime. She examined her hands. "I did hear one thing, however…"

He looked up at her, eyes wide.

"Last night, after you left me here, Mrs. Grant called for tea, and we talked for a while before retiring. Mrs. Grant asked Mr. Crawford whether he had found success with the tailor in Northampton. He looked a bit abashed and made some noncommittal remark, but Mrs. Grant asked again, and a bit of the story came out.

"It seemed that about a month ago, Henry Crawford had the idea to have a hunting coat made."

She paused, but Alexander did not press her. The wealthy did such things all the time. They had the leisure to hunt, the luxury to do so for sport and not for survival, and the great advantage of doing so on their own land. How unlike the starving peasants, for whom a trapped rabbit could be the difference between life and death, and for whom such trespass and poaching could send a man to prison or to the gallows. Furthermore, the wealthy could afford to treat it like a game and to dress the part, commanding a new coat because the old one had lost a button. Still, he waited patiently for Mary to continue. He knew she would; It was not like her to speak of such frivolities without purpose. In a moment, she satisfied him.

"It was to be of a special fabric, one that had arrived at the local tailor and from which Tom Bertram himself had recently had such a coat made. Hunting coats are most often red," she commented. "The 'pinks,' they are termed. But this coat was to be green. I know not why they made such a choice. Perhaps just to set themselves apart."

His eyes widened. This was interesting. "So Henry Crawford had a hunting coat that exactly matched Tom Bertram's?" Mary nodded. "And also like the coat which James Rushworth was wearing when he died?" She nodded again.

"This matter gets stranger and stranger." He cast his mind back to the previous Saturday, when the hunt had gone so terribly wrong. "Stranger still, Henry was not wearing that new hunting coat. I recall him in something deep red, whereas Rushworth's coat was an unusual light green, almost blue. That is how we found where he tried to leap the thicket, for a piece of his coat tore and it stood out like a beacon against the browns and greens of the shrubs."

Now Mary turned her head to face him with a most unusual look, something almost gleeful. "Do you have something else to tell me?" he asked her.

She slowed her steps. "I do! Do you wish to know why Henry Crawford was not wearing the hunting coat he had just had made, most especially for this exact event?"

"I do, and I know you wish to tell me."

"He says," she dropped her voice almost to a whisper and stepped closer to him as they continued their walk, "that he had lost it!"

"How on earth..." Alexander exploded, then lowered his voice. "How on earth does one lose a new hunting coat?"

Mary shrugged and shook her head. "He said nothing, as if he wished to change the subject, but his sister, Mrs. Grant, kept talking of it. She asked whether he had worn it yet, and whether his valet had located it, for the maid in the laundry room certainly had not seen it, and neither was it misplaced amongst Doctor Grant's clothing. I would not have thought anything of the topic, except that it clearly made Mr. Crawford most uncomfortable, and of course, it related to the hunt."

Alexander stopped walking and pulled out his notebook to scribble this information down on the next empty space. "And what did Miss Crawford have to say? Had she seen the coat at all?"

Mary screwed up her forehead. "She was out of the room at that moment, seeing to something about my room, I believe. When we heard her returning, Mr. Crawford immediately changed the subject and began asking me about Hertfordshire. I do believe," she continued slowly, "that he did not wish his sister to know something about the coat. I wonder why that was."

They had by now returned to the parsonage and all such conversation must end. At the moment they were about to enter the house, the carriage was heard rumbling up the short drive. Mrs. Grant and Miss Mary Kate Crawford emerged from the parsonage to oversee the stowing of Mary's luggage, and farewells and great exclamations of appreciation were offered in all directions, and soon it was time to leave. Thus, they prepared to part ways, all satisfied with the other.

Alexander had decided to ride in the coach with Mary, his horse tethered to the carriage so he might ride back after seeing her well settled with his friends. Mary's maid was to make the short journey with them, but she chose to sit on the box with the driver, for the day was fine and the young woman had come to enjoy his company, leaving the two friends together inside the vehicle itself. The proper thing to do, of course, would be to allow Mary to take the forward-facing bench, whilst he sat diagonally across from her, facing the back of the coach. This he did not do. As soon as Mary was seated, he asked if he might move to sit beside her, and the moment the carriage left the small village for the eight-mile drive to Northampton, he moved his seat.

She smiled at him and shifted closer to him. When the carriage hit a small rut on the lane's surface and jolted slightly, he reached out to hold her safe, and when she did not object or pull away, he allowed her to rest along his side, his arm across the back of her shoulders. How very natural this felt, as if it were meant to be. Mary fit. She fit along his side, she fit under his arm. She fit into his life. Images flooded his mind of returning to his home after a day's work to find her waiting for him, ready to listen to his problems and share her thoughts and insights. He imagined her working alongside him, asking questions and discovering things he had not thought to examine. He pictured holding her close and pressing his lips into her soft hair, touching her own lips with his...

Another small jolt of the carriage brought him back to reality. A twinge in his heart warned him against such dreams, for they could never be; she could never be his. But he knew it was too late. He was already in love with her.

All too soon, the carriage entered the town of Northampton and he shifted back to the other bench. The streets grew more and more familiar until they pulled to a stop before the elegant townhouse that belonged to the Meldolas. Elijah was waiting at the top of the short stairs, Hannah behind him, and both came down at once to greet them as the groom opened the carriage door.

There was a great deal of fuss and bustle as Mary was ushered inside and her belongings carried in by a servant. Most of her trunks from her visit to the Darcys had remained safely stowed in the Meldolas' storage sheds behind the house until her return to Hertfordshire, but even for a few short days' visit, a lady required more than a small satchel of personal belongings and suitable clothing.

"I have had the maid prepare the same room for you, if that is acceptable." Mrs. Meldola grabbed Mary's hands and led her into the family's comfortable sitting room. "But first, let us have some tea. Alexander, you will stay?"

"I told my clerk to expect me late, so I could sit with you a while," Mr. Meldola added. "Come, my friend, let us enjoy a few moments with a cup of something hot and a slice of cook's almond cake."

Alexander laughed, "Elijah, how could I not?"

They sat for a few minutes in congenial conversation until Meldola had to return to his business and Alexander to his investigation. Meldola went to find his coat and hat and his wife excused herself for a moment to inquire as to the state of Mary's room, leaving Alexander alone in the room with Mary.

"You will be well here." The statement came out as a question. "Hannah and Elijah will see to your every need. They are the best of people and I shall try to come by each day until this case is concluded."

"It is a long ride. I do not expect that."

He leaned forward to look into her eyes. "It is not too long for you. No distance is too long for you." The words came unbidden to his lips, but he did not regret them. Although they had no future together, she ought to know she was worthy of great affection. He knew how she felt herself to be the ignored daughter, the quiet one, the one who thought herself plain. She had spent her life feeling second best, and if his poorly considered words allowed her to know, just for a moment, that she was a diamond of the first water in his eyes, at least, he would gladly suffer the consequences.

He felt her hands upon his own, and she leaned forward as well. She started to speak, but no words emerged, and her eyelids fluttered. Was she upset at this poor attempt at a declaration? No, it could not be, for rather than recoiling, she had taken his hands. What was it she wished to say?

She looked into his eyes for a moment, and then, so quickly he hardly knew what had happened, she leaned forward that small bit more and touched a light kiss upon his lips. Her face flushed bright red and, without another word, she turned and fled from the room.

Alexander stood there, stunned. She had kissed him. Mary Bennet had kissed him! It had been so quick and tentative, he had no time to react. Now that she had fled in embarrassment, he wished for nothing more than to run after her and kiss her back. It was only with the greatest effort that he kept his feet in place on the ground. His face felt strange, and in the mirror above the mantel he caught a glimpse of himself bearing the largest grin he had ever seen. Mary had kissed him!

Suddenly, every impediment to their future happiness melted away. Every problem could be managed, every difficulty smoothed over with enough effort and willing to find a middle ground. With a comfortable enough income, perhaps Mary would not mind a place in the middle class. Her uncle and aunt Gardiner were more than respectable, and they were of the merchant class. Mary loved and looked up to them, and enjoyed spending time with their family in London. No. Status mattered not to her, after all. There was only one remaining issue...

"Alexander, shall we?" Elijah called from the hallway. The rosy glow over his future dimmed, but that spark of hope remained. After all, Mary had kissed him!

Mary stood in her chambers in the Meldolas' house, shaking. The door was closed, her few belongings half unpacked, her maid sent from the room. Mrs. Meldola had asked what was amiss, and Mary had muttered something about being tired. In truth, she had never felt more awake in her life, although she was shaking, both from shock and embarrassment.

Whatever had she been thinking? How had her good sense abandoned her so? She was accustomed to being in close proximity to Alexander. The touch of his hand upon hers was nothing unusual, the feel of his arm about her shoulders something she ought to be used to. They had exchanged brief hugs in the past, as good friends are wont to do. Nothing should have changed.

And yet, when he looked at her so directly and told her that no distance was too great to travel for her, something deep within her had shifted. That reserve which had defined her for all of her twenty years disappeared, the dam holding back all of her innermost sensibilities suddenly giving way under the pressure of her emotions. And unable to help herself, she had kissed him.

Oh! What must he think of her? What sort of shameless girl made such forward advances to a man? How brazen he must find her to be. She was worse than Lydia, for her youngest sister merely flirted with men; she did not throw herself bodily at them.

To be sure, a kiss was hardly equal to a loss of virtue. Even Lizzy, she knew, had kissed Mrs. Hill's nephew that summer several years ago, when Andrew had come to spend the hot months of the year with his aunt in the countryside. Lizzy had been sixteen and Andrew seventeen and adept at figures. He was training under Mr. Parney, the steward, to learn some skills that might one day allow him to take up a similar position at some great estate. Lizzy had been showing him something in the storehouses behind the main house, and when he had asked for a kiss, Lizzy had offered her lips willingly. Mary, as so often happened, had been nestled in and amongst the crates and sacks where she might read uninterrupted by her mother's demands, and had seen the whole thing. It had only been a kiss, little more than she had just now given to Alexander, and she had said nothing, had never told her secret.

But whilst a chaste kiss might not be a stain on any young lady's character, that was Lizzy! She was Mary, a very different sort of person, and one who held herself and her behaviour above the ways of most. She was Mary, whose tendency towards piety led her to impose a stricter morality upon herself than even those words which she so liberally cast upon her family.

Mary Bennet did not kiss men.

But she had. She had kissed him, and she could not regret it.

She remained in her room for quite some time, unpacking only the very few items she might need immediately, and expecting at any minute to hear Mrs. Meldola at the door, demanding she gather her belongings and depart the house at once, on account of her most improper behaviour. When this did not happen, she tentatively crept down to the sitting room, where her hostess was busy at work on some sewing.

"Miss Bennet. I do hope you are feeling refreshed. This must have been a trying time for you." There was no reproach in the words, no look of scorn in her eyes. Alexander must not have told of Mary's scandalous behaviour.

Mary sat with a smile, and before long was helping her hostess at the sewing, mending torn sleeves and hemming dresses for the local orphanage. As on her previous visits, she found Mrs. Meldola to be excellent company, speaking neither too much nor too little, and having well-formed and intelligent observations when she did speak, and the time passed quickly.

Morning had passed and turned to afternoon when there was a knock at the door and the housekeeper showed her head. "A Mr. and Miss Price to see Miss Bennet, if you please.

Chapter Seventeen

William Price's Evidence

Mrs. Meldola met Mary's surprised exclamation with a smile and a nod. "Would you like to see your friends?"

"Er... yes, if it is not too much inconvenience."

"Not at all." She looked up at the housekeeper. "Please show our guests in."

A moment later, Fanny and William stood at the doorway, to be welcomed inside by Mrs. Meldola. "Please sit. I shall order some tea and cakes. And I must see to dinner, so I shall allow you to visit without my awkward presence. Please, you are very welcome in my house."

As soon as the three were alone, Fanny apologised for their unexpected visit in her quiet, tentative voice. "I do hope we have not intruded upon your visit, but William required some items which were not available in the village and offered to drive me into town to visit the shops. We were... I was very relieved to leave the house. My uncle, Sir Thomas, is not in the best of spirits today."

William rolled his eyes and huffed. "He was a right bear. Worse even than the admiral after a poor showing. Had I but known, I might have delayed this visit to the house, but I was pleased to be able to provide an escape for poor Fanny." He lowered his voice to a conspiratorial level. "I did not really need these items, but I did need an excuse for a long drive. And here we are, and I have purchased my soap and taken my watch in to be repaired. My sister was hoping you might join us for a treat at the tearoom, and then on our final visits to the haberdasher for some gloves and the draper for new cravats. My uncle has determined to have a ball for Fanny, and I have no suitable clothing for the affair."

"Do say you will join us on our errands, Miss Bennet." Mary had never seen such a look of appeal in Fanny's eyes, and she was well inclined to accept. Furthermore, whilst she had been very happy to help Mrs. Meldola, an outing to a tearoom and some shops would make a nice diversion from sewing.

She sought out Mrs. Meldola and put the suggestion to her, which was considered most agreeable. The mistress of the house then invited the Prices to stay for dinner, but this they had to refuse, for they wished to return to Mansfield Park before full dark.

Mary sought her hat and boots and set out with her companions. They found their tea and cakes in a sweet little shop near the high street, and enjoyed pleasant, if unremarkable, conversation whilst they sat. Fanny insisted that Edmund had passed some coins along to her for the very purposes of paying for the treat. Once more, Mary was struck by these little kindnesses Edmund did for his young cousin and she considered again that he was not as indifferent to her as he might think himself.

It was only after they had finished their tea and had set out for the haberdasher that Mary dared to ask William about his sudden arrival in Northamptonshire. Whereas he might be reticent when speaking to an investigator with his notes and pencil before him, ready to record every word, a pleasant question in the context of a light conversation might release some secrets.

"It has been a delight to meet you, Mr. Price. I did not hear how you happened to be in the neighbourhood, but I am very pleased you are. What brought you to these parts? There is hardly a port nearby." She tried a lighthearted laugh, which sounded creditable to her ears.

"Do tell, William! For I have not heard the whole story either," Fanny clutched at his sleeve. "He has only told me that he was in the neighbourhood for matters of business. What can they be? It all sounds so very mysterious."

"Not so mysterious, Fanny. Alas, my dealings were unsuccessful, however." He turned to Mary. "You are in the confidence of Mr. Lyons, are you not?" She agreed. "I trust Fanny with my secrets, such that they are. I believe I can trust you as well." He walked on in silence for a moment, passing shops and shoppers without seeing them.

"I have long since hoped for a promotion in the ranks. Although I have not yet been able to achieve promotion to an officer's commission, such things are, at times, granted through effort and industry. Upon my most recent return to England's shores, I passed my midshipman's exams, and I had settled on speaking to the admiral to plead my case.

"With that in mind, I arrived early one morning at his offices. I was sitting outside waiting for my appointment when two men left the building. They must not have seen me, hidden as I was behind some large crates, for they spoke freely. I heard only parts of their conversation, but what I did hear alarmed me. They were to head directly for Northamptonshire, to 'take care of a problem,' in their words. It became clear that the 'problem,' was a man, and 'taking care' of him involved ending his life.

"They never spoke a word of who this unfortunate man might be, or when they were supposed to execute their duty, but they joked about 'we shall know him by this.' I never saw what 'this' might be, for I dared not show myself; indeed, it might have been a scar or a medal or a wooden leg. It might even have been a particular way of walking or a mannerism, but the men seemed confident in their quarry. It was only when I heard them walk away that I dared to look out from behind my screen. I saw one man of average size, and one very large. I gathered my bravery too late and determined to take my leave and do what I could to find and stop these men."

They had now arrived at the haberdasher. Inside, they examined the various offerings until William discovered the perfect pair of gloves that were within the means of his pocket, and he purchased them. The draper was exactly next door. This shop was large, with an impressive selection of fabrics lining the walls and filling the floor-to-ceiling shelves. Uncle Gardiner would be most impressed. Indeed, Mary considered, he had almost certainly seen this shop himself as he travelled through the country selling his textiles, and she wondered how many of these bolts and piles of lovely fabric had originated in his very warehouses.

There was a sign on a doorway near the sales desk advertising the services of a tailor for alterations to existing clothing, as well as for newly made clothing. "As good as anything London has to offer," the sign boasted.

"William, do see if he can make a waistcoat for you!" Fanny urged. "If Sir Thomas insists on this ball, you must be well dressed. See, the door is open. He must not be engaged with a customer now. Do go and ask him."

He shook his head at her. "I cannot, Fanny. It is a luxury I can ill afford, and I would never wear such a garment again. There is nowhere in my day-to-day affairs where a waistcoat suitable for a ball would be an appropriate garment. But I shall ask about those cravats I wanted."

"Ask him, at least," Fanny begged. William rolled his eyes, but gave her a smile. "I shall ask, but no more than that. Ah, here comes the proprietor. Let me see first about those cravats."

If Mary had wondered why William was seeking to purchase cravats at the draper rather than at the haberdasher, her answer came quickly. Mr. Lennox, who owned the establishment, had a small display with a variety of materials, all of which were suitable for cravats. Some were crisp, snowy white, but there were other colours too, as well as a selection of subtle and elegant prints. A customer could select his favourite material and within a day, the tailor would cut and hem the pieces to the perfect size for his wishes.

"Edmund told us about this shop, for my cousin Tom comes here for his own clothing," Fanny explained in her tentative voice. "He is something of a dandy, as you have most likely noticed, and does love his clothing, and now he has Mr. Crawford purchasing his clothing here too, as well as Mr. Yates." She moved to the material for the cravats and began pointing out selections for her brother.

Mary did likewise, and suddenly her eyes opened wide. There, on one shelf, was a silk print with a cunning pattern derived from Greek letters in a shade only just darker than the pale eggshell of the background. The letters were arranged in such a manner as to look like nothing more than a richly textured cloth. The wearer—and his valet, of course—would know the truth. This appealed immediately to Mary, who had to have one made for her father. This was exactly the thing Mr. Bennet would appreciate. When she looked closely, she found a similar print, but with white upon white, and there was another in two very close shades of dark green, a colour which her father sometimes wore in the mornings.

Whilst Fanny and William were choosing William's neckcloths therefore, Mary made her own selections. She had already bought little things for her mother and younger sisters, who would certainly want presents after her long visit in Derbyshire; Papa seldom expected anything, and likely would not know how to respond if a gift were to present itself before him, but Mary could not deny herself the joy of selecting and making a gift to him of these unusual objects. Mr. Lennox took her order and her money, and assured her that Mr. Gambon, the tailor, would have the finished cravats ready for her by the following afternoon.

Fanny and William were still arguing over the waistcoat, although it seemed to Mary that Fanny would emerge the victor. "It need not be of an elaborate or expensive fabric, William. Here, a simple dark blue will look well with your coat and the white cravat you have purchased, and will be suitable for half dress as well, or any other occasion when you need look a little smarter than if you have only now stepped off your ship. See. Edmund has been generous to me over the years, and I have little use for spending money for myself. Allow me to do this one thing for you. It will make you even more handsome, and it will make me happy."

As the siblings discussed the best choice for the cut and lining of the waistcoat, Mary continued to browse. Here was a beautiful rich silk in a deep purple that would look fine with Lizzy's green eyes, and here a delicate muslin with sprigged flowers that would be fetching on Lydia. There was some lace for a fichu for Mama, and a pale yellow sarsenet that would do well for a day dress for her. She wandered the perimeter of the shop, fingering some of the bolts when the lure became too great to resist, and had all but decided to purchase some mint green silk for a gown for herself when her fingers fell on an unusual green wool, almost blue.

Mr. Lennox was right there at her side. "Does the wool interest you, Miss? We have not very much left, for it has been popular of late. A riding coat, perhaps? No? The silk then, for a frock? It must be for you. Such a lovely colour with your complexion. An excellent choice. Will you take it now? Or tomorrow, when you return for the cravats? Perfect. I shall have it all wrapped and ready for you."

His patter continued until Mary had counted out her coins. At last, the Prices had also come to a decision, and it was arranged that William would return on the morrow to be measured for a waistcoat at last.

The day was drawing to a close, and the three walked the short distance back to the Meldolas' smart house, where William and Fanny would retrieve their buggy in order to return to Mansfield. It was with a strange sort of regret that Mary watched them depart. She was not like her younger sisters with their love of shopping, but she had enjoyed this day and its diversions very much, and she desperately hoped that neither William nor Fanny Price had anything to do with Mr. Rushworth's murder.

Alexander had spent much of the day in Northampton as well, pursuing his own lines of inquiry. His first visit was to the offices of Mr. Framington, to whom Tom Bertram had been rather in debt some weeks before. The man was not pleased to be interrupted from his work, but received the investigator graciously enough.

"I am, you can see, rather busy, and whilst I know your questions are important, I must ask you to be as expeditious as possible in asking them."

"I understand completely." Alexander gave a curt nod. "Let us dispense with the social niceties, then, and begin. Where, sir, do you make your money?"

"Curt and to the point." Framington smiled for a moment. "I appreciate that in a man. Very well. Canals. I have invested heavily in canals, and am engaged as well in building and expanding them. It is not a quick return on funds, should you be so interested, but it is a sure one. No funny business here. We work hard, but we reap the rewards. Our current endeavour is a connection from the River Neve to the Grand Junction Canal. Work is underway and we expect it complete within a few short years. Yes, I have become a wealthy man."

"I am impressed. As a working man myself, I appreciate the value of solid work and I rejoice in your success. I shall assume, then, that any debts owed to you by Mr. Tom Bertram of Mansfield Park are matters of honour and not of survival."

Framington stared at him for several moments. He spoke at last. "Ah yes. I recall. You were there that night he made his spectacular entrance at Elijah Meldola's house. I loaned him enough to save his sorry neck that one time. I did not expect to see my money again, at least until his father returned and honoured the debt, and yes, it was an inconvenience but not a vital one. It was, if you will, a business decision. Whilst I care little for the approbation of such families as the Bertrams, they are influential in the county and they can make my way easy or hard. They cannot stop me, but I would rather have them on my side than not."

"What came of that loan?"

"To my surprise, it was repaid, and all at once. The whole two thousand pounds." Alexander whistled. That was a sizable amount of money to have owing. "I have to wonder whether Bertram applied to his future brother, Rushworth, for the blunt. Rushworth is… or rather, was thick enough that after a time, he may have forgotten about the debt entirely. The man had more shillings in his pockets than thoughts in his head, and wouldn't have missed a thousand or two, if you know what I mean."

This was news! Alexander withdrew his notebook from a pocket and copied the relevant information. "Have you any evidence to support this supposition, that Rushworth paid off Bertram's debts?"

Framington shook his shaggy head. "Nothing solid, other than seeing them both in town the day before Bertram came to me with a draught to cover the entirety of what was owing. They were walking near the bank, but it is in the midst of the town and men pass it every day. I have no reason to think they had business there, other than that welcome repayment of my loan. It is more likely that they were taking some entertainment in town, or paying a visit to the tailor, which they did not infrequently. Bertram does love his clothes. Had a special hunting coat made in a most unusual green rather than usual red, simply because the fabric was rare. No wonder his pockets were always running empty."

Alexander thanked the businessman and went on his way. Framington had little reason to wish any particular ill of Bertram, or of Rushworth, so it seemed. He had seemed frank and honest enough, and if Bertram had relieved him of some money, Rushworth had seen his coffers refilled.

However, a new idea was forming in Alexander's brain: did Tom Bertram somehow wish ill upon Rushworth? If Framington's supposition were correct, did Bertram wish Rushworth's gift not to be known? Was there some condition to the loan, or gift or whatever it might be, that he was determined at all costs to avoid? There was no point in designing plots of murder based on a guess; a visit to Mr. Harris at the local bank seemed to be in order.

Harris welcomed Alexander with a smile that did not reach his eyes. This, Alexander reminded himself, was the brother of the lazy coroner, the lawyer who wished for nothing so much as to avoid his job. Whether the brothers spoke often, or agreed when they did, was something Alexander could not guess, but he had to wonder how much the coroner had set the banker's mind against him. Still, when confronted with sufficient evidence, Harris the coroner had come to Alexander's way of thinking. He might be lazy, but he was not unfair or blind to justice. Alexander hoped the banker would be likewise disposed.

"Mr. Lyons," the banker smiled his actor's smile. This must be part of the man's stock-in-trade, to appear at all times pleasant to his customers whilst keeping his inner thoughts hidden. "How may I be of assistance?"

"I hoped you might have some information for me about some of the late James Rushworth's financial dealings."

The smile vanished from the banker's face. "I am afraid I am not permitted to discuss this."

Alexander reached into his bag and placed a short pile of documents on the desk. "I am officially investigating Mr. Rushworth's death, and have letters to that effect both from Mr. Edmund Bertram and the coroner, who I believe is your brother."

The look that passed across Mr. Harris' face suggested that he and his brother were not, perhaps, as close as two siblings might be. "Be that as it may, I am bound by matters of confidentiality here." Of this, Alexander was not quite convinced. During his legal training in Glasgow some years back, he had studied such matters and knew that a visit by the coroner himself might open some account books, but he hoped not to have to resort to such measures, especially if the two Messrs Harris were not completely fond of each other.

"Perhaps, then, I might provide a narrative, which you may accept or deny."

The artificial smile had returned, accompanied by a sceptical look in the man's eye. "Very well," he pronounced at last. "Tell me your tale."

"I believe that Mr. Rushworth came in several weeks ago—six, or perhaps five—and made a large withdrawal in the form of a draught to be made over to Mr. Tom Bertram. Two thousand pounds, if I am correct." Mr. Harris did not need to speak. His expression confirmed every word. "I further believe that Mr. Bertram was with him at the time; Did you overhear anything that was said between the two concerning the nature of this transfer?"

Harris blinked. "Very well. You seem to know it anyway, or most of it. Rushworth came in..." he pulled out a ledger and consulted its pages, "about six weeks ago, on the thirteenth of September, to be exact. As you said, he requested a large transfer to be made to the accounts of Mr. Tom Bertram of Mansfield Park, as a gift for specific purposes, or so he put it."

"Did you hear anything as to the nature of these 'specific purposes?'" The notebook was in his hand, the pencil at the ready.

Harris shook his head. "I had the impression it was a gift to help Mr. Bertram satisfy some sort of debt, but nothing definite was said." He paused. "There is one point in which you are wrong, though." Alexander's eyes snapped up to the banker. "He was not with Mr. Bertram that day, but with Mr. Crawford, who is now residing with his sister at the Mansfield parsonage. And the two did have some conversation."

Alexander fought to control his frustration at the banker. "Please, go on," he kept his voice light and patient. He could act as well as Harris, no matter how much he wished the man had spoken earlier.

"If I recall, Mr. Rushworth asked several times, 'Are you certain this is the best course?' and Mr. Crawford reassured him that it would be to everybody's benefit. I cannot see how that might help, but it is all I know."

Alexander thanked the banker for his time and took his leave.

Henry Crawford was the one convincing Rushworth to settle Tom Bertram's debts! Whatever could that mean? If he was correct that Henry's interest in this affair was somehow to detach Maria Bertram from Rushworth, how could it be to his advantage to have Rushworth the hero? Better, surely, to have Henry himself make the beneficent offer and save the man's honour and rescue the estate from another great debt. Once, already, Tom's habits had caused his father to make a great sacrifice and sell several assets, including the living at Mansfield, which ought to have been Edmund's...

His feet stopped moving, but his brain was working furiously. A jostle and a curse behind him, from someone whose path he had blocked, set his feet to motion once more, although he was scarcely aware of where he was going.

Sir Thomas had already sold the living to Doctor Grant to pay for Tom's debts, and Edmund had suffered. If Tom were to repeat this ill-considered behaviour and accumulate such debts again, might Sir Thomas be obliged to pay out of his daughters' dowries? Rushworth, with his twelve thousand a year, had little need of Maria's dowry, but Henry might. His own estate brought in four thousand, so Alexander recalled, but to that healthy income, a large dowry might add significantly to the man's wealth.

What sort of dowry might Maria have? He knew that Georgiana Darcy, his friend's sister, had a fortune of thirty thousand pounds. It was in rescuing her from a miscreant wishing to abscond with that fortune that he had first made Darcy's acquaintance. If the Bertram sisters had even a third of that, their husbands would benefit greatly.

Therefore, in order to preserve Maria's dowry for his own benefit, Henry might indeed work upon Rushworth to settle any amounts owing by the Bertrams' estate. But this only made sense if Henry had already planned somehow to do away with James Rushworth.

The pieces were all starting to fit into place, and the picture they formed painted Henry Crawford as the villain of the piece. It was Henry who was in love with Rushworth's betrothed, and it was Henry's uncle, the admiral, who had sent the two ruffians to kill the man. Henry had convinced the dead man to settle Maria's brother's debts, and it was Henry who had purchased a riding coat like Rushworth's—and which had somehow gone missing. How this last piece fit into the whole, Alexander was as yet uncertain, but it surely must be connected.

How he needed to air these thoughts to Mary. What pieces of insight might she have that would clarify the tiny questions that still clung to the edges of his thoughts? He thought to bend his feet towards the Meldolas' house where she was staying. There was, of course, the matter of that kiss. His lips curved to a smile at the recollection of it, and it could not be ignored. He would have to talk to her, explain how their different stations and expectations in life need not impede a happy union. He would have to tell her that one thing he had been avoiding for the past two years, waiting until she could hear it without fleeing from his presence. And then he would sit down and hear her thoughts on the case.

But no sooner had he formed these thoughts than he saw Mary walk down the street some distance ahead of him, in the company of Fanny and William Price. His high spirits plummeted. He could not speak to Mary now, not in the company of those two people, no matter how amiable they might be. And after they had parted ways, he too would have to return to Mansfield immediately, for the moon was still a new crescent and he did not know the land well enough to ride in the dark. Tomorrow. Tomorrow he would speak with her. Tonight, he would relive that kiss.

Chapter Eighteen

The Clue of the Coat

Alexander's path had not led him to his friends or to Mary, but it had taken him to Rollings' tavern, and here he decided to sit for a short time with a beer and a plate of bread and cheese before reclaiming his horse from the stables where the coach was being housed. Rollings himself was at the counter and welcomed him like an old friend.

"Lyons! I was wondering when I might see you again and hear those Scottish tones. Any joy finding the two men you were asking after?" He poured two mugs of ale, taking one for himself and setting the other in front of Alexander. "You look hungry. I'll allow you to pay for the food. What will you have?" A serving girl came from the kitchens to take Alexander's order and then quickly vanished back whence she came.

"Joy, and not joy," Alexander replied, then thanked Rollings for the beer and toasted to his good health. "You have, I assume, heard the sad news about Mr. Rushworth of Sotherton Court."

"That I have. Sad business indeed. A toast, then, to Mr. Rushworth and his immortal soul." Both men drank.

Alexander considered how much to divulge to the tavern's proprietor. He could safely discuss matters that were commonly known, and his own free speech might elicit some new information from his companion. "Much has happened, and you likely know the most of it. Bertram returned of his own accord, pleased with himself and quite unharmed, but only after Rushworth had died. We have identified the two men who were seeking Bertram here in Northampton as two abolitionists hoping to procure his favour, but now it seems there are two others who were also seeking him, and for less righteous purposes."

They sat in silence for a moment. "Hardly seems possible," Rollings said at last. "Rushworth was not here often, for he was the sort to prefer fancier walls than these, but I saw him here in town only last week. I was off to the baker, for I had need of more than my normal amount of bread, and there was Rushworth walking down the street with that young fop—Cranford? Crawling?—talking about what a grand joke something would be. And now he's dead." He lapsed into silence again, which was broken by the serving girl with the platter of bread, cheese, and fried potatoes.

The two men ate in silence for a moment.

"What else have you learned?" Rollings asked around a mouth full of tasty food.

"How can I trust you?" Alexander teased. "For all I know, you are in with the criminals in order to punish Rushworth for taking his custom to Houghton's inn yonder by the square."

"Aye, and for not squandering his coin at my tables."

"In seriousness," he sighed, "there has been some nasty business. A poor fellow was found dead the other day, caught up in some reeds down near Bedford, and wearing Tom Bertram's old signet ring."

"The one his father the baronet swore never to honour?" Rollings' bushy eyebrows rose.

"That is the story Mr. Bertram tells us. Have you news I might have use of?"

"Sounds like Pickins. He used to come by from time to time, seldom had more than a few pennies in his pockets, but liked to see if he could turn them into crowns at the tables. He always boasted about the ring he found—said it was Tom Bertram's with his seal and all, and that it brought him luck. Even when every merchant in town refused to honour markers with the seal, he still refused to part with it, even if selling it would have brought him enough for a few good meals. Dead, eh? Not such luck, after all."

Alexander made his notes. "His name was Pickins? Where was he from? He must have had family."

Rollings scratched his head. "Cannot tell you, that's for certain. He sounded local, but one never knows. Hadn't seen him in a while. I only remember him because of the ring and how proud he was to have it."

The watery light that shone through the clouded window called to Alexander's attention. He thanked Rollings for his time and generosity and explained his need to depart in order to return to Mansfield by dark. When Rollings refused to accept payment for the beer and bread, Alexander slipped some small coins under the plate before departing. Then he found the stables, checked on the security of the coach, reclaimed his horse, and set off down the country lanes towards Mansfield Park.

He had learned a great deal this day, including the likely identity of the dead man down near Bedford, but something felt unsettled in his mind. How he longed to talk to Mary about it all. He felt her absence keenly and cursed Sir Thomas for returning too soon and all but forcing Mary from the house and back to Northampton, all those miles away. How much would he rather sit with her in quiet conversation, examining his notes and discussing what they both had discovered, than sitting in a lonely room at an inn.

Now he must ponder what to do about Henry Crawford. The tale told by the evidence against the man was damning, but it was not conclusive. He needed to set his questions to Admiral Crawford to uncover the exact connection. He needed to find those two ruffians. And he needed to discover what bothered him so much about Henry Crawford's missing hunting coat.

It was deep twilight by the time Alexander dismounted at the stables behind the inn in Mansfield village, and nearly full dark by the time he descended from his room with a freshly washed face and a clean coat that did not smell of horse.

"Mr. Lyons!" the landlord cried as he saw him. "Visitor for you in the private parlour. It's important."

The room, when he entered, was well lit and rather full. At the far end of the large table sat a gentleman whom Alexander recognised from the inquest. He bowed politely. "Sir Hugh." Sir Hugh Hedleigh was the district magistrate, a knight whose property lay on the other side of the village.

"Lyons," the magistrate returned the greeting. "I have found something that may be of interest to you. Or, rather, someone." He looked to the side of the room near to the door. Two large fellows stood guard over a beast of a man whose hands and ankles were bound with fetters. "The magistrate over near Newport, a friend of mine, had him taken both on the strength of your word about Rushworth's death, and also on suspicion of the murder of Adam Pickins in Bedfordshire. This sorry creature is Fred Warren, late of

His Majesty's Royal Navy. He was found drunk in a tavern in Bedford."

Alexander's eyes went wide. How much ale would it take to bring a man of that size to his knees? Warren was huge indeed. It was no wonder this was the aspect that people noticed most about him. He must stand six-and-a-half feet tall without boots, and sported a massive physique that looked all muscle and little fat. His hair was greasy but wild upon his head, all black and coarse, standing out in a hundred different directions. The two men standing at his side must have had quite the time getting him under their control.

"I thank you, Sir Hugh," Alexander bowed. "I do have questions to put to him and thank you for allowing me the chance to speak to him."

"You are working for Bertram, and we are on the same side here. No reason not to use every opportunity to see justice done."

Alexander's grateful smile was genuine. Not every magistrate was so pleased to have a private investigator interfering with a case. "The thought is welcome, sir. I assume you wish to remain in the room. I would appreciate your witness to the interview."

"Me and my bailiffs." Sir Hugh gestured to the two armed men whose glowering presence was doing as much to keep Warren in place as were the fetters on his ankles.

"Indeed, sir." Alexander took a chair and gestured to the bailiffs. "If you and your companion would care to sit? We may be a while." He pulled his ever-present notebook from a pocket and started a new page as the bailiffs helped their prisoner shuffle across the room to the table and chairs.

"Mr. Warren," Alexander began.

The giant grunted. "Ain't no one calls me Mister. Warren will do, or Fred, if you must." His face radiated animosity, but he seemed willing enough to speak. Hopefully he would remain so voluble through the interview.

"Very well Warren. Do you know why you are here?"

"'Cause I wasn't smart enough to run when Giles did." Whether Giles was his companion's first or last name mattered little right now. That could be determined later. Right now, it seemed they had the right man. "Got too far into my cups and thought we was safe. More the fool me. When I catch him, I'll show him!"

"We are interested in hearing about your time here in Northamptonshire. Two men are dead."

"And why should I talk to you? Giles said if I keep my mouth shut, ain't nothing anyone can do to me."

Fred Warren seemed not to be blessed with the greatest amount of wit, and it was most likely that what little he was given by God had not been supplemented by any sort of an education. Did he know that with every word, he incriminated himself? That with these protestations, he informed his listeners that he and Giles had indeed been engaged in nefarious activities? Still, as a common tar on a warship, Warren would need neither intelligence nor the ability to read, write, or reason. He need merely to obey commands. And that, Alexander considered, is what the man had done now. He had obeyed his admiral's commands. Perhaps he could use this to encourage the man to talk.

Sir Hugh, it seemed, had directed his thoughts along similar lines, for it was he who interrupted. "Mr. Warren, we have sufficient evidence to send you to the gallows for the death of Adam Pickins. You might have left him with his ring, but you took some other items that were known to belong to him. His pennywhistle, the embroidered handkerchief he was known to carry...."

"It weren't supposed to be him!" Warren thundered. "'Twas supposed to be that other chap, what we was sent after. And I didn't take nothing. That was Giles, trying to lay it all on me!" He stopped short, seeming to realise for the first time that he had just condemned himself. He sat back in his chair and narrowed his eyes, his mouth a tight line on his face.

"Now, now, Warren," Alexander cajoled, "let us be reasonable men. If Sir Hugh has evidence enough to make you swing, there is nothing to be lost by telling us what you know. Further," he hurried, seeing gates slam closed in his quarry's eyes, "I happen to know some people. If you are of enough assistance to us, I shall do what I can to have your sentence commuted to transportation rather than death."

"Transportation?" Those dim eyes were still leery.

"Sent to Australia to serve a term there, or to the other colonies. Australia is no pleasure trip, but it has been the making of some men."

"And not go back on the ships? No more floggings?"

"There is the initial voyage, but no, no more navy ships. And if you work hard, no more floggings." He hoped he was not lying. "I do not promise, but if you cooperate with us, I shall do what I can."

Warren glared at him through those slitted eyes for a long time. Somewhere in the room, a clock ticked away the seconds, each sound echoing in the silent space. Then a change came over the giant's face and he seemed to come to a decision. With a scowl, Warren started to talk.

"Giles and me was on one of the ships since we was eleven and sent to sea. No fancy officer's life for us. We come from the gutter and will die in the gutter. But the Admiral—"

"Which admiral?" This was important to hear from the man's own lips, and Alexander's legal training made him very aware of the need for an uninfluenced answer. How pleased he was that Sir Hugh was in the room. He looked up at the magistrate, who gave a curt nod. He, too, understood the importance of this evidence.

"Admiral Crawford. Never sailed under the man, but p'rhaps the captain told him about us. He called us to a meeting, just asked some questions the first day, nothing specific-like, not giving us any notion of what he had in mind. But then on the morrow, he called us back again and set this little task before us. Asked us how we would feel about doing some private job for him, one that no one else could ever know about." He blew his nose, and with his hands bound and no cloth to catch the mucus, it dribbled down his face. He seemed not to care. "Least ways, no one would know if we didn't tell." He narrowed his eyes and closed his mouth.

There was more silence. "What was this task?" Alexander asked gently.

Warren glared at him but continued to speak. "Admiral wanted us to deal with a 'personal problem' for one of his kin. I remember those words well. 'Personal problem.' As if the fellow couldn't put on his breeches without help."

"Did the admiral say who, exactly, required help in dealing with this problem?"

Warren shook his head. "No, can't say he did. I think he wanted to keep quiet about that, or maybe I just don't recall. But I don't think he said nought. Just that it was a job to help out one of his kin, and left it at that."

Alexander cast another glance at Sir Hugh and was pleased to see the magistrate taking his own notes. The bailiffs, too, seemed to be listening attentively. Thank goodness the burden of proof would not be placed purely upon his word alone. It was an easy matter to bring a lowly tar to justice; confronting an admiral would involve a much greater burden of proof.

"What, then, did the admiral ask you to do?"

"Asked us to get rid of a man. Kill him, that means. If you get Giles, will he be for transportation too? Or will he hang?"

Sir Hugh interrupted again. "I cannot say for certain, Warren, but you have been helpful to us, and he has not. Furthermore, he left you to our mercy. He, it seems, has none. I would imagine his sentence will be harsher."

Warren seemed satisfied by this and went on with his account.

"We was to come here, to these parts, and look for a gent and see him dead, but make it seem an accident if we could. Don't think the admiral cared too much about us two, but he didn't want stain coming back to him." A penny dropped in Warren's head and he gave a rather frightful smile. "Heh! Guess the stain got on him now." And he started to laugh like a little boy.

It was some time before the giggling stopped and Alexander was able to coax intelligible responses again from the giant.

It came out, in fits and starts, that the two men, upon arriving in Northampton, had come across Adam Pickins. As Alexander had learned from Rollings, Pickins was ever one to boast about his signet ring, invoking the name of Tom Bertram. The admiral had given the name, even if he had supplied almost no additional information about the man. Giles had heard the doomed man crow and without much thought had felt that fate smiled upon him. Who else but Tom Bertram would possess Bertram's signet ring, after all? He had lured the wretch away and had killed him with a rock to the head. Giles and Warren had then dragged the body some distance away from the country tavern where the unfortunate event occurred and dumped it into the river, where it floated along its sad way until becoming caught in the osiers near Bedford. "Only we learned that he was the wrong man when people kept asking about Adam and his ring, and Giles was sore upset. Only reason he didn't leave right then was because he wanted the admiral's coin when he got back."

One question now seemed to be answered, but Alexander had to put it to the suspect. "Who, then, was he supposed to be, this dead man?"

Warren puffed himself up like a pigeon at a bakery. "Our chap was Tom Bertram, of course. We got him later, in the hunt."

So it was true. Bertram was the intended victim, and Rushworth merely the poor fellow who happened to get in the way. But Warren, as yet, had no idea that they had once again killed the wrong man.

Slowly, one detail at a time, the whole story came out. The admiral had known about the hunt and had set his two stooges to use that event to identify and hopefully destroy their prey. They were given the date and location, which everybody in the neighbourhood could have told them, and were informed that Bertram would be one of the party. Giles, it seemed, had decided that a hunting accident was the best way to dispatch the man with a minimum of suspicion if such could be arranged. The two had surveyed the land around the estate to the best of their abilities and located the hedge-like thicket with the field beyond the gully. Then they began to plan their trap.

They had then found a nondescript fellow down on his luck in Bedford and had given him some coin to lure the victim away from his fellows and towards the field where Warren and Giles were waiting. This, Alexander noted to himself, was why no one had known the stranger. He was from a town far enough away to have no reason to travel to the area around Mansfield, but close enough to sound local and to know the general lay of the land. There must be hundreds of such men, and more in every town in England. Alexander doubted they would ever find him; indeed, there seemed little to be gained if they did. The messenger bore no guilt in the matter, for the two tars were unlikely to have divulged their plot.

He needed only to bring Rushworth to a certain spot and then depart with his pockets a little heavier for his effort.

"We set up across the little gully, in the field." Warren then explained their ruse. "It was all Giles' idea, and it worked too. We had the rope set up just under the leaves, and when we saw our man we called to him to come and talk to us, and he tried to jump. There was only one way across, and the nobs like jumping and all, from what we hear. We knew he'd jump. But the horse got his hooves tangled and went sideways a bit and the toff come off his horse. The horse was good enough to run away, and Giles went to see to the man. He was still breathing, but that didn't last long when Giles took that rock to his head."

Alexander looked up at Sir Hugh. "The hoof prints?"

Sir Hugh nodded. "Giles' horse is gone, but the one this fellow rode was still in the stables. I've set men to take prints of its shoes."

There remained one question. Alexander knew the answer, but needed to hear it, and with these witnesses.

He turned back to Warren and asked, "How did you know it was Mr. Bertram you had found? Surely you don't know one of these men from another."

Unaccountably, Warren let loose another guffaw. "That were easy," he chortled. "His coat. Fancy thing only a toff would wear, all those brass buttons and frilly flaps and things. Giles needed me along because Giles can't see colour well, but I can. I always was good with colours. Pa said I should be a painter if didn't do well as a sailor because I know my colours so well. And that coat was a right queer colour that the toff was wearing. Matched exactly the one the admiral showed us before we left the port!"

As soon as Alexander had bid a good evening to Sir Hugh, he dashed up to his rooms to write a note to Mary. The magistrate had taken Warren to the small gaol in the village. The following day, the giant would be returned to Bedford's magistrate with respect to Pickins' murder, before proceedings could begin in Northamptonshire for this second murder. Alexander was pleased to leave the jurisdictional headaches to these men, as well as the pursuit and capture of Mick Giles, but he agreed to support Sir Hugh's recommendation for transportation in lieu of execution. Warren might be guilty of a great deal, but the plan was not of his making and he was dim enough to be a tool in the hands of other, more culpable men. Giles, when he was caught, would not be so fortunate.

The authorities would have to tread more carefully in their case against Admiral Crawford, the result of which Alexander could not begin to guess. For all the assertion that there was one law in England, everybody knew this was a convenient fiction. Regardless, the admiral had apparently worked to help one of his kin, unnamed to the fool he sent to do his work. The hard work would be in finding the evidence needed to arrest and convict Henry Crawford for instigating Rushworth's murder.

With all of these ideas tumbling through his head, he needed to order his thoughts. How he wished Mary were here, to discuss it all in person. It seemed like the entire case, which had seemed so hopeless only hours before, was now resolved. There remained a few small questions, little gnats gnawing at the edges of his conscience, but these he discarded as those inevitable coincidences that always clouded a case. Tom's strange disappearance, Sir Thomas' unannounced arrival, William Price's presence in the neighbourhood—all of these could be explained easily enough. Mary, of course, would also wish to discuss Fanny's seemingly unrequited infatuation with her cousin Edmund, Edmund's requited infatuation with Mary Crawford, Henry's inappropriate attentions to Maria and her equally inappropriate reciprocation, and finally, Yates' besottedness with Julia. How simple it would all be if they could find suitable matches, like his and Mary's was destined to be. The goings-on at Mansfield Park resembled nothing as much as a French farce, rather than the expected decorum of a staid English manor house in a prosperous baronetcy.

Taking several deep breaths, he strove to still his mind, and then settled at the desk to write down his findings and conclusions to the best of his ability. He made a copy of these, included a short letter to Mary in which he said nothing of that kiss, and at last sealed the envelope with a drop of the wax he carried in his bag.

He then wrote two other letters to his colleagues in London, the answers to which he believed would arrive at his London rooms after he had settled the case, and finally took the lot of them down to the landlord, requesting they be sent off at first light. The one to Mary, he impressed, was the most important of the three.

Now there was nothing left to do today. It was too dark to travel, and Henry Crawford must surely believe himself to be safe from all suspicion. He would not seek to escape tonight. On the morrow, Alexander would speak further with Edmund, and try to think of a way to convince Henry to confess to his crimes.

All seemed settled. But as he lay in bed that night, willing sleep to come, he could not stop wondering where Tom Bertram and Sir Thomas had been.

Chapter Nineteen

A Discovery

Mary awoke early. It was both her own personal custom, and that of the house, for Mr. Meldola was no man of leisure, but needed to be at his place of work. She dressed with the help of her maid and made her way down to the breakfast room, where Mrs. Meldola was sitting at her correspondence.

"Good morning, Miss Bennet. Breakfast is set out. My husband has left for his work for the day, but please do help yourself to whatever you would like. Here," she placed an envelope by Mary's seat, "there is something for you. It came by messenger from Mansfield village. I believe it is from Alexander."

Mary felt her face heat with a blush and she hoped Mrs. Meldola did not notice. The lady seemed quite engaged in her own letters, and she said nothing. Mary let out a sigh of relief. She found the tea and took some bread and fried kippers, deciding to leave the scones for her return to the buffet once her plate was empty.

With Mrs. Meldola's attention on her letters, Mary felt no barrier to opening her own, and this she did. There was a brief note to her, and then a longer document that outlined Alexander's new discoveries and his thoughts. He wrote not a word of affection outside of his norm and said nothing about the kiss. Did he hope that by pretending it had not happened, it would pass from both their minds? Or was he too angry with her to speak of it? And yet, were he to be angry with her, he would hardly have taken the time to send her this note and his ideas about the case. Oh, how she both needed and dreaded to talk to him.

Damping her inner turmoil with a restorative sip of tea, she began to read his notes more carefully. She read about the remarkable meeting with Mr. Framington and the news that Tom Bertram's debts had been settled by Mr. Rushworth, and then of Mr. Harris' reluctant verification of Alexander's suppositions and his assertion that it was Henry who had persuaded Rushworth to bestow such a gift.

So it was Henry Crawford, after all.

But the sheet of notes went on. Now she read about the fortuitous capture of Fred Warren by the Bedford lawmen. That they should have found the man, when he remained in the area, seemed almost inevitable, but a part of her felt pity at the fact of Warren's abandonment, with such evidence placed upon him, by his supposed friend.

Mary wondered briefly if the admiral had placed a second task upon Giles, that of leaving Warren holding all of the blame. But that could not be so, for surely if one were caught, both would be held accountable. What was it, then, that bothered her so? The pieces all fit, but the picture they formed was not quite in focus. She read through the notes again and thought hard.

What, she began to wonder, was Henry's motive in killing Tom Bertram? Whilst they still imagined Rushworth to be the intended victim, there were plenty of reasons she could imagine for a man such as Crawford to desire his demise, the first among them being the affections of Maria Bertram. She could imagine Crawford being incensed at Rushworth's planned destruction of the oak grove at Sotherton, or of being swayed to the plight of Oliver, whose irrigation systems would be gravely damaged by the creation of the dam Rushworth wanted.

But Tom Bertram? The only thing to be gained from Bertram's death would be the promotion of Edmund to heir to the baronetcy, and Edmund was much less likely to entertain Henry's amusements than was Tom. Besides which, Sir Thomas was still a relatively young man, full of strength and vigour, and might well remain so for another twenty or thirty years.

Was Crawford, perhaps, a secret abolitionist? Did he hope that Edmund's strong moralistic character might more easily be swayed to the concerns of the abolitionists, and through him, might Crawford hope for some influence upon his father?

Perhaps when they could determine the exact reason Henry had to wish to kill Tom Bertram, they might find those last pieces they needed to have him charged with instigating Rushworth's demise. Something was still missing.

"Is everything well, Miss Bennet?" Mrs. Meldola looked up from her pile of letters.

"Yes, yes, of course." Had she made a sound? "I was merely contemplating some of the information Alexander has given me. There are some aspects that do not quite fit. I do not know how to proceed."

Hannah Meldola poured Mary another cup of tea and passed her the plate of scones and jam. "I sometimes find that when I do not know what to think, I find a different occupation and engage fully in that. Whilst I am at my sewing or visiting friends or working at the orphanage, my brain keeps thinking without me, and then presents me later with the answer fully formed."

"Like Athena emerging from the head of Zeus?" Mary giggled at the notion of her head splitting open and an Idea stepping out, garbed like an Amazonian warrior with armour and spear at the ready and an owl of wisdom perched upon her shoulder.

"Yes," Mrs. Meldola laughed with her. "Rather like that. I do have to visit the orphanage this morning, where I read to the children and take some of the clothing we have been mending. Perhaps you might like to join me. Then we can enjoy some of the shops along Drapery Street or in Market Square if you wish.

"Thank you," she smiled. "I would be honoured to join you."

"In that case, Miss Bennet, may I ask a favour of you? It is not a great imposition. Whilst I speak to Cook about dinner, would you retrieve the box of clothing from the front parlour? It is at the far end of the room by the cabinets. You can leave the box in here; it is not heavy. Then we may depart as soon as you are ready."

This seemed a simple and useful sort of occupation. Perhaps this was exactly the sort of activity she needed to do to allow her brain to contemplate the problem of Henry Crawford's guilt without her telling it what to think. She found the parlour, which was a large and rather grand room facing the front of the house. It was here, she recalled, that the town's merchants had gathered on that first visit seven weeks ago and more, when she had first seen Tom Bertram, insensible with drink. She crossed to the cabinets, and there, as promised, was the box of mended clothing. She pictured the room as it had been those weeks ago. Before, she had stood at the doorway; from this new vantage point, her perspective was different. Who had been here?

She had not known any of the people at that time, but she recalled names: Framington the investor, Harris the banker,

Thompson the mill owner... Try as she might, however, no new insights came to her. She looked around her one more time, hoping for a flash of insight. Instead, she merely saw an elegant and well-appointed parlour.

Still hoping for ideas, she wandered closer to a beautiful and intricate candelabra that sat in one of the cabinets. Perhaps examining this would allow her brain to make the connections it was missing. There were eight small holders along the base... but no, they were not for tapers, but for oil, for that was an oil jug hanging off one side of the ornate back. And there, opposite the little jug, was a holder with a space for another flame. What a curious ornament this was. She must ask Mrs. Meldola about it. Surely the lady would not be angry at her having looked at it, for she had sent Mary into the room alone.

For now, she cast her glance about the room once more, and when no ideas came to her about the case, she picked up the box of clothing and returned it to the breakfast room, then went up to her room to prepare for the day.

The visit to the orphanage was restorative. No matter how sad the plight of the children, left with no parents and no other family to love them and care for them, they were nevertheless sheltered and fed and given an elementary education that would allow them to make their way in the world. Mrs. Lacey, the woman who oversaw the establishment, was a stern but kind woman, and seemed genuinely to care for the orphans. The girls were taught their letters and sums and cookery and sewing, which would allow them to become a cook's assistant or seamstress, a better fate than a cleaning drudge or worse. The boys, beside learning their ABCs, were apprenticed out to local tradesmen in the area once they were of age. An honest trade could raise a hardworking man from the gutter. In reading to the children and passing along the mended clothing to the mistress of the institution, Mary felt the satisfaction that usefulness can give a person.

As they helped to sort and organise the piles of clothing that had been brought to the orphanage in recent days, Mrs. Meldola explained the philosophy of the orphanage. It was funded partly by private donations, but also by the merchants' association in the town, the members of which agreed to a man that keeping children in the gutters was of benefit to nobody. The more pragmatic asserted that trained workers were of benefit to their employers, and that men with some coin in their pockets were more likely to spend that coin on the merchants' goods than those without, thereby helping to ensure good profits. The more tender-hearted, amongst which Mrs. Meldola proudly situated herself, cried the necessity to offer aid, simply because it was the proper thing to do.

"That is a good Christian sentiment!" Mary asserted, her admiration clear. To this, Mrs. Meldola responded with a queer look, but said nothing and changed the topic.

The morning's duties dispensed with, the two set out for a stroll along the shop-lined streets of the town. Northampton was a good-sized town, almost a city, with a lovely church at its centre in the style of Wren, graced with a classical portico and ornamented with eight elegant columns across the front. This was Mary's first chance to explore the town with any sort of leisure, and she begged Mrs. Meldola's indulgence to visit the lovely building for a few moments. This the lady granted, but declined to accompany her inside, stating a desire to visit with a friend at the nearby milliner's instead.

After a tour of the graceful building, Mary found her hostess in the company of none other than Alexander.

"Mary!" he greeted her with the enthusiasm due to dear friends, and she could not help but respond with a broad grin of her own. "I had more business here in the town and hoped to call upon you afterwards, but here I have found both you and Hannah directly. Luck smiles upon me."

"I had just invited Alexander to join us for tea." Mrs. Meldola gestured to an establishment across the busy street. "I am waiting to hear his reply."

Alexander gave a handsome bow, his flecked green-brown eyes shining in the sunshine. "With two such charming companions, how can I refuse? Ladies, please." He offered each an elbow, and they made their promenade down the street.

Soon they sat at a small round table in the tea shop and awaited their order. They talked of nothing of consequence for a while: the weather, the temperament of the horse Edmund had given over for Alexander's use, the comfort of the rooms at the inn at Mansfield, and finally, of the wealth of fine shops in the town. Mary spoke of the unusual cravats she had ordered for her Papa, and Alexander commended her decision, asserting his opinion that her father would like nothing more. With Mrs. Meldola as company to forestall a more serious discussion of yesterday's kiss and with the general and happy tone of the conversation, the awkwardness that Mary had expected did not arise, and she felt more comfortable in Alexander's presence than she had imagined. If he looked at her, now and again, with a particular light in his eye, she could pretend to ignore it. There would be time soon enough when the topic must arise.

For now, however, the serious matter that did raise its head was the case of the murder. The tearoom was quiet, although not entirely empty, and the other parties were at the distant side of the shop. With their voices lowered, therefore, the three could discuss the matter without the threat of being overheard by somebody at the very next table.

Mary raised the subject. "I read your note, which I thank you for sending. I am not quite satisfied with the resolution."

Alexander raised his teacup but did not drink. "I have no way to prove that Crawford is the man behind this whole sad affair. I have every suspicion in the world, but unless the authorities can convince the admiral to speak against his nephew, there is little sure evidence. As it is, it will come down to the word of a respected admiral in His Majesty's service against that of an illiterate tar of questionable understanding." He replaced the teacup and pushed a hand through his hair.

"My concern," Mary sighed, "is that I cannot understand why he did it. I keep feeling so certain that if we can find the reason why, we shall find the rest of the evidence we need, but I just cannot figure it. It all makes perfect sense if Rushworth were the true intended victim, but Tom Bertram…" She furrowed her brow.

"This was bothering me as well." He blew the tuft of hair he had just disarranged from his forehead. "But from Warren's confession, there is no other alternative. Or is there?" He narrowed his eyes in thought.

"You mean the admiral might have been wishing to solve a problem suffered by his 'kin,' but that the 'kin' was not the instigator of the plan?"

Alexander said nothing, but the crease between his brows deepened.

"As I went to retrieve some goods from the parlour this morning," Mary mused, "I stared at the room from a different angle, hoping that a different physical perspective might help me to see the problem from a different angle as well."

"Did it work?" Mrs. Meldola wore an impish grin on her pretty face.

"I did not think so at the time, but now I wonder. I tried to imagine all the people who were there on that night when we travelled north last month, when Mr. Tom Bertram first came to our notice. I was not there, but you were, Alexander."

He nodded. "Most of the men I did not know, but I do recall Mr. Framington, Elijah of course, the fellow with the mills— Thompson?—Harris the banker, and... was his brother there? Harris the lawyer, who is also the coroner?"

Mrs. Meldola confirmed that he was present.

"Strange, those two. They bear little physical resemblance, although if one knows, it is not a surprise that they are brothers, and seem not to like each other very much. But now I seem to recall them both reacting in similar ways when Bertram burst into the room and fell down in his drunken stupor. They looked to each other, not for assurance in their actions, but to affirm that the other was there. The bond of blood is deep."

Ideas were rushing through Mary's head, bumping against each other and whirling about like a leaf in a windstorm, refusing to settle. Eventually, she grabbed enough of them to form a thought.

"Have we been wrong? Are you correct, then, in your notion that Henry Crawford was the instigator of this plan and not, instead, merely the beneficiary of it?" The other two stared at her, and Mary made a great effort to keep her voice low. It would not do for the other customers to overhear this proposition.

"Who was absent at the time of the murder? Who ought to have been there, but was not?"

"Tom Bertram," Alexander supplied.

"And who else? Whose ship had arrived in port from Antigua days before, leaving him plenty of time to make the journey from London to his home and family?"

"You cannot mean Sir Thomas!" Mrs. Meldola gasped.

"I do not know what to think," Mary admitted. "But both men were missing, their whereabouts quite unknown, until after the murder. It is not impossible that they might have conspired to have Tom seem the intended victim, thereby cleansing him of all implied guilt. They might have put about the suggestion of finding Tom's old signet ring, which led the two tars to think he was their target. And if Tom knew about Rushworth's hunting coat, and also knew that he would most definitely not be wearing his own, he could well plan for another man's murder whilst making himself seem to be the intended victim."

Alexander nodded, his brow still furrowed. "But what motive would Tom have? What about Sir Thomas?"

"Tom would have two motives that I can imagine for ridding himself of Rushworth. First of all, he would now not be beholden to the man for the repayment of the loan. Even if the money was given as a gift, there may have been unspoken conditions behind it. After all, no man likes to be indebted to another. The second is Maria. Tom and his father could both well have wished to rid Maria of the obligation to marry Mr. Rushworth. Tom knew the man well, and knew as well how his sister was unhappy with him. Through him, Sir Thomas might have learned of his daughter's certain unhappiness in life. If Tom had left a note at the docks in London for his father..."

"The two men might have worked together," Alexander completed. "Like the Harris brothers, father and son may not have seen eye-to-eye on many issues, but the bonds of blood are deep and not easily broken."

"Sir Thomas might have arranged for the unhappy event with the admiral in London?" Mrs. Meldola asked. "And then remained absent, like his son, in order to remove all possibility of guilt?"

Mary gave a grimace. "It is possible."

"But why would the admiral agree to this? And how are his 'kin' involved?"

"Because," Alexander explained, "with Rushworth no longer alive, Henry could vie for Maria Bertram's hand. And her dowry."

They sat in silence for a moment. Then Alexander looked up as if just now recalling something. "I have one more small piece of information, or rather, lack of information, which I learned only this morning."

Mary looked up at him, waiting for him to continue.

"I inquired of the post office in the village of Mansfield; there was no package that might have contained a riding coat sent from that location over the last month, or at least, not that the postmaster can recall. If Henry, or one of the servants at the parsonage, did send it, it was not from there. I know this does little to further our investigation, but it was a matter that needed learning."

"Yes. Yes, of course." Once again, the case seemed to be fraught with confusion and clues that led nowhere.

The teapot was now empty, and Alexander pulled his watch from his pocket. "I am afraid I have to leave you. I have an appointment with Mr. Harris, the coroner, in a short while. I promised I would keep him apprised of my progress, and he set a rather strict time for my call. If I have time afterwards, I shall call by the house, but do not wait for me. I cannot say how long I may be. Mary," he turned to her and took her hand to press a kiss upon the back of it, "we shall speak soon. I believe we have much to say to each other." His eyes promised what his words did not, and she felt a flush rush over her.

"Until then, Alexander."

He settled the account for the tea and took his leave.

Mary and Mrs. Meldola strolled back to the house, past shops and market stalls, stopping here and there to browse or admire a gown or bonnet or stand of books set out by the open window of a bookseller. They passed a glove maker, the chandler, a bakery whose aromas lured Mary back for a deeper breath, and the main post office for the town.

"Please," she asked her companion. "May I go in, just for a moment? I wonder..."

"Of course," was the response.

Mary was fortunate to find the postmaster free and willing to answer a question or two. She asked if any man or servant had, in the past few weeks, sent a package to London the size and shape of which might indicate a gentleman's coat inside.

The white-haired man wrinkled his nose. "To London, what? Can't say as I recall. So much comes and goes through here, of different sizes and shapes, and so much to London. Not much stays in the mind as notable, you understand. Er..." he wrinkled his nose again, "There was a chap come through about three weeks past with a crate large enough we had to tell him to find a private cart for it, 'twere too big for the coach. I remember that well. Don't know what he had in there. We joked it must be his mother-in-law, or a pianoforte, perhaps. Don't know what happened to it. A lady come by—pretty young thing—with a package of books for her uncle, and a servant in smart livery from one of the estates with a package of letters he insisted on seeing onto the coach himself. If they were so important, don't know why they weren't sent by private messenger. But these all muddle together in my head, you see."

Mary nodded. "I understand completely. Thank you for taking the time to talk with me." She curtseyed her exit and rejoined her companion on their walk.

Two shops down from the post office was a silversmith, whose beautiful work shone with its soft glow in the sunlit window. Mary entered and bought herself a small pair of earbobs with some of the coin her brother Darcy had given for her personal use. Lizzy had made her promise to buy herself something frivolous with the money, and not to spend it on gifts for others or for necessary expenses. "If you need money for daily expenses, we will see to that separately," she had insisted. "This is a present for you." Mary smiled at the thought of writing back to her sister with a description of the pretty jewellery.

As they left the shop, she recalled the silver candelabra in the cabinet back at the house and asked about it. That same odd expression came over Mrs. Meldola's face. At length, she said, "Come, Miss Bennet. Let us sit. The day is fine and the park is lovely, although the leaves are gone from the trees. I believe I have something to explain to you."

This was quite strange. How could a silver candelabra have so great an import that they must sit and have a discussion that involved explanation? Confused though she was, Mary followed the lady into the little park that ran near the street on which her house stood.

"I see," Mrs. Meldola began, "that Alexander has not told you everything." She gave a reassuring smile and continued. "That candelabra is a ritual item, used for one of our religious festivals."

This was particularly confusing now. "But I know of no Christian holy days that require such an object. It is very beautiful, and would honour any saint, but..."

"Miss Bennet," Mrs. Meldola caught her hands. "What I am trying to say is that we are not Christian."

"That is what Alexander said when we first met, but he refused to explain any more. He led me to believe he was an atheist, or perhaps a Quaker."

"We are neither atheist nor Quaker. We are of the Hebrew faith."

Mary stared at her for a moment as the words settled in her ears. "Oh. I see." But she hardly understood at all. In all of her life, she had never met a person who was not in some way Christian, who did not adhere, by faith or by tradition, to some elements of her church. The Papists celebrated the same festivals, even if they did so in Latin, and the Quakers believed in Christ, although they denied the authority of the established Church of England. Even the atheists—although to her knowledge she knew none—found their identity in their rejection of her faith; in that respect, they were anti-Christians.

But the Hebrews—this was something so very different, something with which she had no experience and no knowledge, other than they had a different belief altogether, and could not reject Christianity because they had never accepted it. She had never thought much about it, but had she been asked, she would have imagined a person of the Hebrew faith as being something strange and exotic, vaguely menacing or somehow evil, like Shakespeare's moneylender. Never would she have envisaged this sweet, pretty, and very unexceptionable lady sitting beside her in the park.

"But you are so normal!" she burst out, before checking herself.

Mrs. Meldola gave a slight smile. "We are that. We are busy, active citizens who work hard and do our best to be of value to our society. We merely hold to an older faith."

The idea was becoming less strange. Mrs. Meldola had indeed acted as any well-to-do lady of the middle class would do, as her own Aunt Gardiner did, to be honest. She ran an efficient home, was kind and hospitable, and donated both her time and efforts— and likely money—to a worthy charity in the town. There was nothing evil or undesirable about her at all. Mary allowed a deep breath to escape her.

But then another thought invaded her mind.

"What of Alexander? How do you know him?"

"Did he not tell you?" Mrs. Meldola smiled. "He is my cousin. Our mothers are sisters."

And with that, Mary's world came crashing down about her.

Chapter Twenty

Crisis of Faith

Mary sat on the bench in the park long after Mrs. Meldola returned home. That kind lady sent a maid to see to Mary's wellbeing, and Mary could see the girl sitting discreetly a few benches distant, working on some knitting until her charge was ready to return to the house. Should she be grateful for the concern, or irritated at the presumption? Nothing made sense, and had she been at home, she would have stormed off across the fields as Lizzy had so often done, until exhaustion and hunger brought her to some sort of resolution.

Her first words to Mrs. Meldola, after hearing the truth about Alexander's identity, were, "But that cannot be. He is Scottish!"

At the time, it was the only thing she could think. In retrospect, it seemed a most foolish comment.

"He is that," Mrs. Meldola had soothed, "but by birth and not descent. He is Scottish as much as I am English, both of which are true, but not the entire truth. I have every attachment to England, as much as any other person born and raised here, with a love of my country and my king, but there is yet another part to who I am that guides my heart as well. Alexander, I am certain, feels similarly."

Now she felt ridiculous for her comments. His red hair, his green-brown eyes—these all fit so exactly with her idea of a Scotsman, that she could not imagine him to be anything else. And yet he was. He was so very much something else that she could not reckon with it. Her thoughts whirled, and nothing made sense.

When the whirlwind in her head settled, she was able to direct her thoughts to the cause of this great distress. Where, mere minutes before, she had imagined their lives coming together, now there lay a great abyss, too wide to span, too deep to traverse. This was no movement from class to class, a short step in either direction, whereby a wealthy merchant might buy his way into the gentry, or where the son of a landowner might choose an honest trade in preference to a pulpit or military post he did not want.

Any other objections, to her mind, had been mere formalities, shades of nuance that could be glossed over with a carefully chosen word or twist of understanding. Had he not believed, he could still accept her own deep faith, as long as logic and common sense were not sacrificed at the altar of blind belief. Had he held with the Quakers or some other Christian belief, there could be compromise. No matter that the Church of England had it correct where all others were somehow mistaken, these were most often honest mistakes that could be mended with the proper explanations.

But this... this was so very different from anything she might have imagined. How could one reconcile the two aspects of this age-old division of faith? How could she, good and pious Christian woman that she was, consort with a man who denied the reality of her God, whose own beliefs denied His holiness? Whose religion would condemn him and all his people to an eternity in Hell for refusing to accept the Saviour? The thought of this sent a new pang into her heart.

But worst of all, she realised, she was hurt by the fact that she had learned this from another. He had not thought well enough of her to tell her himself. For some reason, despite all of their discussions and all that they had shared, he did not trust her. Her eyes stung red and overflowed with tears, and she struggled not to weep.

The day, which had started fine, was becoming cool, and her shivers, if not her desires, at length bestirred her to move. She rose from her seat on the bench and hugged her coat about her shoulders, and further along the park, she saw the maid put away her work and rise likewise. She raised a cautious hand to her cheek and found her eyes dry; they might be red, but she would have the dignity not to appear back at the Meldolas in tears.

Mrs. Meldola had been so sweet. She had assured herself as to Mary's heath, and then had suggested that if Miss Bennet, from her unhappy surprise or other reasons, wished not to return to the house, she would be pleased to procure the best available rooms at the inn for her use, or to ask of some of her church-going friends whether they might have a room for Miss Bennet's use until such time as she returned to her family.

Such consideration was unexpected and rather touching, and Mary assured the lady that she had no objections at all about remaining in her house, if she were still willing to bestow such gracious hospitality. Somehow, knowing that this kind family did not share her faith did not trouble her mind; it had come as a surprise, but no worse than that. Her thoughts about Alexander were still too fraught with confusion to bring her any peace at the moment.

"Mary!" The Scottish tones, almost more foreign here than in London, stopped her feet. "Hannah told me you were here. She told me... she told me everything. I have to speak with you. We need to speak."

"Go away Alexander. We can no longer be friends. I will arrange my journey home tomorrow, with Mr. Darcy's coach if possible, and with the post if not. Goodbye."

"Mary..." His voice was low and desperate, and when she turned, so reluctantly, to glance at him, his eyes were shining with unshed tears. "Mary, listen to me, please."

"We have nothing to say to each other." How she wished she were at Longbourn, where she might storm from the room and slam the door, a final punctuation to their unlikely friendship. Having no convenient door, she turned her back on him to stride off. But her feet would not move, and she felt, instead, his hand upon her own, insistent and pleading.

"Please, Mary, let me just speak..."

She spun around to glare at him. "You lied to me! Every time I asked you about such matters, you lied to me. Why did you do it?"

"Mary... I never lied to you. If you had asked me, I would have answered, but—"

His face was tight, his entire body tense as if wound like a clockmaker's spring, ready to burst forth at a touch.

"A lie of omission is still a lie. You did not trust me, and you allowed me to believe.... I do not know what. I can no longer call you friend. Not after what we..." The kiss, that horrible, dreadful, wonderful kiss, loomed before her. She had acted the harlot with a man who could never do well by her. Shame flooded her senses, that wave of blackness that welled up around her, and she felt her face burn red as her eyes screwed closed against the threatening tears. From that dark black pit, anger was born, and it erupted unbidden. She glared at him, jaw tight and brows low, and her voice was choked. "I thought you a decent person with a soul and strong morality, but now I learn you are a—"

"A man! A man, Mary. I am a man. What I am is nothing to who I am. I am a man who works hard and seeks justice and tries to do well by the world. And I am a man who cares more for you than I ought, but I cannot help how I feel and I am not ashamed of it. Can you not see me for who I am?" Now his bottom lip quivered and Mary forced herself to look away.

His words swam in her head. She raised her hands to her ears, as if by doing so she could block all his words from confounding her. She could not think, could not speak, and she knew if she tried, she would sound like a petulant child. At last, her feet were freed from whatever force had held them in place, and she turned and ran, leaving him in the park, the poor maid scrambling behind her.

Her pace soon slowed, but she could not stop moving. Where she walked, and for how long, she could not say. The anger and frustration roiled inside her without forming a coherent thought, but her breathing calmed and her eyes dried, and after a very long time, when she felt quite lost, she turned to find the poor maid still a few steps away, and meekly asked the way home.

They walked in silence, down streets and through parks and along the wandering river, until the streets looked familiar once more and she knew, at last, the path that would return her to her temporary home. "Thank you, Susie," she whispered to her unwitting guide and companion as they entered the house at last. She was tired and hungry and still very confused, and thought to excuse herself from dinner so she might have her solitude to recover from the day's awful revelation.

But fate was unkind, and upon stepping into the white marble vestibule, she found the housekeeper waiting for her. "Miss Bennet, you have a visitor waiting for you. Miss Price is in the back parlour. What would you like me to tell her?"

Mary blinked her sore eyes with surprise. Fanny was here again? How unusual, and how unwelcome. As much as she had tried to befriend the girl, they had not formed any sort of immediate meeting of minds. Still, it would never do to be rude, for the girl and her relations had been kind and generous to her. She forced a calm expression upon her face, burying the turmoil for now.

"Thank you. I shall take a minute to repair my hair and clothing. Please tell her I shall be down in just a few minutes."

The housekeeper dropped an efficient curtsey and bustled off to execute her duty, letting Mary hurry up to her room to wash her face and find a fresh frock in which she could receive visitors.

She completed her task in good time, being well accustomed to taking care of her own toilette, and within a few minutes she strolled into the parlour, face washed and clear, without a hint of red in her eye nor a hair out of place. And hopefully, without her anguish written plain across her face. "Miss Price," she bobbed. "What a pleasure to see you today."

Fanny sat at the edge of a delicate chair, as if poised to spring up at a moment's notice. "Miss Bennet, I do hope my visit is not unwelcome. I... that is, matters are still somewhat unpleasant at the house, and when Edmund asked... that is, Edmund had reason to come into town, and he asked if I wished to join him. He is at his errands, and will join us later, if your hostess does not object. And," she dropped her voice and leaned forward, "there is something more serious I would discuss with you. I should not dare to mention it, for it troubles me so, but since it affects you most particularly, I felt you ought very much to know."

"How alarming, Miss Price. This sounds very dire indeed. Whatever can it be?"

Fanny dropped her voice even further, and the words rushed out of her. "It concerns your friend, Mr. Lyons. I do beg you to leave now and return home and never see him again." Her eyes had grown very wide and her voice quite stern. Never before in their short acquaintance had Mary seen her like this.

Suddenly, every bit of anger that Mary had felt towards Alexander now transformed into something different. She might well vent her anger upon him and wish him to Jericho in her thoughts, but this was for her and her alone. Her anger was now a deep need to defend and protect him, and this she turned upon her visitor.

"Miss Price," she strove to keep her voice even, "I do hope you are not thinking of speaking ill of Mr. Lyons. To my knowledge, he has been nothing but kind and polite to you and your family, and is doing your family a service as well."

"Do not misunderstand me, please. I would never speak ill of someone who has done me no harm, but you must understand, he is not like us. You cannot know this, else I am certain you would never have befriended him. For you are, I know, a good Christian woman, and Mr. Lyons is no Christian!" She spoke these last words with such intensity that Mary thought she might have a spell.

"Do not trouble yourself, Miss Price." It was nobody's place to berate him but her own, but she must remain calm. "Upon our very first encounter, Mr. Lyons informed me of his lack of communion with the Church of England. We have had many arguments about this, but it has not impeded our friendship, I assure you."

"Surely you misunderstand." Her eyes were wide and intent. "He not only does not hold with the Church, but he is of a different faith altogether. He is one of them—a Hebrew! It came out when Edmund made mention that he had not sworn upon the Holy Bible at the inquest, but had requested the Old Testament alone. Edmund must have known since then, but why he did not tell me,

I do not know. I would not have been in company with him at all had the truth been out."

Fanny's words ate at what little remained of Mary's serenity. How old was Fanny Price? She could not be more than eighteen, which had been Mary's own age when first she met Alexander. And now, she had to ask herself, what her response would have been had she learned the truth then. Even now, two years older and so very much wiser, the fact of his background and identity troubled her soul. Back then, barely a woman, really still a child, her mind so rigid and moulded by the religious teachings and sermons she loved to read and spout, the idea of exchanging even a word with him would have been insupportable.

Was she still allowing that mindset to cloud her perception of the man he was now? She must consider this. But later. For now, Fanny's accusations gnawed at her and must be addressed and the anger that Mary had felt towards Alexander transformed into an anger towards Fanny.

"You would not have been in company with a decent man of good family and strong moral fibre, merely because you do not like the way he worships God? I must have misheard you." Her level gaze insisted that she had not misheard at all.

"I... that is... it was kindly meant. We both know that in order to be a truly good, moral person, one must hold to the correct faith, or how can one understand Good if one does not know God? One must attend to one's soul as one attends to one's body. Miss Crawford, although she is very pretty, will never possess true beauty until she discards her contempt for the Church and for the clergy. Every time she works upon Edmund to give up his living and leave the church for a career of greater distinction, she loses more of her lustre.

In an attempt to deflect Fanny's conversation, Mary asked, "Has Miss Crawford done so often? Spoken against Mr. Bertram's choice, that is?"

"Oh yes." She fell over her words. "Upon first hearing of Edmund's intention to be ordained, she argued against it quite strongly. She insisted that men love to distinguish themselves; that in the law or the military, or in politics, distinction may be gained, but not in the church. A clergyman is nothing. I do believe she said those very words: 'A clergyman is nothing.'"

The look of horror on her face was nearly comical, but Mary did not smile. "And then," Fanny continued, "only a short time later, she returned to the subject and declared that Edmund really was fit for something better—as if there might be such a thing! 'Come, do change your mind. It is not too late. Go into the law.' I remember her speaking these words as clearly as if it were just a moment ago." She gave a great sigh of disapproval. "But Edmund would not listen to her. He must not, although she attempts to use her wiles on him.

"Even this play they attempted..." she shook her head. "Edmund had insisted on not being a part of the play. It was wrong, and Sir Thomas would never approve, he told us all, but when Miss Crawford was cast as Amelia and we needed another to act the part of Anhalt, she coaxed him to discard his morals and what he knew to be right and take up the role. I am afraid of her ambition."

Now that Fanny had started talking about Miss Crawford, she seemed unwilling to let go of the topic. Mary wondered how long these thoughts had been festering in her mind, that they frothed and boiled over to such a state that they now cried for release. As long as the topic did not return to Alexander's supposed corrupt morality, Mary chose to encourage her. Fanny did not disappoint.

"I fear for Miss Crawford." She shook her head. "So shortly after we met, when Edmund offered her the use of my pony to teach her to ride, she forgot the time and would not apologise to me for the blunder. How she spoke then. 'I am come to make my own apologies for keeping you waiting; but I have nothing in the world to say for myself—I knew it was very late, and that I was behaving extremely ill; and therefore, if you please, you must forgive me. Selfishness must always be forgiven, you know, because there is no hope of a cure.' Oh, Miss Bennet, what can one say against that? If she would bend her thought to the teachings of the Bible, how much improved she would be."

Fearing a return to the previous disavowal of Alexander, Mary tried once more for a new subject. "And how does Miss Crawford now? I have not seen her since Sir Thomas returned to the house, nor have I heard word of her."

"She has kept to her own home," Fanny pursed her lips. "She dare not attend us at Mansfield Park, for Sir Thomas is quite put out with strangers, wishing to be only with his family." She spoke on for a time about her aunts and how Maria was faring after the loss of Rushworth, and Julia's sudden dejection at the departure of the honourable Mr. Yates. Mary tried to smile and nod and keep up some conversation, but all she wanted was for Miss Price to be gone. It was far later than she would have wished when the housekeeper came to the door and announced Mr. Edmund Bertram. Mary breathed a guilty breath of relief that this visit would soon be over.

The two left shortly thereafter in order to return in full daylight and fair weather. It was an hour's drive to Mansfield, and the clouds that had begun to scuttle across the sky were starting to foretell of rain. Mary ought to remain inside and retire to her rooms to ponder the tumult of the day's discoveries, but her mind would not be still, and despite her long ramble through the streets earlier, her feet cried for activity.

She would, she decided, make the very short walk to the drapers, where Papa's cravats would be waiting for her. She called for her maid Alice, asking if she minded an outing, and then set off with her coat and umbrella at the ready.

The shop was quiet, the looming clouds seemingly having chased the customers back to their homes, but the tailor was not quite finished with the commission. "Take a seat please, Miss, if you care to wait. Says he won't be more than a few minutes." Mr. Lennox, the proprietor, showed her to an armchair upholstered in a lush brocade—which she was certain was available for purchase—and asked repeatedly after her comfort, as well as that of her maid, who also had a chair made available for her use. He was a chatty sort of a man when there was no one demanding his time, and Mary welcomed the unchallenging distraction.

"We have some fine textiles come through our doors, we do." He puffed out his chest. "Finest in the world. Some come through Liverpool or Bristol, lots from London. I order through a fine merchant there, name is Gardiner—"

"Why! He is my uncle," Mary interjected, and at that moment she became Mr. Lennox's best friend. He strutted around the shop, showing her which bolts he had bought from Gardiner's Textiles, and explained to her which prominent members of the local society had used the fabric for their clothing and furnishings.

"Some are more common, like this peridot-green moiré." He called Mary over to let her fondle the delicate fabric. "Others are much more rare. This velvet, hand-embroidered it is, just enough for one very fine waistcoat, or perhaps a set of pillows for an earl's gouty feet, and this muslin, see how fine it is, with the woven-in design. Of course, what one has, others must have too, and it is mighty hard to make a small bolt stretch to clothe a dozen gentlemen.

"Just a month ago, no, more like two, I received in the shop a very fine and unusual piece of fabric in a green that I had never seen before in a textile. Green, definitely green, but verging on blue, and in the softest wool, yet sturdy enough for a coat."

This caught Mary's attention, and she listened carefully. "First, Mr. Tom Bertram had a coat made, perfect for hunting, he said, green enough to feel the part, but bright enough not to be mistaken for an old tree. He was so insistent on having something out of the ordinary, not the usual hunting pinks. In truth, he is a bit of a peacock, always strutting about and preening himself, and the coat was another addition to his plumage. But if he buys my wares and keeps Gambon busy," he gestured to the door leading to the tailor's rooms, "then I have no complaint. And indeed, no sooner had he taken that coat home, than another came in asking for one just like it. They were going hunting together, he said, and thought a uniform would look well against the wood."

"Which gentleman was this?" She had to ask the question, and hoped it sounded like idle curiosity; she did not wish the man to stop talking now.

"Let me think... It was a Mr. Crawford, I believe. He is not from here, but stays often with his sister at a nearby village. But not only he, for only a short time later, another man came in for his own coat, and let me tell you, we scarcely had enough of the fabric left to complete it. When Mr. Crawford had his coat made, we laughed that he had used up all the best part of the bolt, that there was none left for anyone else. But John Gambon is the cleverest tailor I know, and cut those remaining yards so perfectly, it was as if we had ordered exactly the right amount, not an inch too much, nor too little."

This was interesting indeed! She had known about Henry's coat, which had gone missing, only to appear in Admiral Crawford's hands, which he had then shown to the two hired ruffians. Was Henry then the culprit after all? Or was he a tool in Tom Bertram's hands, for Bertram was the one who knew about the unusual length of fabric? However could she discern this? For it seemed the entire crux of the mystery now rested on who had conceived of the idea.

But this thought was brought to a swift halt at Mr. Lennox's next words.

"Fancy that it was Mr. Crawford's sister who was with him that day; she must have been the one to convince Mr. Rushworth to have his coat made as well, for she kept telling her brother what a fine thing it would be to have a coat like Bertrams, in the exact fabric. What did she say? 'A matching coat will do well, but let us not tarry all day, for I have arranged to meet Rushworth at the bank. I know you can convince him.' There—she must have spoken to him that very day. I believe it was all her idea. Remarkable, isn't it? And then, the very next week, Mr. Rushworth himself; Mr. Crawford must indeed have assured him what a fine coat it would be. What a sad thing about him, and dying in that beautiful coat, too. One really ought not to think about this, but my first question when I heard the dreadful news was whether the coat was damaged beyond repair."

Mary's eyes snapped open. The last piece of the puzzle suddenly fell into place, and the picture that now formed was nothing like what they had imagined. She had to get a message to Alexander!

Chapter Twenty-One

Resolution

The moment Mary returned to the house, she begged for some paper and ink and set down her theory, whereupon she inquired after sending an express message to Alexander at the inn at Mansfield. She had enough remaining coins from brother Darcy's generous gift to pay the cost, and this was important. Mrs. Meldola must have seen the look of determination upon her face, for the lady summoned one of the servants to take the note to the main stables at once and to request a fast rider's services. This being done, she retired at last to her room to sit and think, at least until dinner.

How she wished to request a tray be sent to her room, but a moment's reflection put an end to that thought. After her reaction to Mrs. Meldola's information earlier, she must make an extra effort not to seem rude. It would be wrong to suggest by her absence that she was too good to take food with her hosts, even if the impression were incorrect. Mr. and Mrs. Meldola had been nothing but kind and generous and had gone beyond mere duty to a friend to make her feel comfortable in their house.

Mary reflected on the hours she had spent sitting with Mrs. Meldola at the mending, on their pleasant conversations, and on the pleasure with which she had sat reading to the orphans and of the pride she felt in describing the institution which all but ensured a decent life for the children housed within. This was a lady she would gladly call a friend, one who saw good and did good, without a thought to herself.

No, Mary was not too good to dine with the Meldolas; if anything, the shoe was on the other foot, and she ought to feel grateful that they deigned to have her at their table.

One of Alexander's chastisements came rushing in on her: What I am is nothing to who I am. I am a man who works hard and seeks justice and tries to do well by the world. Can you not see me for who I am?

Through Fanny's strange conversation as well, that same notion had arisen again and again—that one ought not to rely on pronouncements or on external trappings to learn who a person was, but to look, rather, to deeds. For a man betrays himself not with his words but by his actions. By this accounting, Mrs. Meldola was unquestionably a good person, no matter her profession of faith. And, Mary realised with a gulp, so was Alexander.

He was, perhaps, the best man she knew. He worked hard to support not only himself, but his mother and sisters in Scotland. He had a fierce sense of justice and would exert himself for the sake of good, whether or not there was compensation at the end of it, and heedless of possible danger to himself. She recalled their first adventure together, when he faced a man with a loaded pistol and nearly died in the pursuit of justice, and the gulp became a sob. To have lost him then, before she even knew him, would have rent her soul in two.

But the facts remained as they were. They were from two worlds more different than ever she could have imagined. They must part ways. After this case, she consoled herself, after he had seen her safely to her family, then they must say their goodbyes and not meet again. Her heart broke at the thought, but it must be done, for there was no other way forward.

Soon it was time for dinner, and then for some songs at the pianoforte, where Mr. Meldola surprised her with his skill at the keyboard and a remarkable voice. She accompanied him for a short set of Scotch airs, which he confessed had been a wedding present from Alexander.

"I have only today learned that Mrs. Meldola is Alexander's cousin," she spoke whilst looking through some more books of printed and handwritten music. "And yet I had thought that you and he were friends. If the matter is not too personal, I would beg to be enlightened."

"You would be correct on both accounts, Miss Bennet. Here, this one." He pointed a wide finger to a short aria from Paisiello's *Il barbiere di Siviglia*. "Then, perhaps, some Mozart, and I have the music from Mr. Beethoven's *Fidelio*. But to your question, Alexander and I were acquainted through our fathers, who were childhood friends, and it was he through whom I met my lovely wife. I also attended university at Glasgow, although I left after my first degree and did not take further training, as Alexander did. I wished to return here to the town of my birth to take up my family's business." He tried a few notes from the aria. "Do you transpose, Miss Bennet? Might we try this down a fourth? I am not in good voice tonight. Ah, much better." And music became the only further conversation of the evening, before exhaustion and a need for solitude took her at last to her bed.

The morning light, when she opened her eyes, bespoke grey skies and rain. She threw back the covers with a sigh and resigned herself to a day of enforced idleness. Surely Mrs. Meldola would have some useful chores that needed doing, but Mary could not be satisfied with knitting or sewing when the solution to poor Mr. Rushworth's death was at hand. She pulled the bell to summon Alice to help her dress and splashed some water onto her face as she waited. She must, she supposed, become accustomed to hearing of these cases from others' lips. If she were to part ways with Alexander, as she still determined to do, there would be no new adventures for her.

"Morning, Miss Bennet." Alice slid into the room. "You'll be wanting your light wool travelling dress today, and the spencer and bonnet, and Mrs. Meldola has arranged for an extra shawl and a muffler for you."

Mary looked at her maid in surprise. "What can you mean?"

"Did Mrs. not tell you? A note arrived back from Mr. Lyons last night, requesting you to join him at the manor. Dronch at the stables has sent over a gig for you with a driver, but it is open at the sides and the air is cool, and you don't want to catch cold. There's also a basket of breads and rolls and a flask of hot tea. The gig is ready for us whenever you wish to leave."

"A gig? He wishes me to join him?" After all she had said to him, and all she had accused him of, he still wished for her to join him? She flushed with shame. She had accused him of being somehow lesser than her, but just like the Meldolas, he was showing by his actions that he was, indeed, the best of men. How could she show her face to him after abusing him so badly? And neither was this the first time. Was this an attempt to cow her with mortification? No, she chastised herself. Never once in the two years that she had known him had Alexander acted out of spite. If he said he wished her to join him, then that is what he meant.

"Then let us ready ourselves," she turned a smile on her maid, "and prepare for the drive to Mansfield Park."

The clouds were kind and held back from sprinkling them with rain for the duration of the journey. The first heavy drops fell just as the gig came to a stop before the inn, where they were to meet before continuing on to the estate. Alexander must have been waiting, for he dashed out of the door and under the gig's small canopy before they continued the very short distance to the manor house at Mansfield Park.

"What is the meaning of this?" Mary knew she and Alexander had a great many more words to say to each other, but with Alice and the driver listening to every word, that conversation must be delayed. At least he looked at her with something like an equanimous expression and the ghost of a smile.

"We have an interview with Mr. Bertram and another with Sir Thomas. I believe there are some minor matters we must clear up before drawing our final conclusions." The rain began to splatter under the canopy and he shifted a little further into the middle, his shoulder nearly touching her own, and though she knew with every ounce of her being that she ought to pull away, she found she could not.

They had so much to talk about, Mary and himself, but Alexander knew they must wait. He had gone over their argument, such that it was, a thousand times in his head the previous night as he lay in his bed, unable to sleep. He wished a thousand things had been different—that he had spoken different words, that she had taken a moment to listen, that he had come a second earlier or later—but mostly, he wished he could undo time. It was not that he wished her not to know of his family and his faith, but that he could have chosen the time and manner of the telling, and that he could have told her himself. And now it seemed that somehow Fanny Price had learned of it as well, for such were the whispers at the inn.

To his credit, the innkeeper's only concern was that Alexander not eat the pork pies that he had prepared, suggesting instead the beef stew or the Italian-style pastels with cheese and vegetables. But the whispers preceded him into every room, and he knew his secret was a secret no more.

But that, too, must be dealt with later. For now, there were details of his case to resolve, and a murderer to bring to justice.

The gig came to a stop by the main doors to the house of Mansfield Park and Mrs. Grey came to stand at the entrance whilst two large footmen hurried out to the gig with umbrellas for the party. Mary's maid Alice would remain with the gig for now and would be taken to the kitchen door, where she could wait until the interviews were concluded and it was time to return to Northampton. The driver, of course, would be comfortable in the coach house and stables with his peers.

Would John be there to keep the man company? For the driver's sake, Alexander hoped so. John was far better company than any of the people with whom he would now be forced to meet.

Alexander had hoped that the first interview would be with Tom Bertram. However, it was only just after nine o'clock in the morning, not at all too early for working people, and the indolent heir to the baronetcy was still in his bed. Alexander sent for Barnaby, Bertram's valet, to rouse him and make him presentable enough for the encounter. Bertram would be in ill humour, he knew, but he would also be off his guard and in his sleep-addled state, would be more likely to confess to his sins.

In the meantime, Alexander and Mary would speak with Sir Thomas, the baronet himself. Sir Thomas awaited them in his study, which was the room off of which the former rehearsal room had led. The great double doors, so recently the proscenium arch for the intended stage, were now closed and chaste, the great green baize curtain nowhere to be seen, the room in perfect order as suited a Great Man of Great Estate. Alexander and Mary had been shown in through a side door and ushered to two chairs before Sir Thomas' desk. There was no offer of tea or coffee.

Alexander took in the baronet. He was tall and vigorous, with a wind-reddened face and hair just more grey than brown. In his features, Alexander could see both of his sons, although in them the strong features were softened by the gift of their mother's beauty into handsomeness. He did not seem pleased to be so interrupted in his morning routine.

"What do you want?" This came by way of a morning salutation and greeting. "I must see you, for the magistrate has ordered it, but do not think I shan't be having words with him."

"Then we shall try not to prolong this discussion. We know when your ship docked from Antigua. You were in England for four days, at some business, before making for home from London in the greatest of haste. Your arrival seemed calculated to occur immediately after Mr. Rushworth's tragic death. It is difficult to imagine these events are not connected in any way."

The thunder that threatened on Sir Thomas' face matched that in the clouds outside. "How dare you investigate my whereabouts, Mr. Lyons. My activities are no business of yours whatsoever, neither them, nor the people with whom I associate, nor the purpose behind them. If I chose to remain some days in London before travelling home, that is my affair and nobody else's."

Alexander refused to allow his steady regard to waver. "With all due respect, Sir Thomas, it is entirely my business. A man is dead—nay, two men. One might have been a stranger, but the other was your neighbour and the man who, save for this dreadful affair, might have been your son. I am bound by my engagement on behalf of the magistrate and coroner, and by my integrity as a man who loves justice, to investigate every thread that makes up this knot. If your story has no bearing on the death of Mr. Rushworth, then it shall be as if you had never told it. But I must have the truth."

"And what of her?" He waved his head in Mary's general direction. "She is under obligation to nobody."

"If your tale is honest and above reproach, there should be no objection in her hearing it. But if you have something best kept quiet, she can leave."

"And have her think the worst of me? Scoundrel. Let her remain."

Sir Thomas still glared thunder, but his shoulders relaxed a bit and he seemed resigned to divulging the entirety of the matter.

"There is no secret. Our ship docked, and before I could make my way off the gangplank and onto dry land, I was waylaid by two curs who would talk to me about my holdings in Antigua. Abolitionists! Pah! Do they not understand that the wealth of the entire empire rests on those black shoulders? Bad enough that my sons have contrary opinions. But these two—Wilberforce and Ottley—young whelps, all high and mighty and full of the fury of God almighty, with not one drop of sense between the two of them."

"This took four days?" If Alexander was incredulous, his voice echoed his thoughts.

"Had it been them alone, I would have sent them packing in five minutes, or into the Thames, better! But no, they were followed in short order by a military man, who I now know is uncle to two young people in the neighbourhood. Admiral Crawford is his name. He invited me to his house for dinner, said we were connected through his niece and nephew, and by one means or another, kept me in London until nigh on the Lord's Day, with not one moment to send a letter ahead of me. Don't like to travel on

Sunday, but when a man has been away from his family for so long, and then is kept even longer, such matters pale in comparison. Don't know why, after every scheme and ruse he could imagine, Admiral Crawford so suddenly let up. He received a message from some fellow named Giles and changed at a moment. Even offered to find me the fastest carriage he knew. Never mind that. I am home and have no desire to leave."

Alexander kept his head steady but flickered his eyes to Mary, who sat at his side. Her upper body was rocking, her eyes narrow, as she did when she was deep in thought. She must suspect what he did: that Admiral Crawford did what he could to keep Sir Thomas from Mansfield until the fatal hunt was over. This they might never know for certain, but it was all but established fact in Alexander's mind, and seemingly in Mary's as well.

Sir Thomas, it seemed, might be guilty of greater transgressions against mankind with his slave-run plantations, but he was quite innocent in the deaths of Pickins and Mr. Rushworth.

"Thank you, Sir Thomas. I appreciate your candour. We shall now leave you to your morning." He rose, Mary at his side, and took his leave, thankful that he would likely never see Sir Thomas again.

They had little time to talk. Barnaby, Tom's valet, found them almost at once and informed them that his master was in the breakfast room.

"Shall he be as pleasant as his father?" Mary whispered. Alexander gave a grimace in response.

Tom Bertram looked like a man who had not spent enough time contemplating the insides of his eyelids. His skin was ashen, his eyes red, and heavily shadowed where their underlids met his unshaven cheeks. He had been up late at some activity, and Alexander suspected alcohol or opium was at the centre of it.

He did not speak, but blinked at the two strangers who had dared to roust him from his bed.

"Coffee, Mr. Bertram?" Alexander asked with a smile. He poured a cup from the pot on the sideboard, then prepared a cup of tea for Mary before turning back to Tom. "Here, have mine. Lots of sugar. That should help with the headache." He added three spoons to the cup, handed it to the bleary-eyed man, and then prepared another for himself.

Bertram gazed at the cup and took a sip. "What do you want?" He spoke as if in a dream, every word vague and dispassionate.

"Merely to know where you were last week, when we all thought you missing, or dead. Also, to satisfy ourselves as to whether you had any involvement in Mr. Rushworth's death. That is not too much to wish to know, surely." The lilt in his voice must be more annoying than his questions.

For a moment he thought the son would echo the father in his reluctance to talk, but Tom merely took another mouthful of the sweet coffee and sighed.

"I suppose I had better, hadn't I?" But instead of talking, he stared glumly at the now-empty coffee cup before him, then rose and poured himself another from the pot and took a small plate of fried potatoes.

"Mr. Bertram, do you understand the serious nature of this matter? That you were so conveniently absent during the hunt in which Rushworth died could well be seen as proof of your guilt. One might suggest that you had set the plan in action and then vanished from the scene so as to give yourself an alibi."

"What? Me? Can you credit it?" At last, his voice held some passion. *Good*, Alexander thought. *Now we might see what lies behind the foppish facade.*

"One might further say that you were distressed enough with Mr. Rushworth's performance in your play that you chose to remove him from the cast in a most permanent manner. Or that you disapproved of him as your sister's husband to an unnatural extent. That you were hiding in the bushes, directing this tragedy, whilst he wore your costume."

"Do you seriously believe this? Do you seriously suspect me of killing Rushworth? I was not even there. You can ask—" He stopped suddenly.

"I can ask whom, Mr. Bertram?" Alexander's voice was soft again. He tried to keep his mien sympathetic.

Bertram's shoulders dropped, his second cup of coffee untouched, and his fingers twitching on the table. "I do not know his true name. He goes by Smokey. He was a sailor on the ships that travelled to China, where he learned not only of opium eaters, but opium breathers. He has a supply, just as our better respected merchants have their lines for silks and spices. Smokey brings in opium to breathe. It is marvellous, really." His voice took on the dreamlike quality again. "One breathes in the vapours, and one is transported... Time has no meaning. There is only pleasure and release and peace and an absolute absence of pain and distress. I..." He looked at Mary and turned red. "Pardon me, madam. I did not mean to talk of such things in your presence."

"She will not be harmed by your words. Miss Bennet is stronger than most men of my acquaintance. Where might I find this Smokey, to confirm your presence in his establishment? I have heard of such places in London, and at some of the other busy ports, but I had not thought to find one in Northampton."

Bertram looked abashed. "There is an inn, down towards Stoke, on the canals. One can ride part way in a cart, under the hay, and then travel the rest of the distance on the barges, and nobody knows where you have been. I shall give you his direction, if he will speak to you." He fell into himself, his secret no longer straightening his spine.

Alexander stood and bowed. "Enjoy your breakfast, Mr. Bertram. I shall require that direction of you in good time, but now Miss Bennet and I have to catch a murderer.

Chapter Twenty-Two

Justice

The rain had abated whilst Alexander and Mary were at Mansfield Park, and they chose to walk back to the village rather than taking the gig. Alexander asked the driver to meet them at the inn later for the return to Northampton. For now, there was no more need for the conveyance.

The lawns were damp from the rain, rendering the usual route through the back parlour inadvisable; instead, they walked the longer distance along the drive and down the lanes, which were not too muddy for walking. As they entered the village, they passed by the parsonage. Edmund was standing on the stoop, talking to Mrs. Grant and Miss Crawford. Alexander waved as they strolled past.

"Mr. Bertram. Well met. Mary and I were about to seek a spot of tea in the private parlour at the inn. Do come and join us. You too, Miss Crawford." He gave a great smile. Beside him, Mary smiled too, although hers seemed more tentative. He had told her his plans as they walked, and she had agreed with them, but she was still not entirely comfortable in his presence. After today's events, whatever they might be, he would sit her down and they would have their words at last.

"That sounds like an excellent plan, Lyons. We shall be along directly." Edmund called back. "You will join us, will you not, Miss Crawford? And bring your brother as well. We shall have quite the party. Mrs. Usher at the inn makes the finest fruit tarts, if you have not had the fortune already to have tried them. Let us walk over together. Meet you there, Lyons, Miss Bennet."

He gave another wave and then walked on, Mary beside him. He had thought to offer his arm, but she hardly needed the support, and he did not wish to force an intimacy she did not want at the moment. Mary kept her eyes ahead of her, intent upon the road and the path along which they walked, flickering only occasionally towards him, her hands firmly at her sides, making no motions to suggest she wished for his elbow. Only her eyes betrayed something of the turmoil he knew she must be feeling. They would have so much to discuss later.

It was only a few more yards to the inn, where Mr. Yates was waiting for them. "G'morning, g'morning! Good job I stayed around, and not head right back to the family, eh what?" He flashed a theatrical smile and then took Mary's hand in the ancient French fashion. "Miss Bertram and Miss Julia have sent their regards, and will be pleased to join us, as you asked. Just got the note from their footman whilst you were out and about; the ladies were visiting some of the tenants and will come by on their return. Jolly good, eh what?"

They moved to the private parlour, there to await the Bertram sisters, Edmund, and Miss Crawford. "Pity Maddox and Oliver returned to their homes yesterday," Yates drawled. "This should be quite some entertainment. Best show of the year! Perhaps I ought to try my hand at writing a play about it."

Any reply that Alexander might have made was forestalled by a tap at the door and the arrival of Edmund and the Crawford siblings, followed immediately by two maids with trays of tea, cakes, biscuits, and the promised fruit tarts.

"Ah, what perfect timing. Come and sit, and let us take tea. Miss Bennet, would you do us the honour of pouring?"

The conversation continued light and friendly for a time. With the capture of Fred Warren, a shadow seemed to have lifted over the company, as if finding the actual perpetrator of the murder, rather than its instigator, was the final stage in the investigation. Alexander wondered how many of the elegant young people here assembled suspected that with Warren's confession, the work had only begun? The conversation touched upon the play—what a pity it had to be abandoned yet again!—and the cool and damp day which had come after so fair an autumn, and whether the gentlemen would travel to Newmarket for the races, which Tom Bertram enjoyed so very much.

Another tap at the door brought the two Bertram sisters in the room, and once they, too, had been provided with tea and cake, Alexander finally decided to turn the discussion to the murder.

"I was wondering, Mr. Crawford," he looked at Henry, "whether you ever found your hunting coat. How very strange it seemed, to have a coat made and then for it to disappear so completely. I find I cannot get that story out of my head."

Henry shrugged and gave a half smile. "I have resigned myself to its utter loss, Mr. Lyons. I was quite vexed about it at first, but it is only a coat; no use losing sleep over an item of clothing."

Alexander suppressed the desire to growl at the man. That article of clothing, so insignificant to him, must have cost enough to pay the wages of a skilled labourer for a month or more; a poor family might eat for a year on the amount Crawford tossed aside so carelessly. Certainly, Alexander himself had never purchased a coat tailored exactly to his form, and in such a superior fabric as the wool he had seen on Rushworth's beaten body. Only a gift from his friend Darcy had allowed him even the taste of such luxuries. For a moment—or perhaps more—he sympathised with Mr. Lennox, the draper, who had told Mary he gave more thought to Mr. Rushworth's coat than to the man himself.

"Then you have no notion of what might have become of it?" Mary asked.

"It is a mystery, Miss Bennet. I thought perhaps one of the maids might have seen it, or my valet or the lady who takes in Mrs. Grant's laundry, but not a soul had any idea at all." At that, Henry Crawford turned his palms up in resignation and leaned back in his chair, the image of an entitled gentleman with not a care in the world.

"Miss Crawford, what about you? Have you any ideas? I admit that whilst your brother is not losing sleep over it, I am kept awake at night by this puzzle." Alexander turned his smile to her and her jaw tightened.

"I... I cannot think what you mean, Mr. Lyons." She sat perfectly still with a stiff smile. "Why should I know what became of my brother's coat? He can be careless and loses items all the time. And why should his coat be so important that you are thinking of it when you ought to be asleep?"

"It simply seemed," he tilted his head, "that this coat is at the centre of the affairs that led to Mr. Rushworth's demise. It was you, was it not, who suggested to your brother Henry to have a hunting coat made exactly like Mr. Tom Bertram's, was it not?"

Miss Crawford blinked. Her voice remained light and teasing, and her smile remained upon her face, but she could not disguise how the blood drained from her face. "It might have been so. I do recall Mr. Bertram being so proud of the fabric he had discovered, and of the hunting coat he had made, and I thought the colour would do well on Henry, too. It quite brings his complexion to its best advantage, and a man ought to look handsome just as a woman should."

"You can be very convincing, Miss Crawford. You convinced Henry to have a coat made like Mr. Bertram's, then you and Henry convinced Mr. Rushworth to pay off Mr. Bertram's gambling debts, and you likely convinced your uncle of some matters as well."

Miss Crawford's face was now quite drained of colour and her breathing grew shallow, although the smile remained. Alexander beckoned to Mary with his eyes to attend the lady should she swoon. But he had more to say.

"Indeed, Miss Crawford, the only person whom you were unable to convince was Mr. Edmund Bertram. That you had set your cap at him is indisputable. No, no, do not go missish on us. There is no shame in fancying a man. But you fancied he would be far better suitable for you were he not to be a clergyman. You tried to sway his ambitions towards the law, or towards a great career in politics, perhaps, but he would have none of it. And so, you decided that if he would not take steps to better his position in the world, you would act for him.

"You decided," he enunciated the words with the utmost care, "that if Tom Bertram were deceased, Edmund would have no choice but to rise to the level you desired him to attain: that of baronet. And you, then, could claim your place at his side as Lady Bertram."

The stunned hush in the room was broken as Edmund leapt up from his chair. "No! This is not so... it cannot be so. Please, Miss Crawford, tell me it is not." But the despair on his face revealed his understanding of it.

"Surely you cannot believe this nonsense," the lady protested. But the habitual sparkle in her eye had disappeared, and the laughter was thin. "What a joke, Mr. Lyons. You must jest. You have taken a child's puzzling game and assembled the pieces all incorrectly." She attempted a chuckle, but the bells were silent.

"No, madam, the picture is complete. I have sent people to London to inquire after your uncle, and the men sent to do his bidding on your behalf have been apprehended." One had, at least; the other would be captured within days. He would let the half-truth stand for now.

"But... I... he could not have told anybody..."

Every last glimmer of mirth on Mary Kate Crawford's face fell away under the realisation that she had just betrayed herself, and she whimpered and slunk sideways on her chair in a dead faint. Mary was at her side and caught her before she might injure herself, and with Henry's help, laid her carefully on the settee that sat against one wall of the parlour.

"Are you certain?" Henry asked as he held her unresponsive hand. "Have you proof? This is my sister! I would see justice done, but she is my sister, and I will not abide such accusations without strong evidence." Like Edmund, his words were fierce, but his face betrayed his understanding.

Alexander gestured towards Mary. She had found the last pieces of evidence and had knit the threads together to form this strange tale. She deserved the telling of it, and the credit for the solution. Alexander was not driven by his pride, and he had no desire to claim glory that belonged to another.

Mary gaped at all the people now staring at her and a pink blush crept across her pretty face. She had always thought herself plain, but she was wrong. Just like her character, seeming at first so quiet and shy but so entrancing upon better knowledge, so was her beauty. When no longer intentionally subdued in favour of her more flamboyant sisters, her features transformed into something glorious, and when she allowed herself to speak, her inner fire broke free of its fetters and lit up the room.

And now, he thought with that pride he could not feel for himself, she was about to set the room ablaze.

"The proof," Mary spoke quietly, "is more a chain of related events than a single great one, at least for now. Mr. Lyons has sent messages to London which will allow us to confirm what we surmise. We believe that Miss Crawford was the one who took her brother's coat. She wished for a coat to match Mr. Bertram's exactly, so she could instruct the killers she had hired as to their target. The colour was unique, and she believed there could be no other coat. She wrote to her uncle, the admiral, of her wishes, and he, being unable to deny her anything, agreed. She then sent him Mr. Crawford's missing coat, concealed in a package of books, and told him the exact date of the hunt. When better for a man to die, after all, than at a fox hunt? Such a death might be construed as an accident, and indeed, it nearly was so, had not Mr. Lyons spoken so convincingly at the inquest.

"Admiral Crawford then arranged for two of his less savoury sailors to take on this commission. They were given a name, and shown the coat, and were told of the date of the hunt. When their first attempt at the murder struck down the wrong man—a poor fellow who had Mr. Bertram's old signet ring—they moved on to this second part of their plan and lured the man in the green-blue coat over the trap they had laid in the hedges. It was plain luck that Mr. Bertram was not present, being," she glanced at Alexander, "indisposed. And it was plain bad luck that Mr. Rushworth had heard of Mr. Crawford's coat that matched Mr. Bertram's so exactly and had his own made. Therefore, the only man who wore the coat these killers were told to find was the wrong one. Their plan worked perfectly. But the wrong man died. That is why Miss Crawford was so amazed when Mr. Bertram strode into the room that day, fit and healthy and very much alive."

"But how," Maria now asked, "did you think of Miss Crawford at all? She has always been so pleasant and gay and not at all serious. I would not once have imagined her capable of this."

The pale pink blush that had coloured Mary's delicate complexion now deepened to red. "It was something that Mr. Lyons taught me: to measure a person by his or her own words and deeds and not on how others wish to portray them. Miss Crawford put on a fine performance and played the light-hearted coquette very well, but at one of our very first meetings, when she invited me to take tea with herself and Mrs. Grant, she made a joke about not wishing to marry a clergyman, but preferring a man of greater distinction. When Mrs. Grant suggested a gentleman of the higher classes, Miss Crawford replied, 'Or a baronet!' She may have intended the comment to seem a froth of a joke, but the idea was surely well set in her mind, and she must have, at some point, made a similar suggestion to Mrs. Grant for her sister to mention it thus.

"When I recalled that, every other action made sense, where no other proposed solutions worked at all. This entire scheme was to rid the world of Tom Bertram so Mary could marry his brother— her baronet."

"And that was all I wanted," came a weak voice from the settee. "I merely wanted to marry a baronet."

"What will become of her now?"

Edmund turned to Alexander with a look of resignation and distress. He had long since replaced his teacup with a tankard of ale, as had Alexander himself. Mary had refused a glass of wine in favour of more tea, but Alexander suspected that she might change her mind a little later. The morning had been a difficult one for everybody involved, and the relief that came with the resolution to the mystery was tinged with sadness and a sense of restlessness. Although the mastermind behind the crime had been found and her confession taken, two men were still dead, and nothing could bring them back.

After Miss Crawford's admission of her part in the crime, Mr. Harris and Sir Hugh had entered the parlour from the side room where they had been sitting and listening to the proceedings. With Henry's reluctant permission, she had been taken to a secure room in Sir Hugh's house on the far side of the village, where she would await a decision on the part of the authorities as to her fate. She had protested but had put up no resistance, and her final words, before departing under Sir Hugh and Mr. Harris' guard, had been, "I suppose I shall never be Lady Bertram now."

"What will become of her, Alexander?" Mary echoed Edmund's question.

He took a draw on his ale. "It is hard to say. In some ways, nothing she has done was a crime. It is not illegal to wish a person dead in one's heart, nor is it to ask a relation for a favour. She was not the one who engaged the killers, and she certainly had no direct hand in either Rushworth's or Pickins' ends. She could be charged with some sort of intent to commit murder, but she might well claim that she merely expressed a frustration to her uncle, who chose to act on it without her direction."

"And the admiral?"

"Now we enter the realm not of justice, but of politics. He will almost certainly be stripped of his commission, but whether this goes to trial or whether it remains a hushed-up affair dealt with in the back rooms of the halls of power, I cannot say. The scandal of an official charge and a public trial would be disastrous to the Navy, and with matters on the Continent still so unsettled, with Bonaparte still on the rampage, those in power might decide that the damage to the institution is not worth the risk. And then, there is the matter of it coming down to the word of an illiterate tar against that of a respected admiral. I do not expect to see anything of this in the newspapers."

"Then Miss Crawford walks free, despite the two bodies at her feet?" Alexander could feel Mary's sense of indignation at this; indeed, he felt it himself. Had she been a farmer's wife or a working girl, she would face the gallows. Her rank and wealth would save her life, and this sat very ill with him.

"We shall have to await the magistrate's decision. I spoke to him earlier and offered what thoughts I had on legal options. But if she is not charged, Henry has insisted that he will send her away. She is wealthy and of age, but he could have her declared incompetent on this basis on this affair, and resume guardianship of her. She might well avoid the noose, and her cage may be gilded, but she will live her life in a cage of some sorts, nonetheless."

"Then," Edmund sighed, "we shall have to be satisfied."

Weak sunshine struggled through the window, bathing the room in a soft watery light. Alexander felt his legs twitch. "The rains seem to have lifted, and I am in need of movement. Shall we find our outerwear and walk a while?"

"Indeed, yes!" Mary cried.

Edmund rose as well. "May I join you? I have something to say, an apology to offer, and I might think better whilst I, too, am moving.

Alexander was thankful for the warmth of his woollen greatcoat, for the air was still damp and the sun held no warmth. Edmund, likewise, was covered from neck to ankle in his own coat, and Alexander looked with concern at Mary, whose cloak and thin pelisse seemed insufficient for the decided nip in the air. But her head was kept warm and out of the wind by her bonnet, and the shawl she had wrapped about her shoulders looked sturdy and thick. She seemed in no distress. Ought he to offer her his arm? He glanced at Edmund and thought not. Not now. She would wish to face whatever it was the gentleman had to say to her as an equal and not as a poor and weak woman who relied upon a man for her strength. Later on, he would offer his arm for other reasons. Now, he would let her walk independently.

They had passed the edge of the village, past the little general shop and the parsonage, and now rambled down a quiet lane. It would, Alexander knew, eventually lead to Mansfield Park, but the route would wind through fields and copses before attaining its destination at the end of the drive. This would allow Edmund all the time he needed to say his piece.

"Miss Bennet, I have done you wrong. I have done you both wrong. I heard, only too late, about my cousin Fanny's purpose in visiting you yesterday. Had I but known, had I only realised, I would have stopped her and would have taken the time to correct her impressions."

He removed his hat and stared at it for a moment, as if it held the answers he needed, before replacing it atop his handsome head.

"No. My fault goes back further. Let me explain something about my cousin. She came to live with us when she was a girl of ten. She was sent by her mother at my Aunt Norris' command, and quite without her consent, I believe. She has always been treated as something of a slave to my aunt, her personal servant. Aunt Norris has never allowed her to forget her place and has, for the past ten years, not missed a day in reminding Fanny of her good fortune in being chosen to live with us, all the while heaping upon her the sort of quiet abuse that can destroy a child.

"Fanny is a good sort of person and one who feels deeply, and she has found her solace by adopting a character as opposite to that of my aunt as possible. Instead of Mrs. Norris' manipulative dishonesty, Fanny has chosen the path of unquestioning and rigid morality. She paints her world in terms of right and wrong, and once the choice is made, it is nigh on impossible to sway her from this choice."

"She is, in many ways, how I was not so long ago," Mary murmured. "I had my sisters' bright spirits and vivacity and beauty as my foils, and I retreated into piety and moralising, where I could find no other independent path." She took a deep breath. "I sometimes find myself returning to these old habits, for they are comfortable and provide guidance where there is none other readily to be found."

Alexander saw her eyes dart in his direction, but she turned them back to the path at once.

"Then you understand my cousin, Miss Bennet."

"But surely," Alexander added, "as a man who has chosen the Church as his path, such sentiments are welcome to you. Yours is, after all, a career of right and wrong, sin and redemption."

Edmund nodded and thought for a moment. "This is true enough. I know Fanny holds affection for me, more so than for one cousin for another. In time, she might make me a good wife. She has the strength of character and goodness of heart. But she is still too young. Her sense of morality is too absolute. She must learn that there are other paths than her own in the world, and she must learn compassion."

"Although," he added after a moment, "compassion has been sorely lacking in her experience at Mansfield Park."

They walked a while in silence. Then, to Alexander's surprise, Mary asked, "Mr. Bertram, after Miss Price's visit and her stern words, I understand you know of Alexander's family, of his faith."

Edmund stopped and turned to her. "Yes. At the inquest... When he insisted on taking his oath upon a different Bible, I resolved to ask him about it, and he told me he is of the Jewish religion." Alexander took a step back. It was awkward enough to be hearing himself so spoken of; being physically present between the two speakers was the epitome of discomfort.

"This did not dissuade you from retaining his services? From having him as a guest in your house?"

"No, not for a moment!" Edmund seemed affronted at the suggestion, and Alexander breathed more easily for it. "The news I had received from my colleague Elton suggested that he was nothing but an excellent man, and the evidence of my own eyes confirmed that. Of course, should he decide at any point to subscribe to the principles of the Church, I would be most pleased to guide his way in, but faith cannot be dictated. It must be felt. I would far prefer a world of good men of no faith at all than a world of pretenders who wave their Bibles but have no goodness in their hearts."

Alexander could not help but think back to their first case together and of the horrid things he had discovered about one particular clergyman; from the expression on Mary's face, she was experiencing similar thoughts.

"Thank you, Mr. Bertram. I respect your words and your opinions."

They began to walk once more; the straight line of trees that edged the road at the entrance to the park now emerged from behind the copse past which they wandered. Mary slowed her steps to wait for Alexander and cast her gaze down at his arm as she pulled at her bottom lip with her teeth. Daring to believe what his eyes told him, he offered her his forearm, and she rested her hand upon it, so lightly at first he hardly felt her touch, but then more firmly, until he felt her fingers give him the slightest squeeze. He smiled at her, and she at him, and they needed no more words.

The End

Historical Notes

A Legal Note

Despite Mary Crawford's pivotal role in the plot against Tom Bertram, she was not necessarily legally culpable, thus her fate was left in her brother's hands rather than legal ones. England distinguishes between conspiracy and soliciting murder, and her involvement seems to be more along the lines of soliciting murder. Furthermore, until 1861, there was no law making the latter a crime. And so, although today she would be charged with soliciting murder, in 1813 when this story takes place, it was just a *really not good idea*. Perhaps a good lawyer at the time could manage to prosecute a charge of conspiracy in this case, but Mary could raise a very good defence, claiming that she merely offered her thoughts to her uncle, who acted on his own volition.

Abolitionists

Jane Austen never says anything specific about the Bertrams and their business in Antigua; however, it seems more than likely that their holdings include sugar plantations, which in turn implies a huge workforce of enslaved people. Furthermore, Austen never voices her opinions on slavery in so many words, but she alludes to it in some of her works. In *Emma*, Jane Fairfax talks with horror about the institution in a conversation with Mrs. Elton.

"...There are places in town, offices, where inquiry would soon produce something—Offices for the sale—not quite of human flesh—but of human intellect."

"Oh! my dear, human flesh! You quite shock me; if you mean a fling at the slave-trade, I assure you Mr. Suckling was always rather a friend to the abolition."

"I did not mean, I was not thinking of the slave-trade," replied Jane; "governess-trade, I assure you, was all that I had in view; widely different certainly as to the guilt of those who carry it on; but as to the greater misery of the victims, I do not know where it lies."

Furthermore, Jane Austen was known to admire the writings of the abolitionist Thomas Clarkson, and later in life, her brother, the Rev. Henry Thomas Austen, attended the 1840 World Anti-Slavery Convention in London, which drew some 500 delegates. Austen also included a mixed-race heiress in her unfinished novel *Sanditon*, which suggests she had a great awareness of racial issues and was sympathetic to the abolitionist movement.

There had been voices crying out against the injustice of enslavement for decades in the British Empire. In 1772, Lord Mansfield of the Court of the King's Bench decreed the capture of an escaped slave unlawful, stating that no legislation existed to establish slavery in England, calling the institution "so odious, that nothing can be suffered to support it."

The judgement was generally taken at the time to say that slavery did not exist under English common law and was thus prohibited in England. One must wonder whether Jane Austen had Lord Mansfield in mind when she wrote her novel *Mansfield Park*.

Laws that began to chip away at the institution of slavery began to appear throughout the Empire. The *Act Against Slavery*, passed in Upper Canada in 1793, was the first law limiting slavery within the British Empire, and in 1798, Chief Justice James Monk in Montreal ruled that there was no basis for slavery or indentured servitude within the law of Lower Canada.

In 1783 a group of Quakers in England founded an abolitionist organisation, whose petition was presented to Parliament by Sir Cecil Wray, and the Bishop of Chester called on the Church of England to end its involvement in the slave trade and to work, instead, to better the conditions of enslaved people in the Caribbean. Africans and escaped slaves also played a huge role in the abolition movement, demonstrating that they were intelligent and sophisticated people advocating for their liberty. Two such men were Ignatius Sancho (c1729–1780) and Olaudah Equiano (c. 1745 –1797). I don't have space to write about them here, but they are worth reading about.

Other efforts to turn public opinion towards the abolition of slavery included the famous Wedgwood Medallion of 1787, which became a sort of badge of the movement, and public talks throughout England by white abolitionists and Black men who had escaped from slavery. The Committee for the Abolition of the Slave Trade was formed in 1787, and its cause was led through a parliamentary campaign by William Wilberforce (1759-1833). Through his efforts and those of his allies, the *Slave Trade Act* of 1807 abolished the slave trade in the British Empire, and the *Slave Trade Felony Act* of 1811 made involvement in the enterprise a felony. While the slave trade was now illegal, it was still permissible for men to own slaves in the colonies. The campaigns continued, and in 1833, Parliament passed the *Slavery Abolition Act*. William Wilberforce was in poor health at the time he but lived long enough to see the act passed.

Canals

The earliest canals in Britain were built by Roman engineers around 2000 years ago. The Fossdyke connected Lincoln to the River Trent, and the Caer Dyke extended about 40 miles to the south of Lincolnshire. These were primarily intended for irrigation and to drain swampland, but they were also used to transport heavy goods. From about 1500, there was an effort to expand the canal system in England, but it was not until the dawn of the industrial age that the great age of canal building began.

From the middle of the eighteenth century, roads were being improved across England, but the coal and steel needed for the new mills and factories were too heavy for wagons. But if these goods were placed on barges, a horse could pull 50 tons of cargo. The smooth motion of the barges also meant that fragile goods like pottery could be transported without the threat of damage.

But rivers did not necessarily go where the goods were needed, and canals proved to be the answer. In 1759, Francis Egerton, 3rd Duke of Bridgewater, commissioned James Brindley to build a canal between his coal mines and the big market of Manchester. The canal was only about six miles long and it took two years to complete. Bridgewater nonetheless still had to borrow £25,000, an exorbitant amount at the time. The gamble paid off, and the canal soon made back that money and a great deal more.

Canals quickly became a focus of investment in the UK, and a great deal of money was made—and lost—in these ventures. A good plan could make a man his fortune, but shady characters selling shares in non-existent canal systems could rob a man blind as well.

By 1840, there were about 4500 miles of interconnected canals crossing the country, but the great age of canals was effectively at an end. With the development of steam locomotives and the construction of a network of railways, there was little more need for canals as a tool of industry.

The UK's canals are still in use, however, mostly for pleasure boaters who enjoy a leisurely tour through the countryside on their barges and riverboats.

DEATH OF A DANDY

More from Mary and Alexander

You can read about Alexander Lyon's first case with Mr. Darcy in the prequel novella, **The Mystery of the Missing Heiress**.

And don't miss Alexander and Mary's earlier adventures together.

Miss Mary Investigates 1

Death of a Clergyman: A Pride and Prejudice Mystery

Mary Bennet has always been the quiet sister, the studious and contemplative middle child in a busy family of five. She is not interested in balls and parties, and is only slightly bothered by the arrival of the distant cousin who will one day inherit her father's estate. But then Mr. Collins is found dead, and Mary's beloved sister Elizabeth is accused of his murder. Mary knows she must learn whatever she can to prove Elizabeth innocent of this most horrible crime, or her sister might be hanged as a murderess!

Alexander Lyons has made a pleasant life for himself in London, far from his home village in Scotland. He investigates missing documents and unfaithful wives, and earns an honest living. Then one day Mr. Darcy walks into his office, begging him to investigate the murder of Mr. Collins and to prove Elizabeth innocent of the crime. It seems like a straightforward enough case, but Alexander did not count on meeting a rather annoying young woman who seems to be in his way at every turn: Mary Bennet.

As the case grows more and more complicated, Mary and Alexander cannot stop arguing, and discover that each brings new insight into the case. But as they get close to some answers, will they survive the plans of an evildoer in the midst of quiet Meryton? www.books2read.com/deathofaclergyman

Miss Mary Investigates 2
Death in Highbury: An Emma Mystery

A Jane Austen-inspired mystery, set in the world of Pride and Prejudice and Emma.

When political chaos in London forces Mary Bennet to take refuge in the picturesque town of Highbury, Surrey, she quickly finds herself safe among friends. Emma Woodhouse welcomes her as a guest at Hartfield, Jane Fairfax is delighted by her love of music, and Frank Churchill can't stop flirting with her. But it is not long before Mary starts to suspect that beneath the charming surface, Highbury hides some dark secrets.

Alexander Lyons is sent to Surrey on an investigation, and at his friend Darcy's request, heads to Highbury to make certain Mary is comfortable and safe. But no sooner does he arrive than one local man dies, and then another!

Soon Alexander and Mary are thrust into the middle of a baffling series of deaths. Are they accidents? Or is there a very clever murderer hiding in their midst? And can they put their personal differences aside in time to prevent yet another death in Highbury? http://books2read.com/deathinhighbury

And, coming soon:

Miss Mary Investigates 4:

Death in Sensible Circumstances:

A Sense and Sensibility Mystery

About the Author

Riana Everly was born in South Africa, but has called Canada home since she was eight years old. She has a Master's degree in Medieval Studies and is trained as a classical musician, specialising in Baroque and early Classical music. She first encountered Jane Austen when her father handed her a copy of *Emma* at age 11, and has never looked back.

Riana now lives in Toronto with her family. When she is not writing, she can often be found playing string quartets with friends, biking around the beautiful province of Ontario with her husband, trying to improve her photography, thinking about what to make for dinner, and, of course, reading!

If you enjoyed this novel, please consider posting a review at your favourite bookseller's website.

Riana Everly loves connecting with readers on Facebook at facebook.com/RianaEverly/

Also, be sure to check out her website at rianaeverly.com for sneak peeks at coming works and links to works in progress!

Also by Riana Everly

Teaching Eliza: Pride and Prejudice Meets Pygmalion

The Assistant: Before Pride and Prejudice

Through a Different Lens: A Pride and Prejudice Variation

The Bennet Affair: A Pride and Prejudice Variation

Much Ado in Meryton: Pride and Prejudice Meets Shakespeare

The Mystery of the Missing Heiress

Death of a Clergyman: A Pride and Prejudice Mystery

Death in Highbury: An Emma Mystery